VICTORIA PARKS

WHEN THE HARVEST DIES BOOK ONE

THE
AWAKENING

When the Harvest Dies: The Awakening / Victoria Parks. — 1st ed.
ISBN 978-0-9948915-9-4

Book Layout and Cover Design by Victoria Parks

DEDICATION

I dedicate this to those who are in their own living hell, the survivors—and especially—those who aren't with us today. These atrocities were barely heard of in the past with little to no support. Present day, we hear of it more with prevention and much improved support. But we're not there yet. Let's hope for complete eradication in the not so distant future.

Abruptly the poker of memory stirs the ashes of recollection and uncovers a forgotten ember, still smoldering down there, still hot, still glowing, still red as red.

—WILLIAM MANCHESTER

ACKNOWLEDGMENTS

Publishing my first novel is a dream come true. I couldn't have done it without the help of a long list of people. Please indulge me while I take a moment to especially thank:

My Aunt Bonnie and Uncle Dale. If it weren't for you, I never would have had a glimpse into what a real family was.

My loving and always supportive husband, Jeramiah. With you by my side, I know I can do anything. Love you, Moroso x

My editors: Angela Brown and Mitchel Bogatz. Thank you for taking my words and helping to make them into the story it is today.

My beta readers, Eric Deschênes and Leeann Haché. Eric, if you weren't so picky, the editors would've had a lot more work to do. Leeann, thank you for your help with the second section and your input regarding how to bring the story to a conclusion. I hope you're able to find whatever it is you're looking for and to finally be happy.

Dan Munn, the best roommate in exchange for a subpar one—not exactly fair, I know. Thank you for putting up with my craziness the last two years.

Dr. Alfredo E. Walker, forensic pathologist at The Ottawa Hospital, General Campus, for your insights on crime-scene and autopsy procedures. The information you provided was invaluable.

And last, though definitely not least, all the amazing people I met in Newark, NJ, while researching my material. Michael "The Intimidator," Tom, Eric, Jamaine, Jimmy, Gerry, Larry, Walter—fortunately there are too many of you to mention. You helped make my multiple trips over the last year and a half incredible. Don't worry; your sociopath will be back to visit soon!

PROLOGUE

Lake Placid, New York
December 1993

THERE WAS NO DENYING IT. Only fourteen years old and I was going to die.

I'd been lucky, in the past, to survive many other dangerous situations—more than I could count.

This time, however, was different.

I hadn't given myself enough time to make my escape. My entire body froze where I stood.

The panic already had its stronghold; it was closing my throat to what felt like nothing more than the width of a single thread. My heart was pounding hard, trying to escape, before my brain had the opportunity to reach the same conclusion as the rest of my body.

I finally managed to turn my upper body, and there they were in all their brilliance: deep flames, visible only through sporadic gaps of thick, dark smoke.

The flames wilted and cracked everything that was once beautiful, turning everything they touched to ash. I wanted to scream so badly, but there was no use. My voice was lost, and the rest of my senses were following.

The red and amber flames were making their way toward me, creeping along the walls on either side with the fluidity of lava, their heat penetrating deeper into my skin with every additional inch they covered.

A boy's voice called out to me: "What are you doing? You have to get out of here!"

That was what I needed, and I snapped out of it. I started to run, but it seemed only to encourage the fire, inciting its competitive side to race. It was an unforgiving entity, quickly closing the gap and licking at my heels, snapping and snarling. I tried to run faster, but I fell. I swiftly got to my feet, but I was having a hard time staying upright.

"Faster!" the boy yelled.

I could barely see the door through the smokescreen that had now completed its descent, and the harder I tried to reach it, the farther away it seemed.

"Don't look back! It'll only slow you down!"

I gasped for air, but let out a rattled cough far larger than my small intake of breath. I was slowing down even more, and I knew I'd never reach the only available way out.

I fell one last time. I wouldn't be getting up again. Almost filled to capacity with smoke, my lungs weren't functioning properly. The lines of reality became blurred... A thousand-pound blanket covered my body, pushing me closer to the floor, and I lost the little strength I had left. I closed my eyes, and I waited for the flames to devour me.

***

I felt someone pull me up by my arms. I opened my eyes and saw the boy. He flung my arm around his neck, and we made our way toward the door.

A support beam crashed to the floor, barely missing us. The fire must have escaped up into the ceiling, which, judging by its creaks and groans, didn't have long. The fear I'd felt seconds before had dissipated. All that remained was my fog-filled mind and a surprising sense of peace.

"Hold on," the boy said. "We're almost there."

The present regained its hold on me once more as the boy crashed through the door, the right side of my body slamming into the frame. Seconds later I was outside, on a snow-covered field, surrounded by darkness. The boy pushed on my chest, and placed his mouth on mine as he forced air into my lungs.

It took a bit of an effort, but soon, between intermittent coughs, I inhaled the fresh air on my own. It felt foreign, unnatural, as it found its way down my windpipe and into my oxygen-starved lungs. I tried to push it past the fire burning in my chest.

"You have to get away from here, as far away as you can."

Confused, I said the only word that came to mind. "Where?"

"Where no one can find you."

The shock of it all enveloped me: the fire; his directives. Once again, excruciating pain radiated throughout my body.

He was right. It was time to run.

CHAPTER ONE

GO TO SLEEP

Newark, New Jersey
October, 2016

"SHHH… BE STILL. Be quiet little one," he crooned. "Soon, you can sleep."

She tried her best to stand motionlessly and be quiet, even though the pain in her head and face was nearly unbearable. All she wanted to do was scream in pain and run… though she knew the punishment would be severe if she didn't comply, she didn't know how much more she could endure. She allowed a single tear to roll down her cheek, past her chin, and drip onto her naked body.

"Now lift your arms for me," he gently said, and she obeyed.

Even though she couldn't see through her swollen, beaten eyes, she could feel the soft silk of the garment as he pulled it over her out-stretched arms, carefully over her head, and finally, smoothly down the length of her body until it rested at her knees. She felt him move behind her—felt him pull at the zipper until it reached her neck, tightening the fabric around her chest. He positioned what felt like a rope around her waist and fastened it midway down her back. He grasped her hand and turned her slowly toward him.

"Almost perfect," he whispered, placing her on a chair.

She flinched as the brush made its way through her hair, and again as it scraped the long renegade strands off her damp skin and away from her face.

He stopped brushing, and she tensed up as thoughts of what might come next entered her mind. She let out a sigh of relief when she felt him tie a simple ribbon around her hair. He then took her hands and placed them softly in her lap.

"My perfect porcelain doll!" he proclaimed, appreciation radiating from his voice.

Apart from her breathing, not a sound could be heard. Was she alone? She had no sense of where he was—whether he was still in front of her, had moved, or had left altogether. A layer of perspiration coated her body, and a sudden chill followed. She shivered as his voice slithered into her ears.

"Are you ready to sleep now?"

All she could do was nod.

"I want to hear you say it," he said in his soothing voice, before repeating, "Are you ready to sleep now?"

Sleeping was all she'd thought about in the last few days. She could sleep forever... No more pain, no more torment—only the promise of eternal darkness to take it all away.

She tried to say what he wanted to hear, but she couldn't find her voice. It had been so long since she'd been allowed to use it without the threat of reprisal... she wasn't even sure she could. With that thought, the tears flowed more easily down her cheeks.

He brought his mouth to her ear and repeated once more, this time, slowly, his voice shaking, "ARE. YOU. READY. TO. SLEEP. NOW."

Then she finally said it. Her voice might have been hoarse and nearly inaudible, but she managed to release the words she so desperately wanted to. "Yes, I'm ready to sleep."

The silence returned, and the fear was quickly on its heels. She was afraid—not of sleep, but that the promise of release would be stolen from her.

A thin, cold wire snaked around her throat, fitting snuggly around her neck. He started slowly, pulling the ends in opposite directions, tightening the wire, wrapping it around her throat, over and over. She could still breathe, but the pressure in her head increased. As he continued to pull, the wire cut into her skin, but she refused to fight it. Her eyes felt as if they were trying to escape her closed lids, and the unmistakable trickle of blood ran down her neck. Her head was beginning to feel foggy, and she knew she would soon succumb to unconsciousness.

What felt like an eternity took about ten seconds. Permanent darkness.

CHAPTER TWO

THE CALL

IT WAS FOUR O'CLOCK on a balmy Thursday afternoon, and I was struggling with a damp blouse that kept sticking to my body, trying its best to merge and become one with my skin. It was mid-October, but the temperature had risen to the eighties, which was unusual for Newark. After five consecutive days of this, with no sign of end in the near future, I could only wonder why the maintenance department refused to switch the HVAC settings back to air conditioning.

Giving up on comfort, I turned my attention to the computer screen where I was putting the final touches on a preliminary report for my upcoming court appearance. The case I was working on concerned a seven-year-old girl who'd been sexually assaulted by her uncle, repeatedly, since the time she turned four. It was the girl's newest pediatrician, who noticed the telltale signs of abuse; she had been fidgety, always backing away when the doctor tried to touch or even approach her... but the most telling sign was the bruising on her legs, and particularly, between her thighs. The doctor noted everything in a single day, the moment he was finally allowed to examine her. When gently questioned, the girl broke down, relayed what was happening to her, and named the perpetrator. How the abuse had gone on for that long, unseen by the family, still baffles me.

It was after Patrick Brook's arrest, that I was called to meet with the victim and the accused. I was asked to make a psychological assessment of Mr. Patrick Brook.

He didn't look at all like I imagined: he was in his mid-twenties, tall, with a medium build, boyish good looks, and not a blond hair out of place. I understood how he could easily fool those around him, but his arrogance slapped me in the face within the first few seconds of my meeting him. His self-assured smile never left his face, and his entire demeanor whispered, *I'm better than you.*

If ever I'd sensed the slightest hint of doubt about the young girl's statement, or the contents of the detective's reports, it quickly dissipated. Patrick's guilt was written all over his face, interwoven with his claims of innocence and the child's supposed need for attention. However, in the end, I knew his type of evil all too well.

I was to present my findings then leave it to the judicial system to do the right thing... as if they would. The longer I did this job, the more cynical I became.

It wasn't that I didn't like my job—I knew I chose the right path. I was doing something I thoroughly enjoyed, without regret. More than that, I had the opportunity to help some of the most vulnerable people in the world—children... but I also had the obligation to dissect the worst of us: those cleverly hiding who they are from the world, those claimed in full by evil. I've made it my mission to expose them for what they are. So I'm more skeptical... I may even be missing the human spark most others have—but I still have my own brand of passion for what I do.

The phone rang, further distracting me from my report. It was Marcus Hudson, a lieutenant with the Newark Police Department, or the "Intimidator," as I lovingly called him. We'd worked on many cases together over the years. It wasn't a social call.

"Isabella, there's something you need to see."

"Where are you?"

"Coordinates already sent to your cell phone." He hung up.

I quickly typed out the last few words and printed everything out. Once it was in my hands, I read through it one last time, shaking my head as I did. I was confident with my assessment, but it didn't prevent the potential outcome from entering my mind. Patrick Brook, like many of the other degenerates who came across my desk, would probably get off. Proof was the burden of the victim, not the perpetrator… but in my opinion, it should be the other way around. Sighing, I put the report neatly in a folder and placed it on the corner of my desk, purging it from my mind for the time being.

I stood up and grabbed my suit jacket from the back of my chair, dreading the idea of squeezing my damp arms into their constricting sleeves. Nevertheless, I knew it would be better than revealing the mess the jacket promised to conceal. Once it was on and it immediately meshed with my skin, I grabbed my bag and left the office.

CHAPTER THREE

THE MEADOWLANDS

OFFICIALLY I'M A FORENSIC psychiatrist in private practice, although I often collaborate with the Newark Police Department, the NPD, on cases that require a psychiatric opinion. For this reason, I already suspected why I was being called in.

Truthfully speaking, whether someone is experienced or not, nothing can fully prepare them for what goes on beyond the door—even I wasn't completely immune to it. However, here there were no doors or entranceways—no thresholds to coax oneself across. This time, faced with a wide-open space, it wasn't any easier.

The Meadowlands consisted of roughly 8,400 acres of open, undeveloped space, in addition to developed areas that were previously a part of the natural wetlands. It was the perfect place to dump the unwanted, whether it be objects or people.

With my eyes closed, I raised my face to the sky and stretched out my arms to the freshly blowing wind. It felt cool and refreshing—a vast improvement from the weather earlier in the day. Finally, some much needed relief.

The sun had almost completed its descent below the horizon, and I watched as the spotlights each took their turn firing up, almost in harmony with the stars above. It did nothing for me from this distance—nor did the uncut grass or the reeds the size of saplings; all simply obstructed my view. I had no choice but to start my approach.

Chain-link fencing lined the perimeter, so I walked to the only place that would give me access to the land. Standing guard at its entrance was a uniform, stick straight with his arms behind his back. He didn't say a word until I showed him my ID and watched his face contort with disgust.

"I hope you haven't eaten, Doc... it isn't pretty."

"That bad?"

"Honestly? Bad would be a bit of an understatement."

***

I found Marcus standing outside the cordoned-off crime scene, and took my place beside him, respecting the silence. I knew better than to interrupt him before he was ready.

After a dozen or so minutes had passed, he finally looked at me... I barely recognized him. What I recalled from the last time we'd seen each other was a strongly built black man in his fifties, rigid and erect in posture. Now he looked like he'd lost four inches and gained ten years in age. His face was ashen, eyes bloodshot, and he had the look of defeat about him. Even his dark-gray suit, typically clean and crisp, was disheveled and caked with mud.

He ran his fingers through his neatly cropped hair for what must have been the tenth time since I'd arrived. He'd seen many things during his thirty years on the force, but this one seemed to have finally cracked his trademark tough exterior.

"Are you ready?" Marcus finally asked, handing me a pair of gloves and latex shoe covers.

I put them on. "Will you be walking me through it?"

"Matthews can do it. I'll be in shortly," he replied, lifting the tape so I could get through.

I ducked beneath. As I was approaching the crime scene, Detective Dean Matthews spotted me, and we met halfway.

Matthews had achieved level three detective before reaching his thirties, and was on the threshold of moving up again. He was definitely good at what he did, but he looked like he belonged in sunny California instead of here. With sandy-blond hair that was a little too long, what seemed to be an effortless year-round tan, and a perfect physique, he was one of the few guys on the force I didn't have to look up at during a conversation.

"Is everyone here?" I asked.

"We are now," Matthews said.

Even though I was closer to the crime scene, I still couldn't see a thing. Multiple black-and-whites, unmarked cars, a portable crime lab, and the medical examiner's SUV were all placed strategically to do exactly what they were doing—conceal whatever it was at the center. The forensic team in their black windbreakers made their way effortlessly through the obstacle course the vehicles had created.

"What are we looking at?" I asked, straining my neck in an effort to find out for myself.

"Children… Better take a look," Matthews said. "Watch your step. It's mostly water. What ground there is is sinking."

Still as statues, three young girls, leaned against three wooden posts. The smooth wood lacked any discoloration—too perfect in the midst of such despair. They hadn't been there long.

"A couple exploring the area found them and called it in," Matthews said. "Don't think they'll be coming back any time soon."

The girls looked like dolls, each wearing white long-sleeved dresses with white lace tied around their waists. White tights covered their legs: shiny black Mary Jane's with heart cutouts. Their hands were folded in their laps. Even though their sleeves covered their arms to their wrists, I couldn't miss the ligature marks peeking through. The final touch was the matching red ribbons, neatly keeping their long hair away from their grotesquely disfigured faces. There were gashes, bruises and sub-surface tissue damage so severe that much of their skin was heavily bloated, especially around the eyes.

Could the disfigurements have been done to make them harder to identify? I squatted to get a closer look.

Except for hair color, they all matched physically: small, Caucasian, and wafer thin from shoulders to feet. If I had to guess, I'd say their ages ranged from eight to ten. Although they leaned against the posts for support, their heads seemed to rest unnaturally. The skin on the neck of one of the girls had ligature marks as well.

"We'll be laying them on the ground as soon as we get the okay."

"That's not going to be easy to do," I started, pointing to her head. "The perp somehow attached this one's head to the pole."

"How do you know?"

"After he positioned them to his liking, he wanted to make sure they wouldn't move, but he also didn't want to ruin his perceived artistry by wrapping a rope around them to keep them secure."

With a gloved finger, I gingerly moved a lock of blond hair near the back of the head that seemed a bit darker in shade than the rest. Now no one could miss the blood on the wood, as well as the coagulated stream on her scalp.

"Are those nailheads?"

"Hook and eye," I said. "I'm thinking he prepped the post before he brought them here, strategically placing the metal hooks in it—and the metal eyes later—into the skull to match up. He probably used pliers to close off the hooks."

"Was she still…" Matthews trailed off.

"There wouldn't have been that much blood flow if she'd already been dead, though he did try to clean up the area as best he could… judging from the marks on her neck, she was dead by the time she was positioned here."

"Strangulation?"

"That's what it looks like."

It was then that the medical examiner, Melanie Scott, joined us. Her long blond hair was completely hidden beneath a cap, and her slim body swam in her oversized windbreaker. We had become friends not long after I had returned to Jersey, and being similar in the way we think—especially when it came to forensics—we also worked well together.

She was now standing beside me. "We're going to lay out the tarp so we can lay them down. We've taken all the shots we're going to need."

"Did you notice this?" I asked, pointing to the girl's head.

"No," Melanie said, leaning in closer and motioning for a technician. "Tom, take some shots of the back of this one's head."

I stood up to give him some room.

"Let me know when you get them down," I said.

Having done what I came for, I made my way back to Marcus with Matthews in tow.

CHAPTER FOUR

THE VOICES

I FOUND MARCUS EXACTLY where I'd left him, though he seemed to have regained some of his composure. Matthews and I were facing him, but the crime scene tape kept us separated.

"I couldn't bring myself to go back down there," Marcus said, fanning out his hand and slowly bringing it down the length of his face, literally wiping the images away.

"Can't say I blame you. I don't relish the thought of returning either."

He looked briefly at the clear indigo sky. "Sorry I brought you into this…"

"No, you're not… and you shouldn't be," I said with a warm smile, placing my hand on his arm. "This is what we do, and it's not meant to get easier with each case. We're supposed to feel like this. It means we're the right people for the job."

He nodded, but said nothing.

When we're regularly exposed to one soul-sucking scenario after another, it becomes imperative to find a way of not letting it consume us; so we learn to compartmentalize, whether consciously or subconsciously, to avoid the discomfort and anxiety. It's an effective defense mechanism, and one I often use myself, though it's usually a temporary fix. The horror doesn't magically evaporate over time into thin air; instead, it lies in wait beneath the surface, opportunistic in nature, always ready to strike.

So what do we do? Some transfer out; others find hobbies to distract themselves. Some turn to faith. Others to sin. However, the moment it no longer fazes you—affects you in one way or another deep within your core—it's time to walk away.

The three girls—or children in general—were the most difficult to wrap my head around, to bury deep enough in a neat little compartment. Seared into my brain were the negatives of the snapshots my mind had taken, and I could tell it was the same for Marcus.

Matthews, on the other hand, was a little harder to read.

"So how do we look at this? Serial? Random? Psychotic? All of the above?" he asked.

"Psychopathic is a given." I said. "What normal, adjusted human being would do something like this? But serial... that's where you guys come in. Can you think of anything in the past remotely like this?"

"Nothing recent that I can recall. Not here anyway. I'll have to dig a bit—and check around in the surrounding states as well—to give you a more definitive answer."

"I'll be honest... even though this screams an experienced killer, my first impressions don't point to serial, despite there being three victims," I said. "It looks like they were killed at approximately the same time, judging by the shape the bodies are in. It wasn't long ago either.

I'll confirm with Melanie, but I don't think they've been here for more than twelve hours."

"Do you think they were killed here?" Marcus asked.

"I don't think so, but again, Melanie will need to confirm that."

Marcus let out a long sigh. He wasn't good with the waiting game.

"How about the two of you take off? Nothing really left for you to do here," I said. "Forensics is wrapping up, and we won't know much more until the autopsies are completed."

"Is that an order, Porter?" asked Marcus, his traditional smart-ass smirk emerging, much to my relief.

"It's a very strong suggestion," I said. "And that's Dr. Porter to you!"

***

When I returned to the scene, I found all three girls lying on a dark plastic tarp, mere feet from the posts they came with. Again, I bent down to get a closer look.

"Glad you weren't here for the removal." It was Melanie, kneeling beside me. "It was easier to pull out the hooks from the post, and believe me, it wasn't pretty."

"I can imagine. Anything else you can tell me? Signs of sexual assault?"

She shook her head. "None that I can see so far. They're fully dressed, and I intend to keep them that way until I get them back to the morgue."

I agreed with her plan. They'd already been exposed enough.

"When will the autopsies be done?" I asked.

"I'd like them to take place tomorrow morning, but realistically, sometime in the afternoon."

"If it's okay, I'd like to be present. I have court tomorrow afternoon, but it might work if you gave me a heads-up."

"I'll give you a call first thing. By then I'll have a better idea of my schedule… Alright, It's time to pack things up and get these babies out of here."

"Agreed."

I stood up, and looked down at the girls one last time before making my way back to my car. Even though it was faint, I could hear the whispers begin deep within my mind.

CHAPTER FIVE

FAMILIAR TERRITORY

IT WAS 9:00p.m., and I knew I should have gone straight home to prepare for court the next day… but I was wired, and decided home was the last place I wanted to be. Instead, I made my way to the Jersey Tavern on Washington Street, a popular spot for various levels of law enforcement to retreat and unwind.

As soon as I'd taken a seat at the bar, Eric, the regular bartender, placed a double whiskey, Van Winkle Special Reserve Bourbon, in front of me: on the rocks, just the way I liked it. I immediately removed the red stir stick from the glass.

"When will you finally catch on?" I asked, handing it to him.

"It's habit," he replied, his Polish accent heavy.

"Yet, you know exactly what to serve me as soon as I walk in."

He placed the stick in his mouth then tossed it into the garbage. "Maybe it's because I don't drink while working, and this is how I get my taste."

"Buzz from residue?" I asked, squinting my eyes at him.

"Something like that." He winked, then walked away to serve another patron.

After a half hour, I sensed someone slip onto the stool beside me. I didn't even have to look to know who it was. The scent of his cologne—lavender and sandalwood—hadn't changed since the day I'd met him. It always made me want to sneeze.

"I figured you'd get here before me," I said, turning toward him. "What took you so long?"

"I had to do some paperwork. But worry not my dear—I'm here now," Marcus said.

He raised his hand to the bartender, and within a minute or two, had his glass of gin and soda.

I heard a thud as a file the size of ten hit the bar space between us.

"A gift?" I asked, grinning. "How thoughtful."

"A new case. It was going to be sent your way before I called you this afternoon."

"What's it about?"

He paused and studied the nearby patrons out of the corner of his eye.

"Want to grab a booth? It'll be easier to talk."

We gathered our stuff and took a booth in the far corner, away from the massive groups of other patrons. Marcus took a seat opposite me and slid the file across the table.

"What can you tell me about this case?" I asked.

"It's pretty bad, Izzy. I'm still having a hard time digesting it," he started, before finishing off his gin and signaling to Eric for a new one. "We have an eleven-year-old girl, Ember O'Reilly, with every type of abuse imaginable, starting at a very young age. They're all male suspects from the paternal side of the family, including the father, Michael O'Reilly."

"Where's her mother?"

A look of revulsion took over his face. "She's there, but she's in denial. Everyone is backing up everyone else."

"Of course. Any siblings?"

"Two brothers. Ember's the middle child. One of the suspects is the eldest one, Cody, her stepbrother. Sixteen-year-old. Ember seems to be the only one of them experiencing any type of abuse."

I started to flip through the pages. "How did it come out?"

"She was about to run away for the second time, but one of her classmates told the officer assigned to their school. After he'd spent a couple of hours talking with her, she finally opened up."

"That's a bit surprising, considering her past relationships with males haven't been exactly positive," I said. "She was taken out of the home, I'm assuming?"

He nodded. "Same day it was reported. The mother is supporting the two suspects, so there was little choice. Ember's staying with her maternal aunt and uncle in Queens."

"Well, at least she has some form of family support."

Just then, Eric came by with another gin for Marcus, and a double shot for me. I took a long sip to help loosen the knot forming in the pit of my stomach.

"I can't disagree with that, but you definitely have your work cut out for you." Marcus sighed. "We both do."

As I continued to skim the pages, I started to see what he meant. I read on until I came across a red rubber stamp from the Jersey PD. "How did this fall into your lap? It's not within your jurisdiction."

He wouldn't look me in the eyes. "It was given to me because it's similar to something I worked in the past. They may be connected. Cases can switch jurisdiction if there's a link. It's not uncommon."

"And they just willingly handed it over to you?"

"There was no convincing needed. I know the detective, and she was more than happy to wash her hands of it."

It still didn't make sense to me as I had never heard of it. However, Marcus didn't seem like he wanted to get into it, so I didn't push.

I didn't realize it was possible, but his voice softened even further. "Regrettably, this isn't unfamiliar territory for you, either. Read the medical report thoroughly, and you'll understand what I mean."

"Can't you just tell me?"

"I don't have to. I can tell it's already simmering in the pit of your stomach."

Unfortunately he was right. Something was tickling my subconscious, something familiar that I hadn't quite been able to put my finger on.

"Well, on that note, I'm heading home. Three autopsies, court tomorrow, and apparently some reading to do."

"I'm sorry, Isabella. I told you before, but I really am," Marcus said, concentrating on the hand that was fidgeting with the red stir stick in his glass.

"And if you say it again, I'm going to slap you." I smirked, stood up from the table and stuffed the huge file into my bag, forcing it to fit.

"Is that a promise?" he asked, his own mischievous smirk returning.

***

I dropped my keys on the credenza near the front door, and reset the alarm to "armed". I dropped my bag off on the floor beside the desk in my office, and made my usual rounds making sure that every possible entrance was locked and glimpse inside removed. The last curtain closed, I suddenly realized how unlived in my home looked. It was extremely neat and sterile, with just the right amount of furniture, all of it meticulously organized—almost as clean as an operating room.

A colleague once told me that, if we can't control the thoughts in our head, we compensate by controlling our surroundings. I'm a perfect example of that, though I wouldn't normally admit it.

Once I was satisfied the house was secure, I went back to my office to study the file. It wasn't long before my head was swimming, and it wasn't because of the bourbon; alcohol rarely intoxicated me, just soothed my inner voices… As I read on, the knot at the bottom of my stomach turned into a boulder that sat heavily in my chest, threatening to weigh me down even farther.

But I had a job to do, and I couldn't afford to let my instincts get in the way—yet.

CHAPTER SIX

I STILL SEE YOU

AS PROMISED, a message was waiting for me when I arrived at my office late the next morning. Melanie was going to begin the autopsies at three o'clock, and I was expected in court at two. I wouldn't be able to make it to the morgue. I called her back and scheduled a time to go over the findings.

After sending off a few emails, I had a moment to call Marcus... but couldn't resist looking over the file one more time. Words were popping out of the pages; it was as if I could catch and feel them between my fingers.

Scarring throughout the body...

Some are as old as she is; others are still in the healing stages...

Signs of sexual torture...

Evidence of previously untreated fractures...

I had to shut the folder; I couldn't read any more. I picked up the phone and punched in the number.

"I was expecting to hear from you a lot sooner," Marcus said.

"I think a warning beforehand would have been warranted. 'Familiar territory' was a severe understatement, and you know it."

"I needed you to see it through your eyes, not mine."

"I would have seen it, regardless."

"No. You would've separated it, just like you do with every other similar case you're handed," he said gently. "But this one... I couldn't let you do that."

"But this case is *more* than similar."

"I think the right term would be 'identical.'"

"It's impossible, Marcus. It's not... I can't make it to the autopsies because of court, but I'll head to the morgue after. I'll give you a call once I know more."

"You know you can talk about this, right?"

No, I never can, I thought, but I kept it to myself.

"We'll talk later," I said, and ended the call.

Funny... not a single apology from him this time.

***

"Dr. Porter," the defense attorney began, "in your sworn testimony, you stated that you interviewed everyone who's had personal contact with Claire Brook. Is that correct?"

"'Everyone to my knowledge.' That's what I said."

"I see... Did you interview her teacher, Mr. Conner?"

"I did not."

"Did you interview her bus driver, Mr. McAllister?"

"No."

"Did you interview the Brook family gardener?"

"No, I did not."

"So *everyone* who has had personal contact with the girl, was in fact, *not* interviewed."

"According to the detective reports," I said, "these men were questioned, but didn't have the opportunity to be alone with her."

"Tell me, are you aware of the assignment Claire turned in three weeks ago?"

"Pardon me?"

"I asked if you were aware of the last assignment Claire was asked to turn in. It was about telling the proper time on an analog clock."

"No. I'm not aware of any assignment."

"Then I'd like to fill you in. According to Mr. Conner, whom you neglected to interview, Claire was found cheating off another student, and when she was confronted, she *lied* about it. Does that surprise you?"

"She was under a lot of stress."

"So it doesn't surprise you that the young girl, whom you seem to believe more than her own mother, cheated off one Katie Borden, then did everything in her power to cover it up."

"Katie Borden didn't rape her!" Before I knew what I was doing, I was standing, clenching my fists, staring into the eyes of that son of a bitch.

"And police reports are never wrong, and seven-year-olds never lie..."

"Objection!" The prosecutor was on his feet in a matter of seconds, but the defense attorney wouldn't give him the satisfaction.

"Withdrawn. No further questions."

"Redirect, Your Honor?" the prosecutor asked. The judge nodded. "Please, sit back down Dr. Porter... I've just one question: who did Claire identify as her abuser?"

"She identified her uncle, Patrick Brook."

"And do you, in your expert opinion, believe she's telling the truth and correctly identified her perpetrator in question?"

"Absolutely."

"Thank you, Dr. Porter. Nothing further."

Once excused from the stand, I made my way to the doors at the back of the room, and out of the courtroom. Across the hall sat Claire and her mother. She held her doll so tightly that her knuckles were ivory white. Her strawberry-blond hair was pulled back into a ponytail, a slight curl at its tip. The emerald-green of her dress matched her eyes perfectly.

"Was it scary?" she asked as I kneeled in front of her.

"A walk in the park, honey. All you have to do is tell the truth."

"Will you come in with me?"

"I won't be able to, but I'll be right here waiting for you when you finish."

"He's in there, isn't he?" she asked, diverting her eyes to the floor.

"Claire Brook?" the bailiff called out.

I gently took her chin in my hand and lifted her gaze back to me. "Yes, but he can't hurt you anymore… Keep your eyes on the person who's talking to you and answer their questions, okay?"

Silently, she nodded and made her way to the bailiff, squeezing her mother's hand as tightly as she'd held her doll. She looked back at me one last time before disappearing behind the thick oak doors.

***

Midway down the courthouse steps, I had to take a deep breath to calm my racing thoughts. I imagined hearing steps behind me, imagined looking over my shoulder as Patrick Brook and his attorney walked by, laughing and slapping each other's backs. My thoughts raced even faster.

Reasonable doubt. I knew he'd be acquitted. He and his attorney were able to convince at least a few of the jurors that he was innocent, and in a federal case, that's all that was needed. My thoughts went immediately to Claire and what would be a long road ahead of her. I hoped her parents would take me up on the offer of additional counseling. Now, more than ever, she'd need it to move on with her life.

I imagined Mr. Brook telling his friends how horrifying it had been to be falsely accused—soaking up their sympathy, sadness plastered all over his face.

"You can fool them…" I muttered under my breath, "but you can't fool me."

CHAPTER SEVEN

FACE OF A MAN

I ARRIVED at the Essex County Coroner earlier than expected. It was 4:30 when I walked into the brown-brick building, presented my ID, and stated my reason for being there. I doubted very much if Melanie had time yet to complete the autopsies. After I'd received the customary, but unnecessary, directions, I climbed the stairs to the second floor and headed for the fifth door on the left.

I opened it just enough to stick my head in.

"Mel, am I too late?"

She looked up from the table and smiled—which felt a bit odd given the circumstances. Instead of her usual field attire, she wore blue surgical scrubs with a disposable gown, matching cap and booties, a chin-length shield covering her face. "No, you made it. Come on in. I'm just finishing up the first one," she said, lifting the shield with her gloved hand. The place was pristine. On one wall was a mortuary refrigerator, capable of holding eight bodies, and on the another, a four-bank x-ray illuminator—the perfect way to catch a movie on a slow afternoon.

I made my way to the center of the room, to the middle of five stainless steel tables, where the first of three girls lay. I'd prepared myself for the Y-shaped incision in her chest, but it was already sewn up. Still, I was shocked by what covered her body: ligature marks, not just on her wrists, neck, and disfigured face, but everywhere.

Melanie put her hand on her hip, slightly leaning to the right as she did. "My expression was exactly like yours when I started undressing her. There's more to this than we originally thought."

"It appears so."

"Jane Doe, young female, Tanner stage two."

"That would make her what… eight, nine years old?" I asked.

"A little older."

"Cause of death?" I was having a hard time taking my eyes of the dead girl.

"Strangulation." Mel pointed to the deep bruising on the neck. "I'd say by a thin rope or wire. There's bruising of the skin as well as hemorrhages in the strap muscles and around the trachea and larynx."

"Do we have a time of death?"

"It's hard to tell. I'm thinking no more than twenty-four hours before they were found, solely on the condition of the bodies."

"Was she sexually assaulted?" Even as I asked it, I realized the question was redundant.

"There's marked bruising to the thighs, as well as the pelvic, anal, and vaginal areas, all in different phases of healing. She was penetrated, but unfortunately we didn't recover any bodily fluids," she said, walking to the illuminators. "I ran a full-body postmortem CT instead of the standard radiology. We also found several healed fractures to the ribs, both wrists, and the ankles, fingers—"

I didn't let her finish. "Long-term abuse."

She nodded. "Yes, and the scarring and sexual injuries she sustained support that conclusion. There's something else... there were no signs of a struggle before she died."

"What do you mean?"

"There's nothing under her fingernails to indicate she fought back, no markings on her neck to show her pulling at the rope."

"Toxicology?"

"Clean, as was the body. Couldn't find a thing on her or her clothes."

"Did she die at the scene?"

"I doubt it," she said. "Livor mortis shows blood settling in on the back of the body, which meant she was probably on her back at the time of death. There were also several white patches on her skin... she was dressed before she was killed."

"Is it safe to assume that your findings will be consistent with the remaining two girls?"

"I don't like to assume, but I wouldn't bet against it," she said, a somber note in her voice.

"Okay. I'll wait for the final report." I turned and started toward the door... but I couldn't resist.

"Do you think she wanted to die?"

Mel began to answer, but stopped suddenly, looking me over.

"Honestly," she said, "I really don't know."

***

I arrived home just as the sun was setting. After making sure the house was secure, I made my way to the basement, hitting the switch at the bottom of the stairs.

If I allowed anyone else to see this place, they might think it was a martial arts studio. All the equipment was there; all that was missing were mirrors on the walls. I headed for the laundry room, and changed into my workout clothes—loose-fitting pants and a tank top.

I tied my ponytail, walked back into the main room, and slipped on my open-palm finger gloves, securing the straps tightly around my wrists. The man-shaped dummy bag that hung from the ceiling looked particularly hittable that day.

I started with a few simple jabs, hooks and a right cross, the dummy gently rocking from the punches. Soon, I picked up momentum, striking harder and harder until it danced in front of me. I imagined the damage I could be doing if it were a real man, the blood that would secrete from his nose, the cuts that would form on his lips—every hit another part of the beautiful mosaic that would form across his face and torso.

My breath became labored, and I stopped to stare once again at the man in front of me. Images flashed from the present to the past and back again. Then I felt it as it washed over me, that numbness that reaches from the top of my head to every extremity of my body. It felt as if I were only partly there; the object in front of me moved farther and farther away.

I ripped off the gloves and threw them to the floor. I launched into a sidekick, quickly changed positions, and landed a round house kick across the dummy's head. Using all the strength I had, I switched between my hands and feet, using the occasional elbow and knee to batter the form in front of me. With my last kick, I hit the dummy so hard, that I was barely able to avoid its smashing into me when it returned.

I was in my own world. The dummy had a real face, one that I recognized—one that continually haunted me, awake or asleep. I smashed it with my fist one last time, causing pain to radiate from my knuckles all the way to my shoulder.

That was it all it took to send me crashing back into the present.

Sitting on the floor, rubbing my tender, swelling hand, I realized, suddenly, that my cell phone was ringing. "Not tonight, Marcus," I whispered. "Not yet."

CHAPTER EIGHT

ANNA

IN THE DISTANCE, I heard the alarm scream for my attention, sounding almost as if it were saying my name. The more I tried to ignore it, to stay hidden within my subconscious, the louder it seemed to get.

Izzy... Izzy... Izzy... Izzy... Izzy!

"All right already!" I yelled back, slamming my hand on the oversized snooze button.

Quiet again. I smiled to myself as I basked in the silence. However, after what seemed like only a few seconds, the assault began anew, this time seemingly louder than before. The clock's screams bounced violently between my ear canals, unable to find an escape, the noises burrowed deeper into my head. I slammed my hand on the button once again.

When I was finally able to pry my eyes opened, ever so slightly, I directed them toward the beaming green LCD display. It was 7:29a.m. The last time I took a glance, it was 5:20. So I'd gotten at least a couple of hours of sleep the previous night... morning. Whatever. I grunted my disapproval either way.

The ringing phone replaced the alarm clock as the most annoying object in the room. I took the receiver from the charging dock, and looked at the number on the display.

"Isn't it a bit early to be calling on a Saturday morning?"

"When I didn't hear back from you last night, I got worried," Marcus said.

"I got a bit distracted. Forgot to call back. I'm fine."

"You sure?" he asked, unconvinced.

"Yeah. So what's up?" I finally sat up and immediately regretted it. My head was throbbing.

"You were supposed to let me know when the autopsies were completed."

"Forgot that too. Sorry."

"Want to meet up to discuss them?"

"It's Saturday," I reminded him.

"I meant after your visit."

"You know the rules. Nothing work related on Saturdays — unless it's an emergency."

"And three dead girls don't fall under that category?"

I hated myself for needing to be reminded. What's more, we needed to discuss the other case.

"How about we meet up for lunch?"

"Sounds good. Where were you thinking?"

"How about I call you back in a bit."

"Okay. Talk to you soon."

I returned the phone to its dock, and turned off the alarm to avoid another round of assault. In one quick motion, I ripped off the covers and hopped out, tensing in the cold air as I made my way to the bathroom.

I turned on the light and looked at myself in the mirror. My long brown hair was a matted mess, and my skin appeared paler than usual, highlighting the dark circles under my eyes.

"You look like shit," I told the reflection. She nodded.

My hand didn't look much better. Even though I'd iced it the night before, the bruises were large and angry looking: purple with various shades of red marbling up and down my fingers, stretching all the way to my wrist.

After I finished my shower, and bandaged my hand, I opened the drapes of the bedroom window. It looked like it was going to be a clear, sunny day… hopefully minus the heat. I stood there for a moment rethinking what I would be doing for the first part of the day, pushing out the rest to make room in my head.

I walked to the bureau and looked at my reflection in the mirror above it. I still looked like shit, I decided. The reflection once again nodded in agreement as I picked up a brush to comb the tangles from my damp hair.

***

Twenty-three years ago.

I was fourteen when I left, taking the train by myself to Rhode Island to live with my now-deceased aunt and uncle. I remember watching the snow-covered trees, fields, and houses, passing at eighty miles an hour, although, to me, it felt like it was closer to ten. I couldn't get away fast enough, and I couldn't wait until I was out of the reach of New York City—and all that it entailed.

Unfortunately, that never happened. After I became a forensic psychiatrist, I often came back at the request of Marcus—and eventually moved to New Jersey permanently. To this day, however, I made sure to keep as much distance between New York City and I as possible... except on Saturdays. Here, I was going in the wrong direction, almost back to where I swore I'd never return.

I was driving over the Brooklyn Bridge when the weight in my stomach appeared again. As always, I was slowly drawn back in as I watched my life rewind before my eyes.

What I wouldn't give for a pause button right now.

Half an hour later, I arrived at my destination, parking along the street not too far away. Soon, I was standing at the property's edge. I tried to urge my legs forward, but it was like coaxing a stubborn ass when he'd had enough. After closing my eyes and taking a deep, cleansing breath, I was finally able to force my iron legs to move toward the gates of Holy Cross Cemetery. When I passed through them, it was as if I were magically fourteen again. The only thing missing was the light dust of snow on the ground.

The ninety-six acres were serene and beautiful, filled with various types of greenery. I was able to pick out at least three types of trees, but the one that stood out the most was the Kwanzan cherry. In the spring it bloomed with pink flowers that closely resembled carnations. Now, in the fall, it grew rich golden leaves that grabbed my attention.

Without giving thought to anything else but her, I was pulled automatically to where she lay. In front of her grave, I went down on my knees, resting my bottom on my heels and my hands in my lap.

"No matter how many times I come to see you, I don't seem to get any better at this," I began, before glancing around to see if anyone else was nearby. "You know, to this day I still wish I would have followed you. Permanently escaped. Things aren't getting any better," I confessed, letting a laugh escape. "My own fault for not staying away, I suppose."

I felt like such a hypocrite. I'd given up my faith long ago, but there I was, in a Catholic cemetery, talking to the dead. I tried to change my thought process, reminding myself that, the day she died, a piece of her remained with me. In a way, she was in fact there. I truly believed that—a part of her was always with me.

Then suddenly the events of that night flooded back in such an unexpected rush that it almost knocked me to the ground. Before my eyes, I saw her tiny body swaying where she hung, her stare bloodshot and blank... her hands twitching the last twitches of death.

I quickly stood up to get a firm grasp on my surroundings. Fight-or-flight mode started to kick in, and I fought... I knew I had to stay. What good was I if I couldn't even follow the advice I gave my clients? "Face it, dead on," I said, forcing myself, to kneel back down where I was—her image vanishing as quickly as it had appeared.

"Oh, Anna, I'm so sorry. I was the older sister. It was my job to protect you, and I failed," I confessed, as the guilt ripened again inside my chest. "The weird thing is, I can actually hear your voice telling me it's all right—that you forgive me, and I should let it go. That's who you were. But I can't give myself permission... I'm not you, though I wish I were... I honestly need to be anyone but me right now."

The wind rustled the leaves as it made its way across the ground. I'm not even close to believing in the supernatural, but I was forced to admit, the wind's timing was impeccable. After a few moments had passed, I felt it was time to take my leave.

"I'm going to go now," I said. "But I'll come back to see you next Saturday. I promise." And then I got up, wiping the debris from my pant legs.

As I walked back, I ignored the grave site just a few headstones away.

CHAPTER NINE

THE MASK

AT NOON, I arrived at Andros Diner, located in the Dumbo neighborhood of Brooklyn, suspecting Marcus wouldn't be too far behind me. It offered good food, reasonable prices and a "family friendly" atmosphere. And in my youth, I could personally attest to that being true. Now, I just hoped it hadn't changed.

After walking in, I noticed the booth Anna and I used to take was free, and I immediately took it.

A rush of warmth flowed through me as I remembered the few precious moments we actually shared as children. Happily seated in the red-vinyl booth, I removed my coat and took a quick look around. I was taken back in time; the place was exactly how I remembered it.

"Grandma" was still behind the counter, speaking in the heavy Greek accent she somehow never lost, loud but always friendly. The owner's daughter, Alex, was now waitressing. A few minutes later, she arrived at my table.

"First time here?" she asked, handing me a menu and placing a glass of water in front of me.

Alex magically transformed from a scrawny little girl to a Greek goddess. Her wavy black hair reached halfway down her back, and she was tall, slender and delicate.

"No, but it's been a while."

She took a moment to study my face. "Isabella? Noooo…"

"In the flesh."

She placed her hands on her hips, contorting her face as she tried to remember. "But it's been what… how long has it been?"

"About twenty-three years," I said.

"Never thought I'd see you again. Shocked really, after every-thing—"

I cut her off, not wanting her to finish her thought. "I was in the area and decided to stop by. It's amazing nothing has changed."

"I keep trying to get them to update the place, but you know Grandma—old school. I'm so glad you came by! How long are you here for?"

"I'm over in Jersey now, so I guess you can say it's permanent."

"I had no idea. I really thought you'd have stayed away after you left. Anyway, we definitely have to catch up," Alex said with a smile, "but for now, what would you like to order?"

"I'll take a latte. I'm meeting with a colleague in a bit, so I'll order the rest then."

"Sounds good. I'll be back in a sec."

I was thankful for the short interaction and that it didn't resume when she brought me my coffee, as she had other customers to serve. Even though I'd known Alex since childhood, not only from the diner but also from school, the need for friendly chitchat was never on my list of priorities.

Human contact always made me nervous—even the simplest of interactions. If it's encouraged, they always seemed to have questions... but even the most innocent of "small talk" questions are tough on me, for many reasons. Firstly, I don't like talking about myself unless it's work related. Then there's the big one: putting on the proper mask. It's not always easy to do on a whim. When you factor in the questions I don't have the answers to, and the ones I simply don't *want* to answer, there aren't a whole lot left.

Like a chameleon, I mimic the atmosphere I find myself in. Happiness, sadness, frustration, excitement—it doesn't matter. I have a mask for it all. However, from time to time, the emotions refuse to engage when summoned, which can produce very awkward moments. To avoid this, I try to avoid the situations whenever possible, keeping only a couple of people close to me.

I counted more than a dozen people scattered about, which I'd say was normal for the time of the day. The place itself wasn't meant to be anything fancy, though Alex was right: it probably could have used a bit of fixing up.

The bluish gray paint pealed from the walls in the places the grease spots hadn't touched. My guess was that the pictures covered the worst of it. The furniture had seen better days as well. Everything felt confined, crammed into a small space. Still, if Grandma were trying to maintain that old-time feeling, she was definitely succeeding... well, except for the flat screen TV in the corner.

"Why is it every time I see you, you look like you're anywhere but where you are?"

My smile was just another mask.

"It's called daydreaming, something I'm accused of often."

"Then stop doing it," he said as he smiled back, sitting down across from me. "So this is your choice of a meeting place?"

"Don't disrespect this diner," I warned. "Sorry if it's not up to your standards."

"No, no, it's… perfectly fine," he said, sarcasm exuding from his voice.

"Childhood favorite. Get used to it. Anyway, how's your morning been?"

"Busy, got a few things ticked off on my to-do list at home. You?"

"Usual Saturday."

Before we got the chance to go any further, Alex was at our table with a glass of water and a menu for Marcus. She didn't waste any time.

"So Isabella, who's your friend?" she asked, unable to take her eyes off him.

"Alex, this is my *colleague*… Marcus," I finally replied.

"Nice to meet you, Alex," he said, that mischievous smile making its appearance.

"Is there anything I can get you?"

I couldn't tell if she meant from the menu or anything in general.

"Just a coffee to start, sweetheart. Thanks." And she pranced away to fulfill his request.

"You definitely made her day," I said, once she was out of hearing range. "You're incorrigible."

"What?" he asked innocently, but he knew exactly what I was referring to.

"Pretty young things have always been your weakness."

"And a great weakness it is!"

I stared him down until Alex brought his coffee.

"Can I get you guys anything else?" she asked, looking directly at Marcus as he eyed her from head to toe.

"That's it for now, thanks. I'll let you know when we're ready to order," I told her, unable to miss the smile disappearing from her face as she was forced to leave. Marcus shook his head in disappointment.

"What?" I asked.

"That wasn't very nice of you, sending the poor girl away like that."

"Won't exactly get any work done if you're distracted, now will we?"

"Fair enough. Now, seeing this is a working lunch, any recommendations?"

"I used to get the prosciutto with fresh basil and mozzarella in a wrap, choice of sides. Still on the menu... I'm sure Alex could happily tell you about it," I teased.

"If I didn't know you any better, I'd say you were jealous. But because I do..."

He stopped, suddenly changing direction—

"Anyway, sounds good. I'll have whatever you're having."

"So, where to start?" I asked.

"Before that, I'd like to know what happened." He nodded toward my bandaged right hand.

"I was working with the dummy last night and hit it the wrong way."

He leaned forward. "I've known you for how long now?"

"Since I was fourteen."

"And you've been into kickboxing for at least half that time, probably could even kick my ass if my guard was down."

45

"If your guard was down? Sure. I'll let you believe that," I said with a grin.

"Mm-hmm…"

"So what's your point? I hit hard. That makes it more likely to injure my hands."

"Fine… So what did you learn from Melanie yesterday?"

I hated the fact that Marcus knew me the way he did—that even to this day I couldn't keep things from him.

"I arrived just as she was finishing up with the first girl… they match, Marcus."

"The three girls? I kind of suspected that."

"I didn't stay for all three. It would have been pointless. We both agreed the results would be the same."

He gave me a confused look. "I'm not following."

"The three girls, the file you gave me—they match."

He sat there quietly for a moment, taking in the words. "You're talking about the physical aspects?"

"Yes."

"Shit."

"That's one way to put it."

"But the staging, Ember being alive… that's completely different."

"Agreed, but things can change slightly and still be the same. Besides, who's to say what would have happened to Ember if she hadn't said anything."

"Okay… I don't want you working this."

"Don't you dare!" I said. "You wanted me on this *because* you had your suspicions. You knew I was the right person to work it."

He shook his head. "That's when I thought it was one girl, not four. Things have changed. The idea that they could be possibly linked... well, it doesn't sit well with me."

"Right now it's a theory, nothing more."

"And last night?" he asked.

I let a sigh escape. "That was my way of working things out. Don't read too much into it."

"Isabella—"

"—I'm serious, Marcus. You're probably the only person on this entire planet who knows who I really am. If I didn't think I could handle it, I'd walk away. You know that."

"Okay, let's say I agree to keep you on this. What first? You usually begin with the victim, don't you?"

"Survivor," I corrected. "And yes I do. I find them to be a good base to build upon. If you start with the perpetrators, it's usually a huge wall to crack through before getting anything productive."

He placed his elbows on the table, his chin in the palm of his hands. "Yeah, yeah. I know. When would you like to meet with her?"

"Tomorrow, if possible. I'll give myself some time to process it, and then I'll use the week for the remaining interviews."

"All right. I'll see if I can set it up with the aunt and uncle."

"I'll also need to speak to the original officer and the detective to see if their views differ. Too hard to tell on paper. Facial expressions, body reactions, tone of voice are what I need. You can't hide as well within those parameters."

"I'll set up a time for you to meet with Officer Anderson. The new detective, Matthews, you already know."

"Sounds good."

I motioned for Alex, and she quickly appeared. I placed our orders and also asked for another latte and a coffee refill for Marcus. When she was off again, we got into our work, making an outline to help us navigate the mess we were about to dive into.

CHAPTER TEN

EMBER

ONCE I GOT the okay from Marcus to meet with Ember O'Reilly, I headed out to fight with my fellow, Sunday afternoon commuters. He had offered to come with me, as he'd met with Ember, her aunt and her uncle several times, but I declined. It wasn't that I wanted them to be uncomfortable, I just didn't want them to have someone familiar to lean on. I think Marcus understood. I also told him I'd let him know if I'd be up to debrief him later that evening. By now he should have known that debriefing wasn't my style—yet, still, he tried.

My drive took me to the historic Sunnyside Gardens in Queens. I turned onto Skillman Avenue and found the house I was looking for: a two-story brownstone, halfway down and on the left. I parked a block away, and made my way back.

When I arrived, I was surprised to find a man sitting on the front steps, seemingly waiting for me. I hadn't noticed him when I first drove by. He stood up as I approached.

"Dr. Porter?" he asked.

"Please, call me Isabella," I replied, taking his extended hand in mine. "Mr. Donnelly?"

"'Dale' will be fine as well. If you don't mind, we'll begin this up there" he said, pointing to the window-enclosed porch.

"Wherever you want is fine."

I followed him up the steps, and into a small area which led us to the main door of the house… for now, that door would remain shut, as he indicated that I should take a seat at a small wooden table in the far corner. I understood why the porch had been renovated from a standard landing to an enclosed sunroom, and it was beautifully done—but if it weren't for the windows, I could see it quickly becoming a claustrophobic situation for me.

"It's unfortunate we have to meet under such dismal circumstances," Dale started, looking at the floor and playing with his fingers.

"Regrettably this is how I meet most of my clients. But we won't dwell on that. We'll see what I can do to help going forward."

He offered a weak smile. I could tell this was hard for him. He'd gone through it a few times already, but that didn't make it easier. From his thinning gray hair, I judged him to be in his mid to late forties. He looked at me with his tired, kind eyes, and I couldn't help but don the mask of empathy—one of the hardest masks to fit into.

"We'll start off slow and see how it goes from there. Does that sound okay, Dale?"

Early on in my career, I got into the habit of asking permission. I felt it gave a sense of empowerment to the person I was talking to. Ironically, I was met with less resistance in the end.

"Yes… thank you."

"So you're Ember's uncle. Is that by marriage or blood?"

"Her mother is my sister, Katherine," he started. He seemed calm at first, but suddenly, his demeanor shifted. "I told my sister to stay away from that family! They were no good. But she wouldn't listen to me—"

"Dale, I don't mean to cut you off, but the last thing we want to do is inject too much emotion in the beginning. Remember? Slowly…"

"I'm sorry. Just thinking about what that poor girl endured—you have to understand."

"I absolutely do, but things go easier if we have room to build. Still, your anger toward the situation, the people involved, is completely natural. Ember is lucky to have you and your wife."

"Bonnie and I would do anything for her. We'll be here as long as she needs us."

His statement reminded me of my own aunt and uncle. I could tell it was genuine.

"Is your wife here today?" I asked.

"She's visiting with her family. I stayed behind for Ember."

"Eventually, I'd like to meet her."

"I'll make sure she's here the next time you come," he said.

"Thank you. Now, it's my understanding that she's been with you since it first came out?"

"Yes. We were the only family she had left."

"Can you tell me how she's been since she arrived?" I asked. "Her temperament in general?"

"Quiet… distant, I would say. But she's always been a quiet child, and now we understand why."

"Her sleeping and eating habits, school… have they been affected?"

"She's been out of school for a couple of weeks. We thought it best for the time being, especially since she's out of the district," he explained. "Her appetite is almost nonexistent, and she has problems sleeping. Since day one, Bonnie has stayed with Ember during the night. The nightmares…"

"Nightmares?"

"She either falls asleep and is woken up by these terrible nightmares, or she's too afraid to try to sleep at all," he explained.

Night terrors.

"Does she remember them? Meaning, after she wakes?"

"Usually not, no."

"Okay, now we're going to get into a bit more if that's okay."

"Y-yes."

"You obviously know what happened to her?"

"I do."

"Who first told you?"

"I received a call one evening, a couple of weeks ago, from my sister. She said Ember was making up some stories, and she had to leave the house. She wouldn't go into any details, even when I pushed her for an explanation. It wasn't until the social worker brought Ember over, that I got the whole story."

"And has Ember herself spoken about it to either you or your wife?"

I was trying to gauge in advance how receptive she might be.

He shook his head. "No. From what I know, she hasn't said anything since she spoke to the police officer. She barely said anything to the detective. Bonnie and I try ourselves sometimes, to get her to talk about it, but we don't want to push her."

"You're doing it exactly right," I confirmed. "Does she know I'm here today?"

"She does."

"And the reason for my visit?"

"Not exactly…"

His response was precisely what I was afraid of.

"Is there a reason you didn't tell her?"

"Look, she's been through a lot in her short life—things I couldn't even imagine on my own, without someone telling me first." Getting defensive… "I don't want to put any additional stress on her."

"It's okay, Dale. Like with you, I'll start slowly and monitor her reaction. It's all in the approach, and I've done this countless times. But if I see that it's affecting her too much, I'll handle it appropriately and stop."

Dale sighed. "I don't know how you do it. I can't imagine doing what you have to do: hearing about these horrible things."

I gave him a reassuring smile. "It's unfortunate that this job has to exist, but I'm glad I'm here to do it."

"Do you deal with all victims or just children… if I may ask?"

He needed assurance as to my abilities.

"My specialty is with children. They're the only cases I handle." Little did he know how much of a specialty it really was.

"Okay. If it's the way it has to be, please, do what you can to help her."

CHAPTER ELEVEN

THE STORYTELLERS

DALE TOLD ME that he would allow the interview to take place in Ember's room because it was where she was the most comfortable… and because she didn't leave it much.

We stepped through the porch door, and into an expansive living room, dining room, and an open-concept kitchen. It didn't look nearly so large from outside.

"Ember's room is the one at the end of the hall," Dale told me as we reached to top of the stairs.

I asked if he'd go in with me, but he felt it best I go alone.

When I arrived at her door, it was closed. I knocked softly.

"Come in," a nearly inaudible voice said.

I gently opened the door and peered inside. It was a medium-size room with the same hardwood floors as the rest of the house. In place of a window, French doors draped with sheer curtains opened to a terrace. There was a single bed along one wall and a dresser against another. The La-Z-Boy recliner placed in the far corner was where I suspected Bonnie had been spending her nights. The walls, painted a soft white, had a few pictures hanging on them that didn't reflect Ember's age. Aside from books and a couple of dolls, there were no signs of personalization in the room.

Ember lay on the bed, book in her hands, looking up at me.

"Hello, Ember. I'm Isabella. Would it be okay if I came in for a while?"

She nodded, and I slowly walked in and took a seat in the recliner, the furthest possible seat from her. I took another quick look around before looking back at her: her head was now lowered; back to reading her book as if I weren't even there. It gave me the opportunity to observe her for a moment without making her uncomfortable.

She had medium-length light-brown hair and hazel eyes that resembled mine in both color and shape—almost identically. I also noticed a kindred spirit of sorts reflecting back, as if I were looking in a mirror. Ember looked very young for eleven. She wore jeans and a plain amethyst-colored T-shirt, and as it was sleeveless, it revealed the marks and scars noted in her medical report.

The knot was forming again; I forced it back into submission.

"You're a doctor, right?" she asked in her tiny voice.

"Yes, I am."

She looked confused.

"But I'm not sick."

"Oh, I can see that. I'm also not exactly that kind of doctor. Do you know what a psychiatrist is?"

She shook her head.

"Well, even though I have my medical license to be a doctor—like the one you're thinking of—I also have a degree in psychiatry. This type of doctor works with the mind part of a person," I said. "I also have some legal training, so I work in the courts, mostly with people like you." The look of confusion only set itself in deeper. I have to remind myself sometimes that I work with children and not always older teens and adults. "A little confusing, huh?"

"A little bit, yes," she said with a giggle. A good sign.

"Well, when an attorney or a policeman needs help with evaluations or testimonies, they call me."

"So Marcus called you?" she said, finally giving me her full attention.

"Yes. He feels I can help in the court case that's ahead of you." With the mention of that, her face took a downward turn. "Ember, I'm not here to make you do or say anything you don't want to, or make you feel uncomfortable in any way. Just remember that I'm here to help, and I'm going to make sure that what we talk about is okay with you first. You're in control here, not me."

That seemed to help. Her body and face noticeably began to relax. Sometimes, my inability to deal with human interactions even bled into my work environment. I decided I needed to add a bit of humanity to make this work with her.

From the corner of my eye, I noticed a shadow cast in the hallway. Dale.

"So you've been living with your aunt and uncle for a couple of weeks now. How's that going?"

"I really like being here. They're really nice to me."

"I'm happy to hear that, Ember. Things weren't so nice before were they?"

I waited for her reaction and saw nothing that set off warning bells. She simply shook her head. I decided to push a little further.

"Those marks I see on your arms... may I ask where they come from?"

"My aunt and uncle would never hurt me!" she said quickly.

Her defenses were going up; she grabbed the sweater that lay at the edge of the bed and started to put it on to conceal what I'd just pointed out. I knew exactly what she was doing.

"Really, it's not necessary to cover them up. I believe you. Earlier I spoke to your uncle Dale and found him to be a very nice man." I decided to take a different approach. "Would it be okay if I came a little closer so I can show you something?"

Ember hesitantly stopped what she was doing and nodded. Very slowly, I got up, keeping the same pace as I walked toward her bed. Soon, I was kneeling on the floor, raising one of the sleeves of my sweater.

"These are mine, and I think I got them in the same way that you did." I was showing her the various scars that ran up my arm, all the while knowing, it was only under these special circumstances that I would ever do so.

She dropped the sweater and cautiously moved off the bed to finally kneel in front of me. With a trembling hand, she ran her fingers over the various marks. Some were thin and flat against my skin; others were large, protruding... angry.

"We match," she said, again in that nearly inaudible voice. She seemed almost mesmerized, unable to take her eyes off what she was seeing.

"Yes, we do, Ember. It also means I understand," I explained. I half expected her to go back to the safety of her bed, but she remained where she was, continuing to explore the road map on my arm. "Did you know scars have stories to tell?"

"Really?" she asked, disbelief in her voice. She finally raised her head to look into my eyes.

"Mm-hmm. If we listen very carefully, we can hear them. Would you like to listen?"

Hesitantly nodding yes, she placed her hand over mine, matching her small fingers to my larger ones. Together, we allowed them to run over the ones on her own arm.

Some appeared to be as old as she was, but then there were others that had only just started to heal. Everything was as reported. We sat in silence until Ember asked the question I knew she would.

"What are they telling you?"

"That you've been hurt, very badly but through no fault of your own. They're also asking for your help in finishing. You see, they're very young and inexperienced. You're stronger than they are right now. They know you can help them."

"I don't know if I can…" she said, cautiously rubbing her arm and shivering.

"We'll start very slowly and stop any time you want or need to. It's absolutely in your control," I reminded her.

She again nodded.

This was why I showed my scars to these children—children who'd been branded like I was: to show them that they weren't alone, that someone out there understood the pain they'd endured—and continued to endure. It helped them open up more easily.

However, it wasn't foolproof, and still had to be taken step by step. At this point, Ember let go of my hand and returned to her bed, though she surprised me when she patted the space in front of her, motioning for me to join her. I sat across from her, not saying a word, waiting until she was ready to begin.

"It started with my dad when I was really little," she began. "At first he used to just hit me, really hard for no real reason. But then it turned to more."

"Can you tell me what the 'more' is?"

"He would… ask me to touch him… in places I shouldn't be touching."

"And how did you know that?" I gently asked.

"At first it just felt wrong, you know, like it was something I shouldn't be doing. But later in school, they told us it was something bad."

"Did he ever touch you?" With that question, a single tear made its way down her cheek then quickly multiplied. "It's okay. Take as much time as you need, Ember."

She waited a few minutes before continuing. "Yes, he touched me. And then the rest started."

"What do you mean by 'the rest?'"

"My uncles, other relatives, my stepbrother… they all did the same things to me, sometimes all together."

"That's-" I paused. "Keep going as long as you can. You're doing so well."

CHAPTER TWELVE

THE BRANDING

ABOUT AN HOUR LATER, I left Ember's room, but not before she made me promise to come see her again. Making my way downstairs, I was surprised not to come across Dale. I found him on the porch with a look of shock on his face. He didn't so much as breath as a took the seat across from him.

"How much did you hear?" I asked, finally breaking the silence.

"I had to leave when Ember was halfway through. I couldn't listen to it anymore," he said, hunched over, with his elbows propped on his knees, staring at the floor. "I was originally given the PG version of what happened..."

"It's always harder to hear it firsthand, from the one who's been abused. Can I ask you something?"

"Of course," he said, now looking at me.

"Do you plan on going to the court appearances with Ember?"

"Absolutely. Bonnie and I both do." He sounded as though I'd insulted him.

"Then can I offer a piece of advice?"

"Anything that'll make this easier."

"To be as supportive as possible, and to avoid the risk of walking out of the courtroom during testimony, I suggest you get accustomed to what's going to be discussed. I'm in no way saying you should accept it, but you'll need to get used to it. It'll be repeated many times by many different people."

Dale nodded and looked me straight in the eyes. "That's why you're an expert. It's not solely because of education or work experience but actual life experience."

Life experience... it happened so long ago, yet the simplest of things could bring it back to the present in a second: a sound, a smell... even talking about it the way we were now, I could feel the tingling on the surface of my skin begin to awaken.

"Dale, please don't take this the wrong way, but I'd rather not."

"You already did. With Ember."

"To an extent, because I know from experience that if a trauma survivor knows I went through something similar, it helps them talk. It shows them I understand the hell they're going through. They'll get no judgment from me."

"You said 'survivor...'"

"If you treat or refer to Ember as a victim, that's how she'll perceive herself. She is, in fact, a survivor."

"The scars telling their story... where did you come up with that?"

He sounded genuinely curious.

"I didn't come up with anything—most scars will tell their story. You just have to give them a chance to."

"Most? Why not all?"

I couldn't get into it with him right then, so instead, I said the only thing I could think of that would satiate his curiosity.

"Ember's still young, and hers are speaking. She'll get the help she needs, and she'll get through this."

"How can you know for sure?"

Dale's eyes were pleading with me now.

"Like you said, actual life experience."

I really needed to get out of this house. I saw a lot of Anna in Ember, which was making it difficult not to make this personal. The voices were screaming at me, making it harder for me to think straight, and the last thing I wanted was for Dale to notice how much this was affecting me. I confirmed a second appointment, asking if Bonnie could attend the next session, then made my leave.

As I walked down the street toward my car, I finally admitted to myself: *this is going to be a lot harder than I thought.*

***

At home, I needed to get my thoughts in order; the knot in my stomach was rising to my chest, threatening to crush me from the inside. I needed to silence the intensifying whispers. I was lost.

After locking up and ensuring everything was, as always, secure, I called Marcus.

"Izzy. I was wondering when I would hear from you."

"Sorry. Got a bit distracted. Listen, I don't think I'll be able to meet up with you tonight."

"Okay… is everything alright?"

"Everything's fine. I just want to get my report started while it's still fresh in my mind," I lied.

"I can understand that. If you need anything, let me know."

"Thanks. I'll come by to see you tomorrow."

I turned off my cell phone, and pulled the plug on the landline.

Walking to the bathroom, I started to shed my clothes, letting each piece fall to the floor as I went. By the time I stood in front of the mirror, I was naked.

Ember not only made me think of Anna, but also of myself. With my head slightly cocked to the side, I examined the reflection thrown back at me. What I had showed Ember earlier was but a quarter of what I could have... and I knew it was the same for her.

Then there were the three girls in the morgue, sharing in our branding of sorts. The only difference between them and us, was that they didn't survive.

"Branding," I said out loud, becoming suddenly fixated on my inner left wrist.

It had faded with the passing years, but I still felt it when I ran my fingers across it. It was something that could easily be missed—hidden by other markings or bruises, nearly impossible to detect if you weren't looking for it in the first place. But even though it was small, one could still make out the words, if they knew what they were looking for.

And I did.

"*Enim aeternitas tibi pertinent ad mihi*" formed in the shape of the infinity symbol. It was in Latin, but I knew what it roughly translated to.

For eternity, you belong to me.

CHAPTER THIRTEEN

SAVE THE FAMILY

LAST NIGHT'S RITUAL once more silenced the whispers, and opened me up to the task at hand. I decided to start the report for the case, taking some information from the notes on yesterday's meeting with Ember and Dale, but taking most of it from my memory: Ember's branded body, what the scars had told me, whom it reminded me of… I tried very hard not to make it personal. But honestly, it was becoming increasingly difficult to separate this case from my own experiences.

My cell phone went off for the fifth time since I'd turned it back on. This time, I decided to take the call.

"Marcus, what's so important that you had to call—"

He didn't give me the chance to finish. "Meet me at Mount Sinai Hospital in Queens."

"What's going on?"

"It's Ember. I'm already here. Come now."

"On my way."

I ended the call rushed and panicked like I hadn't been in years. As I said, it was becoming increasingly difficult to separate the two the deeper I dove in.

***

I had just parked my car at the hospital when I spotted her. Was she trying to escape?

"Ember!" I called out, scrambling to my feet, but I wasn't close enough for her to hear me. I started to run, trying hard not to fall in my heels. When I was closer, I called out to her again.

She stopped dead, her hospital gown blowing in the breeze, waiting until I closed the gap between us.

Taking off my coat and wrapping it around her, I brought her toward my body to warm her up more quickly; it seemed the weather was finally matching the season.

"What are you doing out here?"

"They're coming," she said, looking toward the hospital entrance, immediately starting to cry. "The nurse told me they were coming. I had to leave before they got here."

"Who was coming?"

"My mom... and dad. I didn't do what they asked properly," she said through labored breaths. "They'll be angry."

"You can tell me everything once I get you back inside." I led her toward the entrance without resistance, but her eyes screamed betrayal.

Once inside, I sat her down on a couch in the reception area. Taking the seat beside her, I pulled her close to me, this time noticing the bandages on her wrists.

"What exactly did your parents ask you to do?"

"My mom called Uncle Dale last night. She wanted to talk to me," she started. "It was the first time she'd called since I first told, so I took it. When I got on the phone, she told me how disappointed they all were in me... she said I had to end it."

"How?" I pushed, but the answer was obvious.

"She told me I had to disappear. She said I couldn't be here to do this to *her* family."

"Tell me how, Ember."

"I had to wait until my aunt and uncle were asleep. I was supposed to search the house for something... I can't remember the name of it," she squeaked. "But once I found it, I couldn't do it. It tasted so bad... so I... there was another way. I took a knife from the kitchen drawer—
"

"It's okay... You don't have to go any further. I understand," I said into her hair, squeezing her harder. "You're safe now and will be from now on. I promise."

I looked up to see the figure of a strong black man getting off the elevator, making his way toward us.

"Where were you?" I shouted at Marcus, when he was within ear-shot.

"I know. I'm sorry. She waited until I was in the bathroom to sneak out. I was here."

"No... it's... it's fine, I've got her."

Is she okay?"

"She will be now. We have to get her back to her room, and get one of your officers here."

"What—"

"Now, Marcus," I said, then got Ember to her feet and headed toward the bank of elevators.

Marcus was a step behind us, already on his cell phone to fulfill my request.

***

"I see… none of us had any idea her mother drove her to do it," Marcus explained outside Ember's room once we'd gotten her back into bed. "She hadn't said a word to anyone since it happened last night."

"Why wasn't I contacted?" I asked angrily.

The anger wasn't directed at him but myself. If I hadn't needed to quiet the whispers, I could have met up with Marcus last night.

"I tried, Izzy, multiple times, but you didn't answer."

"I didn't…" I pulled out my cell phone and noticed not only the missed calls from today but last night as well. He did try. "I'm sorry, Marcus. I shouldn't be taking this out on you."

"It's okay. You're here now. There was nothing you could have done to prevent this."

"I know, but still… When will the officer arrive?"

"Shouldn't be long. I was told by NYPD there was a cruiser in the vicinity."

He spoke to me, but he stared off into the distance.

"What are you looking at?" I asked, but a turn of the head made the question unnecessary.

Ember apparently took after her mother's side of the family; she was a spitting image of her. Mrs. O'Reilly was now headed toward us, no doubt after receiving directions from the nurses' station.

"I want to see my daughter," she said angrily, trying to force her way past Marcus.

I had to stifle a laugh that was trying to escape. She was a mouse of a person, and the fact that she thought she could actually get past him amused me. Thin and frail looking, Katherine O'Reilly had an air that screamed confidence, though it didn't seem to fit her physical appearance. In her early forties, she dressed in what was current and expensive. It didn't seem like she wanted for anything.

"Mrs. O'Reilly, I'm afraid that isn't possible right now," he informed her, holding her back by the shoulders.

"She tries to kill herself, and you won't let me see her? I don't think so!" she said, again trying to get past him.

"Mrs. O'Reilly—" I began. "I'm Dr. Porter, the psychiatrist assigned to your daughter's case."

"I don't care who you are," she spat back. "Who the hell are you to tell me I can't see her? Any of you?"

"After what she disclosed to me, there's a lot more we could be doing right now," I replied, fighting to gain control of my racing thoughts.

"Oh, yeah?" She was now standing within inches of me, face-to-face, causing the tiny hairs on the back of my neck to go on high alert. "What tale did my little angel tell now?"

Marcus stood between us just in time. I wasn't sure how much longer I was going to be able to hold back.

"Mrs. O'Reilly, why don't you go with Dr. Porter into one of the quiet rooms? She can explain further there. As of right now, no one is entering this room."

She opened her mouth as if to say something, but suddenly changed her tune.

"Fine, but this isn't over," she said, and walked off.

"It definitely isn't," I agreed under my breath, noticing a police officer, flanked by hospital security, down the right hall—likely the reason she suddenly became so compliant. "Do you have a pen and legal pad in your bag? I want to record what she says."

"Good luck," he said, fishing them out and handing them over. "If you need anything, we'll be right here."

"Thank you."

I caught up with Mrs. O'Reilly and directed her to the quiet room.

CHAPTER FOURTEEN

GHOSTS OUTSIDE THE WINDOW

AS I SAT on one of the couches with the legal pad resting on my knees, I watched Mrs. O'Reilly pace back and forth, looking at the window each time she passed it. Was her husband, Michael O'Reilly, out there?

"You do realize this is all bullshit, don't you?" she finally said. "You're a shrink after all. You should be able to see right through all of it!"

"I'll be honest with you, Mrs. O'Reilly—"

"Katherine."

"Sure, Katherine. If it's all bullshit as you say it is, that's a pretty incredible pile for an eleven-year-old to come up with by herself, wouldn't you say?"

She shrugged. "She's always had an overactive imagination."

"And her imagination made the scars I saw?"

She was about to say something then stopped herself, her pacing becoming even faster. Something was holding her back… perhaps the thing she kept looking for outside the window.

"Why don't you take a seat, and I'll tell you what Ember told me when I first arrived?" I wasn't really expecting her to; pacing was a form of stress relief some individuals used, so I didn't wait before I continued. "She told me you called her last night."

She nodded.

"I did."

"Was that the first time you called since she came out with what was happening to her?"

"I told you that was bullshit," she fired back, now taking a seat on the opposite couch.

"Yes, you did, but I'm not here to discuss the validity of her claims right now, Katherine. I want to speak about last night specifically."

"Fine. Yes, it was the first time we'd spoken in weeks."

"And what did you talk about?"

"That's none of your business."

The whispers were getting louder. I put the pad down beside me, folded my arms across my knees, and leaned in toward her.

"Oh, but that's where you're wrong. She told me what the conversation was about, what you asked her to do—told her she *had* to do," I said, eerily calm. "So I'll ask again: what was the conversation about?"

"No! I told her she needed to stop this nonsense, that it was hurting the family."

"What else? The case is already in motion. How did you want her to stop?"

I practically heard her mind at work as it searched for a plausible answer, but I knew she wouldn't find one. She sat there twisting her fingers, looking everywhere but at me.

She couldn't look at me, but she could still look over her shoulder toward the window.

"I'm not scared of you," she said, finally.

"What are you scared of, Katherine? What scared you enough that you told your own daughter to kill herself?"

"Bullshit," she said through clenched teeth. "I'm done talking to you."

"All right, you're free to go," I said, motioning toward the door. "But let me make this perfectly clear. Last night was the last time you'll have any unsupervised contact with your daughter."

"You have no right to make that decision," she huffed. "She's my daughter."

"Oh, but I have the power to persuade the people who can... And before conveniently throwing around the daughter card, remember that you're the one who decided you weren't going to support *her*." I would have preferred strangling her with my bare hands... but I did feel a tinge of release.

"You'll regret this."

Katherine glared as she rose from her chair, but as she walked out the door, she didn't so much as look back.

"I highly doubt that," I told the empty room.

I threw the legal pad into the wall, and watched as it crumbled, landing on the floor, its pages sprawled.

I remembered the window. I walked over to it, leaned up against the wall, and waited. There was something out there. Now I just needed to see it too.

"Well, apparently you're the biggest bitch in the world." It was Marcus.

"Really? I thought I restrained myself quite well," I told him, keeping my focus outside the window. "And she's not to have unsupervised contact with Ember."

"Yeah, I think she mentioned that."

"Mm-hmm."

"Are you okay?"

"Yes."

"Then why aren't you looking at me?"

"Ember's mom never stopped looking out the window. I need to see what's out there."

"Her husband's probably outside. I was surprised, really, when you said they were both on their way, as he's already restricted from seeing Ember."

Then I saw it: Katherine exiting the building, a man walking up to her. Squinting to make out his features, I suddenly envisioned what it would feel like to run into a brick wall—headfirst. My body trembled, and the voices all spoke at once.

"No, it can't be…" I said under my breath, unable to fully believe what my eyes were showing me.

"Isabella?" There was concern in his voice.

"I'm sorry, Marcus, but I have to go," I replied as I walked past him, grabbing my coat and heading toward the door. "I'll call you later."

"Izzy, wait!"

But the door was already closing behind me.

***

My head was fracturing into a million pieces, and no matter what I did, I couldn't seem to bring the pieces back together. The voices were competing for dominance, talking over one another. Their message wasn't clear. Everything I knew—or rather thought I knew—no longer made sense. What I thought I saw couldn't be real. He was gone wasn't he? He had to be—I'd killed him.

I returned to Holy Cross Cemetery and made my way to the gravesite I'd purposely ignored when I'd gone to see Anna. Once I reached it, I stared at it, willing it to answer the questions that were seeping through the fractures my discovery had produced. I tried to concentrate so I could clearly read what was written on the headstone—

JONATHAN BALDACCI

1956-1993

LOVING HUSBAND AND FATHER

Well, there he was—where he had been for the last twenty-three years. It didn't matter that Ember's father looked like this man… right? You see it all the time: two totally unrelated people resembling each other; our appearances aren't as unique as our fingerprints. So it didn't mean they were the same person. Even more, I'd seen the man at a distance… it was too hard to be sure from that far away.

But what if I was wrong?

I was getting nowhere with this circular argument. *What if? What if?* … It wasn't helping. I had to get my thoughts straight before trying to tackle these questions. At that moment, I was completely useless.

I abandoned the gravesite for my car, deciding there was somewhere else I needed to visit.

CHAPTER FIFTEEN

THE HOUSE

IT WAS A LITTLE past three o'clock that afternoon in Brooklyn Heights, when I pulled onto the street I'd been avoiding for most of my life. However, there I was, willingly making my way up to the two-story house at the end of the cul-de-sac. A FOR SALE sign on the front lawn caught my attention. After parking my car off to the side, I came back to call the realtor listed.

I learned that, since our departure, only one other family had occupied the home; for the last few months, it had been on the market, with the current residents having to leave the country suddenly. After declining her assistance, several times, for the visit, I was given the passcode to the lockbox, 8733, permission to look around, and of course, to call her back if I had any questions.

As I approached the front door, the undeniable stench of regret surrounded me. The front porch was in extremely poor condition. The white paint had almost completely peeled off, and the boards creaked and bent with every step I took. The exterior of the house wasn't much better. The vibrant reddish-brown bricks had turned to a dull greenish-black in many spots. In its entirety, it was in a state of decay... which

I thought fit the house quite well. On so many levels, I dreaded what I would find inside. It took me minutes to punch the code into the lockbox and retrieve the key from it.

I soon stood frozen at the threshold, amazed at the fact that nothing—not a single thing—had changed. Sure, there were unknown pieces of furniture thrown about to make the place more appealing to a potential buyer, but the interior itself, aside from a coat of paint or two, was precisely as I remembered when I was a child. It was exactly as if I'd never left: even the familiar feeling of extreme discomfort picked up where it had last left off. I closed the door behind me and slowly moved out of the foyer and into the living room.

There were only two places I wanted to see—my bedroom and the basement. The rest of the house was simply part of the facade my parents had built, and meant nothing to me.

I headed upstairs and turned right toward the bedroom. The door was open and the blinds drawn up to let in the light of day. It differed from the main floor only in that it had no furniture, probably to exaggerate its size. Everything again was original except for the paint on the walls. Knees suddenly weak, I sat on the floor in the middle of the room, trying hard to keep the knot in its place.

I was about to get up when I noticed something in the far corner. On hands and knees, I made my way toward where my bed used to be. Bringing my face closer to the floor to get a better look, I realized what I was seeing, and with a trembling hand, I gently ran my fingers along the five lines that were etched in the wood. Then I looked at the nails on my left hand, many of which never grew in right again.

Hide! *the inner echo screamed, but it was already too late.*

I was plucked from my bed, carried out of my room, to be brought to his "office" in the basement. I couldn't catch my breath, and in fear of suffocating under his deadly grip, I fought with all that I had, and then I fell to the floor with a thud.

Hide now! *the echo screamed at me once more, and this time I attempted it.*

On hands and knees again, I crawled across the floor, to the closest possible refuge: beneath the bed. Though I could no longer see him, his taunting laughter followed me under, completely encasing me, bringing to the forefront the undeniable reality that there was no escape.

"Please..." I managed in a soft voice.

Soon after the word left my lips, a hand clenched around my ankle. I could feel my body being dragged.

Fight! *the echo commanded.*

I kicked at the hand with my free leg, but I knew I was only delaying the inevitable—actually making it worse, going on experience. But I still felt like I had to try. What would I be if I didn't try?

He finally got hold of my second ankle. With a tight grip on both my legs, he gave a strong, solid jerk, and I easily slid on my belly as he ripped me from beneath the bed.

I tried to stop him by clawing at the floor but only succeeded at tearing off portions of my fingernails, leaving a bloody trail as I went. With his final pull, my head hit the bottom of the wooden bed frame on my way out. I felt my skin tear, followed by a rush of warmth as blood oozed from the fresh wound through my hair, finally making its way along my neck. I actually heard as the drops hit the floor intermittently, forming a crimson puddle beside my head. He grabbed me by the arms and picked me up once more, but this time I was too weak to fight.

I came back to myself, confused, disoriented, and tenderly rubbing the scar on my scalp that was concealed by my hair. I hadn't even realized I'd made my way down there, following along with the flashback I was trapped in… his marionette even to this day. The basement was cold, damp and reeked of mildew. I noticed that it remained as it was, bricks still exposed and unfinished.

Once I regained some of my bearings, I noticed the basement was completely empty, with no traces whatsoever of what had transpired there long ago. This was his office, where he liked to carry out his "hobby." It was also where Anna had taken her life, choosing death rather than unwillingly participating one more time.

Once I was fully aware of my surroundings, I looked around and tried to remember where we'd hidden the box before her death. I recalled how angry he had been, as its contents once belonged to him, stolen one evening when I was confined down here. It was to be Anna's and my way out, hidden behind the loose bricks until the time was right.

That moment never arrived, as my life took a different course after she was gone. Now that so much time had passed, I wasn't sure which of the bricks once concealed it. For all I knew, it could have been repaired.

I searched around for a good half hour, pulling on bricks to no avail. I finally decided to leave for now; there was still time to find and retrieve it before the house was sold. I climbed the stairs to the main floor, determined to come back and search again.

Once outside, I retrieved my cell phone. Just my luck, I had 3 missed calls. Dialing the number, I knew what was coming and braced myself for it.

"Do you have any idea how worried I've been?" Marcus practically screamed.

"Marcus I—" But he didn't let me finish.

"For the first time in your life, just shut up and listen. Without a single word as to what was going through that head of yours, or the slightest indication where you were going, now I finally hear from you—hours later. We're partners in this. The two of us, Isabella. What if something had happened to Ember? I know you care about that little girl. You need to get your shit together!"

"Marcus, I'm sorry. I have a theory about Ember's case, but I wanted to check out a few things before I said anything," I told him quickly to avoid another blasting. "I'm still not certain, but can we meet up at your office to talk about it?"

"When?"

"Are you still at the hospital?"

"Yeah, stuck around to make sure the mother wouldn't be showing back up."

"And how is she? Ember, I mean."

"She's fine, and she'll be guarded, like we requested."

"Good. I'll head to the precinct now if that's okay."

"I'll see you there," he said, and then his voice lightened. "Oh, and Isabella, if you ever do that again, I'll kick your ass."

"And I'll let you do it, promise," I said, smiling.

"Wipe that smirk off your face."

And with that the call ended.

Looking again at the house, I suddenly felt nothing... as it should be. If I ever expected to find what I came for, I had to completely shut down.

And I would find it.

CHAPTER SIXTEEN

ALWAYS AT THE SURFACE

"LARGE COFFEE, BLACK," I said when I entered Marcus's office, extending the peace offering so that it was within reach.

"Have I told you just how much I love you?" he replied, taking the cup.

"Recently? No. But please, do go on."

"I was talking to the coffee…"

I let a laugh escape.

"Do the two of you need a moment alone?"

He pointed to a chair. "Now that I've got you here, sit down."

"Yes, Sir!" I gave a short salute before taking the seat across from him. "Please tell me I'm not in for another tongue-lashing."

"No, you're not, but you are going to tell me what the hell that was this morning."

On my drive over to the precinct, I was trying to think of what to say—how to explain something I didn't completely understand. Now here I was, still unsure what to tell him.

"Katherine O'Reilly really got to me, and I was disappointed in myself for that."

He held out his hands in exacerbation. "And? Don't hold back. You saw something out that window that freaked you out. What was it?"

"I don't get 'freaked out.' I was just surprised to see Ember's father. That's all."

"And that made you leave in such a rush? Disappear for hours without a word?"

"He reminded me of someone from a while ago, and it threw me off a little."

He raised an eyebrow. "A little? Isabella, it was like you saw an axe murderer."

"Okay, fine, it threw me off a lot," I admitted. "Can you help me with some research?"

"Nice change of subject… but yes, I can try. What do you need?"

"Any information you can find for Jonathan Baldacci. Born 1956, died 1993. Born and raised in Brooklyn. He was a defense attorney."

"I don't understand. Why do you need this?" he asked. "You don't need to know any more than the fact that he's dead. Oh, and what's this theory of yours?"

"Marcus, as much as I trust you, it's not something I want get into right now," I explained. "Now I'm asking you to put trust in me, maybe more trust…and I know it's not fair, but I promise you, I *will* tell you everything the moment I feel I'm ready."

"It's somehow tied to the O'Reilly case, isn't it?"

"Marcus…"

"Fine, when you're ready." He sighed in resignation. "When do you need it?"

"Yesterday?"

"Yeah, yeah… Have you eaten?"

"No, but I'm not that hungry. Maybe in a bit."

Did he hear the rumbling that just came from my stomach?

"Let me gather what you asked for and we'll go grab something. Give me a couple hours?"

"You've got it."

***

Marcus and I, deciding we'd traveled enough for the day, headed over to a deli across from the precinct. It wasn't Andros Diner, but it was still a nice place. We grabbed one of the tables next to the window, and after the waiter took our order, we sat in a kind of awkward silence, something that had rarely happened to us before. After trying unsuccessfully to get him to participate in small talk, which he knows I hate, I finally gave up.

"All right, out with it yourself!" I said, knowing something was brewing within that sharp mind of his, but he was still hesitant to speak. "Seriously, Marcus, what's wrong?"

"That information you had me look into… it brought a lot of things back up to the surface."

"Welcome to my world. It's almost always at the surface."

His face dropped. "I'm sorry, Izzy."

I allowed my body to relax. "Don't be. You're the one who helped me finally escape. Thank you."

He finally produced a smile. "That's probably the gazillionth 'thank you'… and you're welcome, but we both know I only played a part."

I remembered the day we first met as if it were yesterday. He was only twenty-seven years old, but even then, he had an aura about him that scared the shit out of me. Back then he was a wet-behind-the-ears detective: passionate, hopeful. I rather blamed myself for how he turned out: his tough exterior, his inability to allow anyone to get too close. He never married or had children. His work became his life. I couldn't help fear that, upon retrieving me from my neighbor's house, what he learned about my life had damaged him.

"Earth to Izzy! Hellooo… hey, welcome back."

"Sorry."

"It's fine. Now enough with this mushy stuff."

"Did anything else of interest pop up?"

"The one on top is the complete file I had on him and his wife. And after calling in a favor, I received the files for the cases he worked on up until his death." He pointed to a hefty stack of folders on the table.

"Have I told you how amazing you are?"

"Tell me again; these files weren't easy to get."

"Beyond amazing!" I said with a smile.

"I didn't say exaggerate." I thought I might have caught a smirk, but it was gone before I could be sure. "Are we now at the point where you expose your theory?"

"No… well, maybe."

"Izzy. If you can't trust me, you're alone in this."

"I don't like to be threatened."

"You know me. I wouldn't threaten you. That's just a fact."

I took a deep breath and began.

"After what I saw at the hospital, I went to two places. The first was Jonathan's grave site. The second was the house."

"Why in the world would you go back there?" he asked, shaking his head.

"There are just too many similarities, Marcus. But there's also something else I'll need to reconfirm with Mel to be able to connect the two cases."

"Okay, so what does that have to do with Jonathan? Why are you asking me to dig up his information?"

"Because to tell you the truth, after what I saw today, I'm not entirely certain what's buried under there anymore."

"I don't really understand, but I'll leave it be for now."

"Thank you, Marcus."

Our meals were just being served, so I grabbed the files from the table and stuck them in my bag. I'd read them once I got home.

"Are we still on for tomorrow?" I asked before taking a bite of my salad.

"Yep. First thing, nine o'clock sharp."

He gave me what he must have thought was a knowing look... but the funny thing was, I was actually looking forward to it.

CHAPTER SEVENTEEN

THE FALL

THAT NIGHT WAS SPENT mostly within one memory or another; perhaps it was my mind's way of trying to sort out my suspicions while I read the files Marcus had given me. Unfortunately, I never got the answers I was looking for, only more suspicions from Jonathan's client list. I would definitely have to explore different avenues.

Newly cleaned and dressed, as I reached for the bag under the entryway table, I noticed a folded piece of paper on the floor.

"Leave it alone before it's too late."

Whoever left this for me had no idea what they'd just done. For the first time in a long while, the voices were now banding together, speaking to me again in unison, and their message was clear.

***

Today, I met two of the accused in Ember's case, an uncle and the older brother. Unfortunately, I wouldn't be meeting the father until later in the week, and I was now regretting how I had scheduled the interviews. I couldn't get him out of my head.

I released a deep exhale before opening the precinct meeting room door. On the other side of the table sat a young man named Cody, Ember's sixteen-year-old stepbrother. At first glance, he appeared confident, his well-dressed, well-groomed body at relaxed attention, his hands folded on the table before him; upon closer inspection, however, a hint of nervousness was beginning to show itself. I took the seat across from him.

"Hi, Cody. My name is Isabella. Is it okay if we talk for a bit?"

"I thought I didn't have a choice."

"Well, you had to present yourself here because of the court order, yes," I said. "But I can't force you to talk, right?"

"I guess."

"We'll just start and see how it goes, okay?"

He shrugged. "Sure."

"Do you understand the reason you had to be here?"

"My sister has been telling you some things," he replied. He ruthlessly began to pick at a hangnail on his thumb. Stone-faced, he caused it to bleed.

"And is there any truth to what she's been telling?"

"Sort of…" He seemed unable to look me in the eye. His words and his manner caught me off guard.

"That's a little different from what you told the detective before, Cody."

"What she said I did to her… it's true."

He still couldn't look at me. Something wasn't right.

"What about the rest of it? The other people involved?"

He ran his hand through his thick brown hair. "I'm not sure why she'd say any of that. They had nothing to do with it. It was all me."

His answers reeked of rehearsal. He made the right movements, but his voice was robotic, void of any feeling or emotion, as if someone were speaking for him.

"So you were the only one," I repeated. "I'm having a hard time understanding, Cody. What was it that you did alone?"

"I already told you!" he said.

"No, you said that it was 'only me,'" I told him. "I need to know what you meant by that."

He just sat there, staring blankly back at me. Perhaps he hadn't expected that question, and was at a loss for words. When the picking of his torn skin began again, I handed him a tissue. Immediately he folded it and wrapped it around his thumb.

"Cody, what did you do to Ember?"

The air seemed to leave the room as a small prick of blood soaked through the tissue. He leaned in. "I took her. I raped her in every way a little girl can be raped. She liked it too—I could tell in the way she cried as I fucked her."

"I- Did-... was anyone else involved besides you? Tell me the truth."

"No."

"Cody, give me a minute."

He resumed his relaxed demeanor. The son of a bitch even shrugged. "Sure."

I got up from the table, and went straight to Marcus's office. "They're making Cody take the fall for it!"

"What do you mean? He admitted to it?"

"He's claiming he was the only one involved."

"And your instincts are telling you what?"

"That he's a fucking psycho… but as good as I am, I'm not good enough to get him to confess within minutes of starting. His family is putting him up to this. It makes sense. Who would have the least to lose by pleading guilty?"

"Cody?"

"Mm-hmm."

"It's his first offense… with a good lawyer, probably a short stay in a juvenile detention center, released at eighteen," he said. He shook his head in frustration. "I think you're right. The family's stories are going to get a lot more focused from now on."

"I'd bet anything you're right. I'm going to go back to him now. Next is the uncle."

"I'll get him down here right away," he said, picking up the phone.

"I'll leave Cody in the room once I'm done."

I left before Marcus could say anything further.

When I entered the room again, I didn't take a seat. Cody was supposedly back to his nervous state.

"The detective who interviewed you initially is on his way to take your new statement. Should you, for whatever reason, decide not to comply, just know that our previous conversation was recorded," I told him. No reaction. "Though I do have a few more things I have to ask you before I go."

"I've told you everything you need to know," he said, flat as can be.

"Not quite." I took a seat. "All this came out weeks ago. At that time you denied what Ember told us. You said you and the other accused were innocent."

"Yeah, so?"

"Why now? Why now are you suddenly changing your story, taking the full blame?"

He squirmed in his chair. "I don't... understand what you're asking."

"Ember tried to kill herself at the request of your mother. The goal, at that point, was to end the proceedings in an effort to save your family. And since that's failed, you're now saying it was you and only you." I leaned in, the same way he had earlier. "Is it just me, or does the timing of your confession seem a coincidence... little too perfect?"

He lowered his head, playing with the tissue I'd given him. "I don't understand what you're talking about."

"When you sit in your damp, dark little cell, you might realize that the important thing is that *I* understand," I told him. "Now wait here. The detective will be in shortly."

I left again. I liked to believe I saw fear in his eyes.

Now it was time for uncle Drew, who was waiting for me two rooms down. From what I'd read in the report, he, like Cody, seemed to have played a much smaller role in what had happened to Ember. Newly recruited or something to that effect. It didn't matter; big or small, they were still involved.

I entered the room and took a seat across from him at the table.

"Mr. O'Reilly, I'm Isabella. I'm here to ask you a few questions, if that's okay with you."

"You can call me Drew. And sure, I have nothing to hide."

He was a big man, in his forties, tall, heavyset and bald—either naturally or by choice, but something told me it was natural. He dressed like he was from the sticks: stained blue jeans, a red plaid shirt, combat boots and a drawl to match.

"Fantastic. So you know why you're here?"

He leaned back in his chair, far enough to lift its front legs from the floor. "Ember has been coming up with some pretty wild accusations, and I was named."

Total opposite of Cody. Had I not had a view of the white light dangling over the table, he could've been lounging at the beach. This seemed like a waste of time, but it still had to be done.

"Why do you think she named you along with the others?"

"Why not? She caught someone's attention, and she wanted to see how far she could go. Simple as that."

"And her suicide attempt?"

"From what I've heard, if you don't succeed, it's a cry for attention. A trend of hers, it seems," he said wryly.

"Right, a trend…" How was I going to stop myself from jumping across the table and attacking him? "So the marks on her body… another one of her trends?"

He sat there for a moment, contorting his face as if trying to recall something. "What do they call those kids? Cutters, I think."

"Not all are cuts… and some of the scars are as old as Ember. Are you suggesting she put those there when she was an infant?" He acted like he had all the answers, but he couldn't be asinine enough to believe they actually fit.

Drew made a show of scratching his head. "I'm not sure about that. I've only been around the last couple of years."

"And where were you before that?"

"Down in Texas. Came back when I lost my job."

That I could believe. "Why'd you lose your job?"

"Cutbacks," he said, annoyance making its appearance. "Now look, why are we even doing this?"

"What do you mean?"

Just say it.

"The boy came in today to admit to what Ember accused him of."

"So you knew about that?"

"Yeah, received a call this morning," Drew confirmed. "So if he confessed to doing it all, why are you still questioning me?"

Thank you, Drew. You're helping to prove my suspicions. "Just because he says he's fully responsible for everything doesn't automatically void what Ember disclosed."

He slammed his fists on the table in front of him. "And why the hell not?" Now came the anger. "I never touched that girl; I don't care what she said. And now you have someone who's confessed to all of it, so leave me the hell out of this!"

"There's no reason to get angry, Drew," I said in a soothing voice. "Nothing has been proven... yet. Don't you agree that every case, regardless of who it involves, should be thoroughly investigated?"

"No. You have your person."

"We have one person... and his confession is telling me that your family's accusations concerning Ember's honesty are inaccurate."

"You know, Katherine warned me about you," he said with a smirk, leaning back in his chair once again.

"How so?"

"You have a one-track mind, won't listen to reason," he replied, setting the front legs of the chair back on the floor. "Oh, and that you're a bitch. I'm done here."

He got up and walked out of the room. Being court mandated to appear, I could have prevented him from leaving. But being uncooperative wasn't going to get us any further than we did. It will at least be noted in the file.

I was making my way back to Marcus's office when I crossed paths with Cody and Matthews. The boy was now in handcuffs and presumably on his way to lockup.

Your family will join you soon, I thought. *The truth will come out one way or another.*

"Heading out to see Mel. I'll be back shortly," I said from Marcus's doorway.

"Aren't you going to come in?" he asked. "I want to know how it went with Drew."

"They're a scary family, I'll give them that… He pointed the finger at Cody. I'll talk to you about it more when I get back. See you soon."

And I left as quickly as I'd appeared.

CHAPTER EIGHTEEN

INFINITY

ONCE AGAIN, I peered through the autopsy-suite door to find Melanie sitting at her desk, stacks of paperwork surrounding her on all sides.

"You really have to stop doing that, Isabella," she said, a smile forming on her face.

"How did you know it was me?"

"You're the only one who pokes her head in. Usually people just open the door."

"Well, I never know what I might be walking into…"

"Waiting for a formal invitation, or are you going to come in?" she asked with a laugh.

I walked through the door and made my way over to her. She was still dressed in her blue scrubs, which matched her eyes under the lighting. Her blond hair was scruffily gathered behind her head with a clip. She slid her chair to face me.

"What can I do for you?" she asked.

"I promise I won't take up too much of your time. I just need to check something."

"You want the autopsy reports?"

"Actually I want to view one of the girls."

"Okay…"

Mel walked over to one of the counters to grab a cover gown and gloves. "Care to elaborate?" she asked, handing them to me.

"Something may have been missed, and I just need a closer inspection."

"I'm not sure if I should take that as an insult, but knowing you, I'm sure you have your reasons." She pulled open one of the doors and rolled out the body of the girl I'd seen a few days before.

"Certainly not meant as an insult," I assured her. "It's something that easily could have been missed, if it's even there at all."

"Well, she's all yours," Mel said, standing back to give me room.

I turned the girl's right wrist to face up. Through the bruising and now the progressed decomposition, I wasn't sure I'd find it. I gently ran my gloved fingers along her wrist, but found nothing. Moving to the other side of the table, I did the same thing with her other arm, several times, but this time I paused.

"Did you find something?" she asked.

"Not sure. Do you have a magnifying glass?"

She went to her instrument table and came back with a pair of glasses. I put them on and brought my face closer to the area of interest.

My breath was trapped in my chest.

"Izzy, what is it?"

"Infinity."

***

"Judging by your demeanor, you found what you were looking for."

I was sitting across from Marcus in his office. I didn't know where to start.

"I have confirmation that the perpetrator was the same in two cases."

"So we have a definite link between Ember and the three dead girls?"

"No, that's not what I said. Two cases… one of them being mine." I barely believed the words coming from my mouth.

Marcus's expression turned stone cold. "What?"

I slid the enlarged photograph of the young girl's wrist across his desk. As he looked at it, confusion washed over his face.

"I'm not sure what I'm supposed to be seeing."

I took the photo from him and circled the mark with a red sharpie.

After a few moments of silence, he finally spoke. "A tag? The number eight? Is that what I'm looking at?"

"It's an infinity symbol," I said. "When was the last time you saw that?"

He grabbed my left arm, ran his fingers gently across my wrist, then turned to the photograph. "Impossible…"

"Now you're where I am."

"And Ember?"

"That's where I'm headed next."

"Well, you won't find her at the hospital. She's already been released."

"So soon?"

"Once the doctors determined she was no longer trying to hurt herself, they let her go with her aunt and uncle," he explained.

"She's still not safe, Marcus!"

96

"Way ahead of you. She's on twenty-four-hour surveillance."

I should have known better and allowed myself to relax. "Okay, well, I'm heading there now."

"Want some company?"

"Yes, please."

***

I was relieved to see an NYPD police cruiser in front of the house. Marcus and I were walking toward it when I noticed Dale; would've been déjà vu if not for the woman with him. "How is it that you always know when I'm arriving?" I asked with a smile.

"Call it instinct," he replied with a wink. "Hello, Marcus. Isabella, this is my wife, Bonnie."

"Nice to meet you," I said, extending my hand.

She was a bit younger than Dale, probably a little taller than me, with graying but still predominately brown curly hair. Her bright eyes were accentuated by thick-rimmed glasses.

"Likewise," she replied with a smile, taking my hand in hers, leading the way to the enclosed porch.

When Bonnie excused herself to check on Ember, everyone, save Marcus, took a seat.

"How's she doing?" I asked.

Dale shrugged. "A bit better…" He paused. "Actually, that's a lie. She hasn't left her room hardly at all… but who could blame her? How would you react if your family wanted you dead?"

"They won't get their way. We'll make sure of it." Things got quiet. I struggled for something to say.

"When I found her, you were the first person I thought of. I wanted to blame you for making her talk about what had happened to her," he confessed. "And with her saying nothing, I honestly thought it was because of your interview earlier that day."

"It's okay. It's a fair assumption."

His expression changed to one of guilt. "Still, I'd like to apologize."

"Really, that isn't necessary." His face was gray, and he slumped over to avoid further eye contact. This was obviously eating away at him. I finally conceded—

"It's accepted and appreciated. Thank you, Dale."

He felt a guilt that I knew I couldn't take away completely. Though it wasn't his fault, the fact was, it had happened under his own roof.

"I appreciate how devoted the two of you are," he said, "and also the police lookout outside."

"If there's anything else you and Bonnie need, please let us know. And don't worry, that officer will be out there until this is all figured out," Marcus told him.

Dale turned to me. "Marcus told me earlier that my nephew confessed. You apparently have a way of making people talk."

"Unfortunately, it's not the end of this," I told him. "I hope you realize that."

He let out such a deep sigh, it reminded me of someone holding their breath for too long. "I know. Marcus explained the theory to me."

I wondered just how much of the theory he had explained, and I gave him a disapproving look.

I was surprised when Dale grabbed my hands in his. I wasn't used to that kind of affection. He gently squeezed. "You'll get to the bottom of this, Isabella. Just don't give up… please."

Strangely enough, that was exactly what I needed to hear. I gave him a warm smile and squeezed back. "That's definitely one thing you don't have to worry about."

***

Leaving Marcus with Dale and Bonnie I found Ember in the same position I'd seen her before: sitting on her bed with book in her lap. The only difference was the bandages on her wrists. I knocked on the doorframe to make my presence known.

"Isabella!" she yelled, quickly rushing from her bed and wrapping her arms around my waist.

After a moment, I put my arms awkwardly around her shoulders.

"I'm so glad you're here!" she said, taking my hand like her aunt and leading me to the edge of the bed.

"How are you feeling?" I asked.

"Okay... I should be able to get the stitches out by the end of next week. I can't wait. They're so itchy."

"I bet. Oh, and before I forget," I reached into my bag and pulled out a book. "You're almost done with *Miss Bee*, so I thought I'd get you *Boats in the Sky*. It's the sequel.... I hope you don't already have it."

She shrieked with excitement, taking the book in her hands. "I don't. Thank you so much!"

"You're very welcome. Let me know when you're close to finishing it, and I'll get you the next one." She smiled broadly. It was nice to see there was something I could do to bring back some life into Ember's eyes. She needed some light moments before the trial started.

"I also wanted to give you this." I handed her my card.

I'd given one to Dale when I first visited, but she was the one who needed it.

"If you ever need anything, even just to talk, don't hesitate to call me, no matter what time it is. It can double as a bookmark." I gave her a wink.

"Thank you, Isabella." She reached over and hugged me again.

The weird thing was, this time, my body had no negative reactions whatsoever to the show of affection. I hugged her back, placing a kiss on the top of her head.

Now wasn't the time to check her wrists for branding, and I doubted I'd be able to see anything through the stitches—that is, if the new scarring didn't already erase it. I wouldn't know anything more about that until at least next week.

But this isn't the only avenue to explore.

CHAPTER NINETEEN

SUBTLE THOUGH SEEN

AS MARCUS AND I arrived back at the precinct, I spotted Dean Matthews. I didn't get the opportunity to see him very often, as he was usually out in the field. I jumped on the chance to speak to him regarding Ember. After a brief explanation to Marcus, I caught up with Matthews, just as he was about to round the corner.

"Hey, Dean, got a moment?" I asked.

He looked a little tense, which was unusual for him.

"Everything okay?" I asked.

"I'm fine. What can I do for you?"

"I was wondering if we could go over the report about Ember O'Reilly."

"Dr. Porter, could we possibly do this another time?

He was fidgety, shifting weight from one foot to the other. It looked as though he needed the restroom. Calling me "Dr. Porter," which he never did, was also pretty suspicious.

"You know about her recent suicide attempt, right?"

"I heard something about it," he said casually.

"Come with me. I promise I won't take much of your time." I put my hand on his back, giving him little choice as I directed him to one of the interrogation rooms.

We sat down, and I pulled out his file on Ember, along with a pad and pen from my bag. The nervous ticking of his legs sent pinging vibrations through the metallic table.

"You seem to have a lot on your mind, Dean. I'm here if you want to talk about it."

"So you want to shrink me now?" He was obviously annoyed.

"No. What I said was that if you wanted to talk, I was here," I corrected. "Otherwise we can just get started."

"Honestly I'd rather just get this over with."

"*Over with*… Correct me if I'm wrong, but doesn't that seem a little inappropriate for an active investigation?"

"Perhaps," he started, his deep-blue eyes expressionless. "But it's an investigation that Marcus took away from me without my say, so really I have nothing to do with it anymore."

"I'm sorry. I didn't realize that." And I didn't. Marcus hadn't mentioned it to me. "Did he give you a reason?"

His voice was as stiff as his posture. "He said he wanted me to concentrate on the three girls, wanted to take this one himself or something to that effect."

"Well, it obviously pissed you off, and I can understand that."

He shrugged. "It's an incredible case, could do a lot for his career once it's solved."

"So is the case of the three dead girls," I reminded him, deciding there was no need to tell him the cases might be connected.

"It's also at a standstill right now. There isn't a single witness or even a possible suspect." He let out a sigh of frustration. "We can't even ID the girls because we're getting zero return from the missing-children database."

"I understand. But because you were the original lead after the NDP took on the O'Reilly case, I'd like to get your perspective."

"That wasn't in my report?"

"Dean, you know this is how I do things… it's no different than any other file I'm handed."

Finally giving in, he relaxed in his chair. "Yeah, I know. Ask away."

"So you took over not long after Officer Anderson initially met with Ember. How long was it before you met with her yourself?"

"Around two days after I received the file."

I watched closely for any change in demeanor.

"What was your first impression?"

He looked at me as if my question were a joke. "I didn't have much of an impression at all. She wasn't very forthcoming regarding what allegedly happened to her."

"And you were surprised by this?"

"Yes. At first I chalked it up to me being a man, and that my gender made it uncomfortable for her."

"But you obviously changed your mind about that."

He nodded as he sat back in his chair. "I did. Anderson is also a male, so in the end, it didn't make sense to me. Anytime I'd ask her anything, she'd fold into herself and remain quiet. Getting her to answer even the simplest of questions was frustrating, to say the least."

Was his interviewing style the reason for the difference in Ember's reaction? I knew how Matthews could sometimes come off when interrogating a suspect, tough and intimidating—sometimes teetering on police brutality. But I didn't want to believe he would use the same tactics with a child.

"You know, I had the same reaction when I first started talking to her," I told him.

He looked at me skeptically. "And you got her to eventually talk?"

"I did, yes."

"What's the secret then?"

"No secret. It's all in the approach," I explained. "From what I read, it took a couple of hours before Ember opened up to Anderson. I don't know the specifics of what happened, but sometimes it just takes time and the patience to notice the little clues they give and to use them."

He didn't respond—just stared blankly as though I weren't even there.

"Dean, do you believe Ember's allegations?"

He stiffened again and leaned in toward the table. "I believe something horrible happened to her," he started. "But I can only gauge that by what I read in the initial reports, not from a single thing I got from her."

"And what about Cody taking the blame? What about everyone else Ember named?"

He shrugged.

"I've spoken to each and every one of them, and Cody was the one I knew for sure was hiding something. Sure, the others were acting nervous and uncomfortable, but they weren't as easy to read. Anyone who's accused of something could act that way, guilty or not."

I nodded. "I can agree with that."

"So you got him to confess? I guess you do have a way of getting people to talk."

"I was in the room with him for no more than five minutes, Dean. It was nothing I did; he just came out with it."

His curiosity was now showing through. "Really? Then why did he confess?"

"Still trying to figure that out, but I've got my theories."

"Care to share?"

I didn't feel comfortable sharing my ideas with him and not because he was taken off the case. I was definitely picking up on something—I just didn't know what.

CHAPTER TWENTY

ON THE EDGE

IT WAS TO BE a full day of interviews, and Katherine, being mandated by the courts, was the first one scheduled. Looking back, I wished I'd set the interviews at the family home… but wishing never changed a thing.

When I arrived at Marcus's office, he was hard at work, the piled papers enclosing in on him—higher and higher on his desk each time I entered.

"As requested," I said, placing a cup of coffee on his desk.

"You do know I was kidding, right?"

"I can always take it back."

I went to retrieve it, but he snatched the cup away before I could follow through. "Want to keep your hand?"

We both laughed.

"How was your meeting with Matthews yesterday?" he asked before taking a sip of coffee.

"Can we talk about that later? Think you could find a way of squeezing Anderson in today?"

"You don't think you have enough on your plate already?"

"I need to get him when I can, and it would be easier if you arranged it, being in a different precinct."

"I'll see what I can do about getting him here, but for now Katherine O'Reilly is in room three."

"Thanks." I was about to leave when he stopped me.

"Izzy… you look like shit."

"And I spit in your coffee," I said with a wink and left his office.

I started to make my way down the hall, but decided to stop at the restroom first. I had to agree with Marcus—I did look like shit. My hair was haphazardly done, and my skin was paler than usual, bringing the dark circles under my eyes to the forefront. I'd get nowhere with Katherine if I looked like this.

But how would she react to something she wasn't expecting?

From my bag, I pulled out concealer for the circles, fixed my hair, and rolled up the sleeves of my sweater. I left the bathroom and resumed my journey to Ember's mother.

Walking into the room with my confidence fully restored, I hung my coat on the rack before taking the seat across from the woman herself, who looked at me in pure loathing. I didn't say anything as I grabbed my notepad and pen from the bag, resting my arms gently on either side. When she began to shift uncomfortably, I turned to her.

"Hello, Katherine. How are you this morning?"

She couldn't take her eyes off of my arms, almost as if she were in trance. She twisted a lock of brown hair around her finger, almost to the point that it was pulling at her scalp.

"Katherine?" She finally looked at me. "Is everything okay?"

"Y-yes. So much is going on right now," she explained, her voice sounding weak.

"Yes, you have a daughter who tried to commit suicide and now a son who suddenly has confessed to abusing her."

She shook her head as if trying to clear the fog from it. "I'm sorry?" She looked confused.

For a moment, I actually felt bad for her.

"How are you doing with everything going on?"

"I'm fine. I'll get through it."

"Okay… well, I'll try my best not to keep you too long," I said, as I made a note on the pad. When I looked back at her, she was staring at my arms again. "I'm sorry, is something making you uncomfortable?"

Her face turned pale, and her body began to tremble. "What are those?"

I looked where she was pointing. "What are what?"

She looked as if she were holding back tears. "You know what I'm talking about! Those marks… on your arms. Did you put them there on purpose?"

"I didn't do these to myself."

My scars were doing exactly what I wanted them to do: put her on edge.

"They have to be fake," she said, mostly to herself.

"They aren't, but you're welcome to touch them if that'll help ease your mind."

She had no interest in what I was suggesting. "What are *you* doing here?"

"Well, I was asked to be here to give my assessment of your family. I'm here today to get your insight on what's been going on."

"Why won't you listen?"

There was an urgency in her voice.

"I'm not sure I understand… Listen to what?"

The urgency intensified. "Just walk away from this."

"I will, once I'm done," I told her.

This wasn't the same woman who, fire in her eyes, had said, 'this isn't over'. The woman I'd met on Monday was strong and confident; the one before me now was weak and scared. "Katherine, is there something you want to tell me?"

She suddenly derailed from the track she was on. "It's very sad that my son did what he did to my daughter. I'm sorry I doubted her on that, but it's time to put the rest to bed."

"You know we can't simply ignore everything else that Ember disclosed. The medical reports, her suicide attempt… correct?"

She seemed unable to blink, and her eyes were no longer shimmering. "There's nothing there, Dr. Porter. I may have missed what happened between my son and daughter, but I missed nothing else."

"I'm going to ask you the same question I asked you on Monday. What are you afraid of?"

She looked me directly in the eyes. "Can I give you a bit of advice?"

"If you feel it necessary."

"I'm not the one who should be afraid," she said, in a voice suddenly so void of emotion, it felt as if I'd been talking to three different people since the interview began.

"Is that what he told you?" I asked, leaning toward her. "Don't make the mistake of misreading my scars… I assure you they're far from being a sign of weakness."

"Then what would you call it?"

"Perseverance."

***

The rest of the interviews that day were uneventful. Leave it alone. Watch yourself. Same old stuff, but it at least confirmed what Marcus and I were thinking.

I walked into his office and found him as before, sans coffee.

"How did everything go?"

"Tremendously well," I said, making sure the sarcasm couldn't be missed.

"Glad to hear it," he said with a wry smile.

"Were you able to set up that meeting with Anderson for me?"

"He's here now if you want to talk to him."

I had been about to take a seat, but stopped myself midway. "Please. Could you ask him to meet me in room four?"

Marcus picked up the phone. "I'll send him your way."

As I started to make my way to the room, I realized how tired I actually was. Even without the lack of sleep and nonstop thoughts, hearing the same information for hours on end can be draining.

Plopping myself on the chair, I was relieved this would be my last interview of the day. I was readying my things when I heard a knock and watched as the officer walked in.

"Dr. Porter?"

I wasn't in the mood to make it informal, so I nodded. He extended his hand.

"James," he said. "I understand you wanted to go over my initial report regarding Ember O'Reilly?"

I shook his hand. "Yes. And thank you for agreeing to meet with me on such short notice."

"Not a problem. Anything I can do to help with the case," he said, taking the seat across the table from me.

Immediately, I noticed the differences between Dean and James. First was the age. James couldn't have been past his late twenties, and still had that rookie look to him, yet he appeared extremely approachable. I think it was his soft voice and deep-amber eyes: inviting, nonthreatening. He had military buzzed reddish hair, was well over six feet tall and had a strong-looking physique. In addition, the fact that he was willingly here to help in whatever capacity he could, on a case he was no longer working, spoke volumes about his character. I couldn't help smile at him.

"I'll try not to take up too much of your time," I started. "There are just a few things I want to clarify."

He settled into his chair and clasped his hands in front of him on the table. "Take all the time you need."

"Thank you. Besides for the two of us, Ember hasn't been very forthcoming when it comes to talking about what happened to her."

"I can't blame her. Putting myself in her shoes, I was surprised she said anything at all. Especially after I met the family."

Dean said he couldn't read anything from the family except for Cody; James obviously had a different point of view. "Would you be able to explain what you mean by that, about her family?"

He took on a serious look. "You know when you get that gut feeling when you first meet someone?" I nodded. "Well, something just didn't seem right. They shrugged off Ember's accusations like they were nothing, with no concern at all for what was being presented—what they were being accused of. Their explanation was that she's an attention seeker."

"From what I understand, it took quite a while before she started talking to you about it. Is that correct?"

"Definitely. Yes."

"How did you first approach the situation?"

He settled back into his chair like he planned on being there for a while. "Well, I was originally asked to talk to her because she told a classmate she wanted to attempt to run away again," he said. "Children don't usually run for nothing, especially at that age, so I tried to get her to talk about the reason why. All I kept getting was 'Just because' then silence."

"I'm assuming you then decided to take a different approach?"

"Absolutely. I put it aside for the moment and started asking simple questions I knew she'd be comfortable answering."

"What kind of things did you ask?"

He raised his hand and started counting off. "You know, just basic things, like what her favorite subject in school is, what she likes to do in her free time... questions about her friends."

"And she was receptive to your questions?"

"She had absolutely no problem speaking about those things. Honestly, her entire composure changed."

"How so?"

He took his hand and ran it through the little hair he had. "When I first took her into the classroom, she was fidgety. Her anxiety was obvious: like deer in the headlights," he explained. "But once we started talking about her and her alone, she didn't seem any different from any other child her age."

James was good. He was able to easily notice the signs and modify his approach accordingly. It brought me back to when I'd first met Marcus.

"Concerning your original line of questions: when did you try again?"

"Not before Ember was providing information without being asked, asking her own questions even."

"That's surprising to hear."

He offered me a wry smile. "Well, she didn't magically change and start spilling everything. The hesitation never went away, but she started to speak about what happened... in parts. She first said she wasn't happy at home. She went further into it when I gently encouraged her, until I got it all."

"Once you knew the reasons she wanted to run away, what were your impressions?"

His expression then turned to one of anger. "Honestly, after hearing what she told me, I almost had to walk away. It took everything in me to stay where I was and not immediately head out to arrest her entire family."

"And when you finally met with the accused, what did you think?"

"I had no doubt in my mind, whatsoever, that what she'd told me was true."

"James, thanks so much for taking the time to go over this with me. I can't imagine it was easy."

He sighed, and his face dropped. "No, it wasn't. If had a way to erase what I know, I'd jump at the chance. But I can't. I'll just have to deal with knowing there are people out there as evil as this group."

His choice to describe them as a 'group' was interesting. Satisfying even.

"If you ever need to discuss that, professionally, please come see me."

"Thank you, Dr. Porter. I appreciate that. I might take you up on that offer."

"Don't hesitate," I said, before handing him my card. "And you can call me Isabella."

"Well, Isabella, it was really nice meeting you."

"You as well."

He got up from the table and headed for the door. "If you need anything else, please don't hesitate to come and find me."

"Thank you again, James," I said, as he walked out.

Now it wasn't hard to understand why Ember had opened up to James but shut completely down with Dean. Nevertheless, something still told me Dean needed more than a refresher course on how to deal with a victim.

CHAPTER TWENTY-ONE

CRIMSON TEARS

MARCUS AND I HEADED to the Jersey Tavern for some much-needed drinks — although we needed them for different reasons. To make it easier to talk, as we often do, we grabbed a booth in the corner, away from the rest of the patrons.

As always, Eric was at our table within minutes, our drinks already in hand. We downed them quickly.

"So seriously, how was your day?" Marcus asked.

"Honestly?"

He gave me a perplexed look. "Always."

I sank deeper into the booth. "Draining."

"How have you been sleeping?"

"Nothing has changed in that department, but I'm making it work."

"Are you really, Isabella?" he asked. "I'm beginning to worry about you."

"Beginning? When were you not worried about me in one way or another?" And as I did best, I changed the direction of the conversation. "Why did you take Matthews off Ember's case?"

He sat back in the booth, letting a laugh escape. "That came up when you two talked?"

"You can't honestly think it wouldn't have."

"You're right… He was pissed at me for it, and I'm sure he gladly made that known to you." He laughed again.

I gave him the least humorous look I could muster. "Marcus, it's me. I want to know why you did it."

He finally wiped the smile from his face. "Once I began to understand the scope of the case, I wanted to take it myself."

"Why?"

Marcus shrugged. "Reminded me of you, thought maybe I could work it better than Matthews."

"So you're making this personal." It was more of a statement than a question.

"And you're not?" he scoffed.

"I'm sorry?"

I raised my hand to Eric for another drink.

"You don't think I can see what these cases are doing to you?" Marcus pressed.

"So we're back to that now," I said with a sigh. "You can't say you didn't know beforehand that this would affect me a bit."

He raised a hand to emphasize his point. "A bit, yes…" He paused when Eric arrived then picked up when we were alone again. "But I wouldn't say it's just a bit. For fuck's sake, you're looking into your dead father!"

"And you think I'm wrong with this train of thought? That there isn't actually something there?"

Sitting back once again, he folded his arms across his chest. "Fine then, out with it and don't hold back. What exactly do you think is going on here?"

"What if it is Jonathan? Or if not, someone he knew who's taking over?" I started. "What if it went beyond just Anna and me? What if there's a group out there hurting these girls?"

His voice softened. "Your father's dead. He died in a fire at Lake Placid. In his cabin. You know that. We read the report."

"How do you know it was his body in the cabin?" Even as I said it, I knew how it sounded, but I didn't care.

"Izzy... he's dead and buried. Nothing—"

I didn't let him finish. "The pieces started to come together at the hospital: how Ember tried to kill herself; Katherine; the man out the window. We more than matched, Marcus—Ember was retelling my story."

I waited for him to say something. When he didn't, I continued. "The man outside the hospital, you were right... but instead of an axe murderer, it was like I'd seen a ghost. Even after all these years, I'll never forget his face."

He looked at me skeptically. "You do honestly think Jonathan is alive."

"Yes," I said, nodding. "I mean, realistically, I knew the chance of finding anything was slim. He was a defense attorney, a good one. He had the connections he'd need to make Jonathan Baldacci disappear and for Michael O'Reilly show up in his place."

"I'll say this again, Izzy—he's dead. That said, the idea that the abuse may go beyond you and your sister isn't implausible." He sat there, apparently mulling over the idea, before continuing. "And if that's the case, or if there's even a possibility, you're off the case."

"Marcus, you can't—"

"I CAN, and just did," he said without looking at me. "If it's at all related to Jonathan, I don't want you anywhere near this."

"You can't force me to back off," I shot back. "Do you really want me to pursue this case without the support of the precinct? If you take me off, you'll be putting my life at risk."

He slammed his fist on the table, forcing a wave of whiskey out onto the hard wood.

"Why the hell are you so hardheaded?"

"I could ask the same of you!" I snapped. "Bottom line is you can't force me to do anything, any more than I can force you. Do what you think is best for me, but it changes nothing."

"You're a right pain in the ass… But I'll be damned if I'm going to stand around and watch you add to your already enormous collection." And with that he nodded in my direction.

Words weren't needed for me to know what he was implying.

"Well, Marcus, I knew you could be an asshole, but I didn't think you could go beyond that." I downed the rest of my drink and got up from the booth. "I'll e-mail you my report once I finish compiling what I have. Goodnight."

I grabbed my coat without saying another word, and left Marcus to clean up his mess.

***

I headed straight upstairs and into the bathroom, ignoring my usual routine of locking up and checking the house. After turning the shower to the hottest setting, I began to get undressed, and was unable to avoid my reflection in the mirror.

The scars were all there: pulsating and ugly, watching me, screaming. It felt as though, with combined will, they were trying to escape my body—punishing me for whatever misdeed I'd committed. I finally pulled myself from the image in front of me and into the shower, closing the door behind me.

I drenched the loofah in soap and vigorously scrubbed, making sure to hit each and every voice as they screamed out in protest. I needed to silence them, to rid myself of the film of filth I felt coating my body.

I didn't notice it immediately, but soon it was hard to miss—

Around my feet was a sea of crimson, at first diluted by the falling water, then overpowering it, becoming brighter. I looked down at my body. I had ripped them open. They were crying in shame. I quickly turned off the shower and stepped out. The white towel I wrapped around me was also soon spattered in crimson.

I leaned against the wall and slid down it until I reached the floor. I hugged my legs, trying to fold into myself as much as I could.

"I can't escape who I am..." I softly reminded myself, my gentle rocking only further causing my wounds to bleed.

***

In a soft cotton bathrobe, I gently eased myself onto the bed and turned on the TV, dropping the remote beside me. I didn't care what was on; I just needed the background noise to fill the silence. A half an hour later, I heard a knock at the door. As I made my way downstairs, I heard it a second time: louder, harder.

Making sure everything was covered, I walked to the door—still unlocked—and peeked through the peephole. Marcus was standing on the front porch in the rain.

I cracked the door and told him it wasn't a good time. As I tried to close it again, he stopped me.

"I need to see you," he said, pushing his way in.

"Okay, well, now I see I don't have a choice here." I commented as he closed the door behind him.

"Stop talking."

"What the fuck, Marcus—"

"Seriously, stop talking," he repeated, then grabbed me by the shoulders and pulled me to him.

I tried not to flinch in pain from his roughness; instead I thought it better to follow through with the movement to ease it. He kissed me.

"M-Marcus, I..." But he was serious—no more talking.

He brought me closer to his body, hugging me tightly. This time, though, I couldn't hide the pain. It escaped my lips when I no longer had a choice but to pull back.

"Isabella, I'm so sorry. I didn't want to hurt you," he said, the regret quickly washing across his face.

"You can't... Why did you... It's not you," I replied, beet red, flustered as can be. I then turned my back to him.

"What's that on your bathrobe?"

I looked in the mirror on the wall in the front hall. There were a tiny crimson spots on my shoulder.

"It's nothing," I replied, quickly dismissing it. I walked toward the minibar in the living room and poured myself a drink.

"You're lying," he said, following me.

"Don't push it, Marcus…" I said softly, turning to him and taking a long sip of whiskey.

He looked at me for a moment then glanced up the stairs. "What have you done?"

"It's nothing really," I said, but it was obvious he wasn't taking me at my word. He slowly made his way toward me, stopping just a foot short of me in my bathrobe, bleeding.

"Tell me," he demanded… but he didn't sound angry. He sounded worried. When I still didn't answer, he took the drink from my hand and placed it on the bar. He took the ties of my bathrobe into his hands. "Don't take this the wrong way, but I need to see."

"You really don't want to…" I said, barely audible.

"You're wrong," he said. He undid the tie, and once opened, the inside of my bathrobe showed a preview of what was to come. Everything was splattered with blood.

Unable to look at him, I turned my head to the side. I felt his hands on my shoulders as he gently pushed at the edges of the robe until it fell to my feet. I couldn't see his expression, but I heard the gasp as he took in what my tank top and shorts weren't hiding.

"I was wrong. You didn't do this," he said, now speaking in a whisper himself. "I did."

I looked at him, confused and sad. I shook my head. "I told you it wasn't you."

"I didn't physically do it, but I did it."

"Marcus, you're not to blame for this."

"Would you have done it if I hadn't said what I did?" he asked, his eyes beginning to water.

"Yes, it still would have happened," I told him, and I was being truthful, though his face shone in disbelief. "Scars have stories to tell, and mine have been trying to get theirs out since the first day I came home."

***

Deciding there was no longer a reason to keep my robe on, I lay beside Marcus on the bed. After convincing him that using the vitamin E ointment was more reasonable than rushing me to the hospital, he generously covered every wound and scar he found. I had to admit it felt good; Marcus actually had the ability to be gentle.

"How's that?" he asked.

"Perfect. Thank you."

Removing his fingers from my arm, he said. "All right, now turn over."

Immediately, I obeyed, carefully turning onto my stomach.

"You know I'm not getting off this case, right?"

He sighed. "I know."

"You also know this has to be done my way."

"I'm putting it on the record that even though I'll no longer fight you on this, I wholeheartedly disagree with it," he said, then added, "You're important to me, Izzy. I'll never stop worrying about you."

"Noted." Marcus blew softly at the wounds on my back. I could hardly believe it: as his fingers ran up my spine, I actually started to doze off. For the first time in forever, I felt completely relaxed.

"Marcus?"

"Mm-hmm?"

"You're going to stay, right?"

"I'm not going anywhere," he said softly.

With that final thought in my mind, I allowed myself to fall asleep.

CHAPTER TWENTY-TWO

LAKE PLACID

I WOKE UP just as the sun was rising, and through sleepy eyes, looked up. Marcus, wearing nothing but a T-shirt and boxers, lay asleep with his arm draped over my waist. Careful not to wake him, I gently slipped out of the bed and into the bathroom.

As I usually did in the morning, I looked at myself in the mirror. Vitamin E is an amazing thing. Even though it didn't mask anything, it helped tremendously in calming the fury of my wounds and scars. I decided it prudent not to take a shower, so I just brushed my teeth and left. Being as quiet as I could, I picked out my clothes and was about to return to the bathroom when I was interrupted.

"Cute... you trying to be all stealth-like."

Marcus was mid-stretch, a huge smile on his face.

"If you want to leave this room alive, you'll never use the word *cute* when referring to me again."

"Right. What was I thinking?" He laughed. "Were you planning on saying good-bye before you left, or should I start my walk of shame?"

I wanted to, but I didn't know how to respond.

"Want to grab some breakfast?" he asked.

"Can't. I have something I need to do this morning. But I'll be in your office this afternoon."

He looked at me suspiciously. "Where do you have to go this early?"

"Marcus, new rule. Don't ask, and I won't be forced to lie. Deal?"

He began his sad climb out of bed. "Okay. But the fine print to that new rule is that you'll let me know if you need anything."

He dressed, and now was putting on his shoes. Grabbing his coat, he made his way to me. "So we're okay?" he asked.

"Yeah, we're fine," I told him with a smile, and he kissed me on the cheek.

"All right, see you this afternoon," he said. Then he left.

It's incredible what one night's sleep can do. My mind was clear, my determination fully restored. If the answers weren't going to willingly come to me, I'd do whatever was necessary to force them out of hiding.

***

I'd grabbed a blueberry muffin and a coffee, and was now sitting in my car, waiting. Down the street from where I was parked was the O'Reilly home. It was 9:00a.m., and for all I knew, I'd missed him already. Still, two vehicles were parked in the driveway. I continued to wait.

A half hour later, there was movement, and he emerged from the house with a bag in his hand. After throwing it into the backseat of the SUV, he climbed in and backed out of the driveway. I started the engine and followed him, trying to maintain far enough distance not to be noticed.

Where are you headed, Mr. O'Reilly?

He got on the New York State Thruway north, then exited onto the 24 in Albany. I followed him on the 87 to exit 30. I merged with him on Route 9. It may have been a while since I'd been there, but I knew then exactly where we were headed. As predicted, we grabbed off-ramp 73. I called Marcus when it was confirmed.

"Hey, where are you? It's past one," he said.

"Looks like I'll be out of the city for most of the day. Can we reschedule?"

"What? You said reschedule? The reception is terrible."

"I know. I'm driving, and the hands-free option is lousy," I explained. "So tomorrow?"

"How about dinner tonight?"

"I'll have to see what time I get back. I'll let you know."

"Either way, call me when you're back in Newark."

With that, we got disconnected.

At least he didn't ask me where I was or what I was doing. Now that I knew where we were headed, I pulled into a truck stop to fill up and get something to snack on for the duration of the trip.

I was standing in line to pay for my purchases when Ember's uncle, Drew, walked in. How could I have been so stupid?! Of course, Michael wasn't going alone.

I put my head down and tilted it slightly to the side to keep from being recognized. He was only two people behind me.

"Miss, do you also have gas?" the cashier asked, clearly annoyed.

"I'm sorry. Yes, I do. Thirty-five dollars. Pump three," I replied.

"You got it... that'll be forty-seven, forty-three."

I handed him the money, grabbed my bag, and left the store. I doubted if I was seen. I was wearing sneakers, jeans, and a hoodie—

far from my normal getup—and my hair did a good job of hiding my face. After filling up, I drove away as quickly as I could.

* * *

Lake Placid. The last time I was here was when Jonathan brought me after Anna's death. I was supposed to die that night, not him. At least, that's what I thought I knew.

I parked my car in one of the picnic areas not far from the cabin and decided to walk the rest of the way. I made my way down toward the lake, through the thick forest and underbrush, and after almost an hour, finally made it to where our lot would have been. Standing by the lakeshore, I looked up and got a glimpse of a new structure. As before, it was built into the side of the mountain, so I would have no choice but to climb to get to it. Anna and I had done it many times, but at least back then, we could use the precarious, old stairs. Thankful I was dressed for the trek, I made my own stairs—carefully, I fought my way through the rocky terrain using dead trees, exposed roots, and rocks protruding from the ground.

At the top, I stayed hidden in the trees as I scanned my surroundings. I spotted Mr. O'Reilly's SUV, Drew's car, and a number of vehicles I didn't recognize. I was in the right place.

This cabin looked little like its predecessor: its long ranch style had been replaced to that of a woodsy two-story log cabin, and judging by the condition of the logs, it had been erected quite a few years ago.

Hearing voices, I crouched and hid behind a tree.

"It does matter. How can you be so cool about this?"

"Look, even if it was her, what do you think she'll do? She'd be out here alone."

VICTORIA PARKS

The first voice was definitely Drew. The second was probably Michael's... it sounded familiar, but I wasn't sure if he was Jonathan.

"You know what she's after. That doesn't worry you?"

"Why should it? The Brotherhood made sure the connection won't be made. Don't worry. It'll be taken care of soon enough."

That explains the note, as well as Katherine's warning. If Michael were indeed Jonathan, the plan would be to finish what he'd started more than twenty years ago... And I had an idea what that was. Unfortunately for him, he had no idea who I'd grown up to be.

Once they were back inside, keeping low, I crept up to the cabin window. Through a slight crack where the drawn curtains should have met, I managed to catch a glimpse inside.

From what I could tell, there were at least a half dozen men, not counting anyone in the adjoining rooms or on the second floor. I couldn't make out a word that was being said, but it was obvious some sort of meeting was taking place. Michael had mentioned "The Brotherhood" earlier. The term *group* was beginning to make sense.

The sun was starting to set, and I had to make my way back down to the lake before I was surrounded in complete darkness.

Do I tell Marcus what I've learned, or do I keep it to myself?

I definitely didn't want the authorities all over this... not that they would be. Anyone else would see a bunch of men getting together at a cabin. I saw a group of child rapists... and maybe worse. What exactly went on in that cabin, I could only imagine.

***

"It's after eleven, Izzy," Marcus, the angriest voice-clock in history, told me over the phone.

128

"It is. Takes five hours to drive back from Lake Placid," I said, carefully checking to make sure everything was safe and secure.

"Jesus! Lake Placid... What did you find out?"

"Think tree house, but for grown men."

"Why would he rebuild at the exact same location?"

"If it's really Jonathan, I wouldn't put it past him. He thinks he's untouchable."

"What'd you see?"

"A half dozen men, Michael O'Reilly and Drew among them. I heard them talking outside, and they mentioned 'The Brotherhood.' Does that mean anything to you?"

"In what context?"

"An organization I think. Michael said something like 'The Brotherhood made sure we couldn't make a connection.' I think they were talking about Jonathan being found out... but I don't want to go there yet.

"I don't get it. Why would Jonathan stick around? It's just too risky."

"Marcus, what else could it be? It's got to be some kind of pedophile ring; maybe even more than that... Think about what Ember said. 'My uncles, other relatives, my stepbrother... they all did the same things to me, sometimes when they were all together.' What else would you call that?"

"Breakfast tomorrow morning?"

"I'll be at your office by eight."

"Great. See you then."

Something had been eating me from the inside the whole way back to the city. There was something I wasn't remembering, something my mind refused to recall. Growing up, Anna and I had been at the mercy of our father, but was there any time, even a single instant, when more people could have been involved? I found it hard to believe that if Michael was in fact Jonathan, he just now had gotten involved with these individuals, whoever they were.

For all my theories and ideas, I couldn't tackle every obstacle at once. I hated the very idea of finding that stupid box. I didn't want to be reminded of what was inside. I'd put it off for too long… but it was time to pay the house another visit.

CHAPTER TWENTY-THREE

THE FIRST TIME

AFTER BREAKFAST, I called the real-estate agent to schedule a second visit, refusing her persistent offer to show me around. She went into the usual agent spiel: a great deal of interest in the house and I should act quickly et cetera… I told her I understood and would contact her if I wanted to put in an offer. She finally conceded.

I pulled into the driveway a little before 10:00a.m. It seemed the initial shock of being there finally had made its way through my system. It seemed a little easier the second time around.

Once inside, I decided to look around the whole house, hoping to unlock whatever my mind was hiding. Somehow I knew that, like the lockbox, there was a code that would reveal the hidden memories. I just had to remember. Every step was steeped in memory. Even the air felt the same as it had back then—as if I was breathing in what I'd breathed out all those years ago.

After Jonathan's death, I wasn't immediately sent to live with my aunt and uncle. I lived in this house for a while after.

I was fourteen, and it was just my mother and me. That's all I could remember as I made my way up to the second floor, starting in her room, the first one off the stairs to the left. Not unlike my own, it was empty. I walked to a door in the far-right corner, and opened it to find a bathroom I'd forgotten was there. When I entered, I saw an antique claw-foot tub and a pedestal sink, with a toilet across from it. I took in my surroundings then closed my eyes, willing for something, anything to come to me.

My mother was in this tub, her dark-brown hair tied in a disheveled bun atop her head, with a bottle of vodka close by on the floor, more than half empty. She was drunk and yelling at me.

I opened my eyes and took a seat on the floor, pressing my back against the porcelain. I ran my fingers along the edge, taking in the cool smoothness. I closed my eyes again.

"What is wrong with you? All you had to do was leave things alone. But no, you couldn't do that, could you?"

"I'm sorry..."

"You're sorry? You don't know what sorry is. I should have killed you myself, but he wouldn't let me."

"Why do you hate me so much?"

She left my question unanswered. "But he isn't here to save his precious daughter anymore, now is he?"

I opened my eyes, unsure if I wanted to continue. I was starting to remember that night, and what it was leading up to. She was a plump woman, no taller than I am now, but even at that age, I knew there was no messing with her.

"Hand me the bottle. See if you can get that right." I handed it to her and watched as she took a long drink. *"Now get undressed. You need to get ready before he arrives."*

"Before who arrives?"

I stood up and paced the floor, trying to remember without having to go back there. Who could she be preparing me for? It wasn't Jonathan... we both thought he was dead. I sat back down beside the tub and forced my eyes closed.

Once again, she ignored my question, so I did as told and undressed. Standing there naked, I stared at her.

"Well, what are you waiting for? Get in!"

Very carefully I put my foot into the water. She'd been in there for a while. The water was cold. When I made the mistake of complaining, she grabbed my arm and pulled me in the rest of the way, forcing my head under the water. Even though she was drunk, she could still overpower me, leaving me gasping for air every time I resurfaced. She finally let me go, then laughed as I wiped hair from my face and coughed out the water I'd inhaled.

"Now here, get rid of the hair. You need to be smooth. Everywhere," she said, throwing a razor my way. She took another long drink from the bottle, this time finishing it off. "I'll be back, and you'd better be finished by the time I am." She was probably going to fetch another bottle.

It was one of those razors that had the full blade inside. I started to quickly disassemble it, allowing the blade to drop between my legs and into the water. I tried to put it back together just as quickly. Once my task was completed, I held it in one hand, with the blade hidden in the other. She stumbled back in, dipped her toe in the water, and removed it quickly.

"I guess you're right. It is a bit cold, isn't it? Don't budge..."

I was sitting right in front of the faucet when she turned only the hot water on. Knowing what would happen if I screamed out, I kept as silent and still as possible, bringing my mind somewhere other than the present. I almost missed it when she finally turned it off to climb back in.

"Now that's better," she said, as she put a leg on either side of me, boxing me in. Then she noticed my legs. "Did your hair fucking magically grow back? What have you been doing in here?"

"There's something wrong with the blade. It's not shaving the hair away," I lied, showing it to her with a trembling hand.

She grabbed it from me and, squinting, looked at it. Something changed. In that moment, I felt the hot blood in my ears. I was driven by a sudden irrepressible thought: this was the only chance I had. Placing the blade between my fingers, I cut her deeply, first on one inner thigh, then on the other in quick succession. She screamed out in pain, but by the time she reached for me, I'd already gotten out of the tub.

"What have you done?" she asked, grasping at her bloody legs, slipping in the bathwater. She was getting weaker by the second. She struggled slowly, inelegantly, like a flopping fish on the wharf. Pushing down on her shoulders, I made sure she stayed where she was.

As the life drained from her eyes, I whispered into her ear—

"I'm finally doing something right."

***

I remembered everything now. What I did to her in the bathtub that day was meant for me. I'd wanted to follow Anna, so I'd learned the quickest route there—through the femoral arteries on the inside of the legs.

Ironically, if Jonathan were still alive, she would have been my first kill.

I stood up and left the bathroom. Not soon enough. I was now re-membering how I'd calmly gotten dressed and then run to the neighbors' house, telling them how I'd found my mother in a tub full of blood. They called the police, and that was when Marcus arrived— the first day we met. Her death was ruled a suicide. My aunt and uncle were called on my request, and I was put on the train a couple days later. I never found out whom I was being prepared for. I probably never would.

As I made my way through the rest of the house, bits and pieces continued to make themselves known... But I still couldn't remember if anyone else had been involved. I was in the basement when I heard someone call out from the first floor. I went up to meet with the real-estate agent.

"I know you said you didn't need my help, but I was in the neigh-borhood and thought I'd drop by," she explained. She was holding a folder under her arm, trying to readjust her glasses, which had slipped to the tip of her narrow nose.

"I understand. I'm actually done here, but I'm glad you stopped by. There are a few things I'd like to discuss."

CHAPTER TWENTY-FOUR

CONFIRMATION

I MADE IT to the precinct just in time for my meeting with Michael O'Reilly. I was heading to the interview room when Marcus stopped me in the hall.

"What happened to you?" he asked.

"What do you mean?"

"That ax murderer look from the other day... it's back."

I hadn't realized it would be that obvious. If Marcus noticed it, Michael surely would too.

He placed a hand on my shoulder. "Sure you're up for this?"

"I'll be fine. I'll come see you once I'm done, but I have to go—otherwise I'll be late."

"Okay, you know where I am if you need anything." He gave me a reassuring look and started back toward his office.

However bad I looked, I was still sharp. Marcus didn't just happen to catch a glance of how bad I looked just sitting at his office desk. He was worried about me... hell, I was worried about me too. Who could blame him?

I had my hand wrapped around the knob to the interview room before I felt sick to my stomach. As much as I wanted to charge my demons head on, I decided to head to the viewing room first.

It felt like I'd been punched in the stomach. Leaning onto the observation desk, I shifted my weight onto my arms, doing everything I could to alleviate that horrible feeling. But my breath only quickened, and the numbness overtook my body, distancing myself from my surroundings. As I faced the dark glass, I stared at the man on the other side, sitting at the table. I no longer could deny it. Staring back at me through the mirror was my father, Jonathan Baldacci.

Twenty-three years older, his hair had gone completely white. Every facial feature had ripened with age… but I knew it was him. He wore his hair the same as before: short and neatly styled. As always, he was impeccably dressed in the finest suit money could buy. His eyes were different than mine—his blue with a permanent squint, mine hazel and wide. Looking at him, you wouldn't even know we were related.

I deposited myself in a chair, so the thousand-pound weight on my shoulder wouldn't break my back. I was fourteen again, regressing to a point in time when I was weak and vulnerable. When I couldn't save Anna.

Anna, the three dead girls, and now Ember. I had to snap out of this if I wanted to help them. I closed my eyes and tried to convince myself that I was here, in time and place. I was no longer that little girl; I wasn't fourteen but thirty-seven. I could prevent the same fate Ember now faced—I had to.

I removed my coat, placed it over my arm, and walked into the interview room.

"Mr. O'Reilly, sorry to have kept you waiting," I said, as I walked into the room. After hanging up my coat, I took a seat across from him.

He waved off what I said. "No apology necessary. I cleared my entire afternoon for you."

"This shouldn't take up that much time, but I appreciate your willingness to participate."

"That said, I do have a question before we start."

"And what's that?" I asked, making a show of readying my supplies.

"How long do we continue this? Pretending we don't know each other?"

He caught me off guard with that. I knew we'd eventually come to who he truly was, just not now.

"You don't like to waste time. I can appreciate that, because neither do I," I finally replied, looking at him.

He purposefully crossed one leg over the other. That's how he did everything: purposefully.

"Well, actually, I was hoping we'd be reacquainted by now, so I was a bit disappointed that our meeting was among the last." He briefly closed his eyes as a smile washed across his face. "Of course, I understood. You needed to make sure before voicing your theory."

He had a way of slithering under my skin.

"What should I call you?" I asked, scratching a note on the pad.

"Whatever you want. Mr. O'Reilly, Baldacci, Jonathan, Father…"

"Okay, Michael," I said, hiding the twisting pain the word 'father' brought me. "Why do you think Ember has named you as a participant in the allegations she's made?"

"We already have the answer to that, don't we? Cody admitted to inflicting what you saw."

"Even you are going to hold to that bullshit?"

He nodded his agreement. "It's the truth. You won't find out anything more than you already have."

"When Detective Matthews spoke with your wife, she hinted that you might not be the biological father of the children."

"The older boy isn't mine. He was the product of Katherine's previous marriage. Though Ember and Brian are my children... I guess that means you have siblings again, Isabella. I'm happy for you."

Until that point, my mind had neglected to connect the dots. Ember and her younger brother were related to me. Of course, I knew the worse that could happen to Brian was that he would follow in his father's footsteps. I still had hope that, if caught early, Brian's path could be changed... but suddenly I knew the real fate Ember faced.

I wasn't sure if I was getting what I needed. It was impossible to separate the three cases, and I didn't know how to proceed. Jonathan was who he was, and he would jump on every opportunity to make sure I knew it.

"I think I have everything I need for now."

"We've only just begun."

The subtle threat was perfectly executed. I leaned in a little closer.

"What do you hope to accomplish here today?"

"We have some unfinished business. We're going to have to come back to that eventually."

"I don't disagree."

"So when's better than the present, Bella? The promise of settling of old scores... gets the blood going, doesn't it?"

"Don't call me 'Bella,'" I said through clenched teeth. "And things will be settled, *Michael*. But not here and not by you."

He leaned in himself, all but closing the gap between us.

"That's where you're wrong," he said, eerily calm. "If anyone is left standing at the end of this, it'll be me."

"Strong words... but you're getting old. I'm not sure how many burning buildings you have left in you."

***

I sat heavily in the chair across from Marcus's desk. He looked up at me, but neither of us said a word.

He was the first to break the silence. "That well, huh?"

"I'm pissed off," I said, taking out my pocket recorder and giving it a satisfied shake. "But with this we can take him down."

"That's great! Congrats Izzy!"

"Thanks," I said, beaming.

"So was it Jonathan?"

I didn't want him to know, for many reasons.

"You didn't come into the viewing room to check things out?" I asked, avoiding the question.

"I made a promise to trust you, and I meant it."

"I'm still not entirely certain..." If I didn't feel like shit before, I definitely did now. White lies were one thing; what I had just told him, was nowhere near the color or purity of snow. I lowered my head to examine the floor, unable to meet his gaze. I felt dirty.

"Listen, head back home, and take a long, relaxing shower—minus anything abrasive this time—and I'll pick you up around eight to celebrate."

"Why?"

"To celebrate! Instead of trying to overanalyze things, try to do as you're told."

"Okay," I said hesitantly, as I got out of the chair. "Can you at least give me a hint?"

"No, it's a surprise."

"You know I hate surprises."

"And that would change things because…"

"I hate you," I replied, finally able to produce a fraction of a smile.

"I love you too. Now get out of here. I'll see you soon."

CHAPTER TWENTY-FIVE

THE LONE MAN

MARCUS PICKED ME UP at eight o'clock. He'd made me close my eyes in the car, so I had no idea where we were. He walked around, opened my door, and walked me a few feet before he gave me permission to open my eyes. It was just starting to rain, and the drops were falling on my face as I looked up at the sign—

ANDROS DINER.

"Oh, Marcus, it's what I've always wanted. A diner!"

"Calm the sarcasm, Izzy."

"Sorry," I said, unsuccessfully holding back a laugh. "But this was the big surprise? This is literally my favorite diner."

He looked at me sheepishly. "Well, I know it's your favorite. That's why, after the way I disrespected it the last time, I thought I'd give it another shot."

"You're such a trooper!" I said again sarcastically. I finally stopped once I realized he was taking it seriously. "I really appreciate it, Marcus. Thank you."

"You're welcome."

He kissed me and I melted. Suddenly, I loved everything about him: his corny jokes, his sarcasm, the way he always took care of me.

"After you," he said, holding the door open. "I called ahead to make sure your booth would be available."

I raised an eyebrow playfully. "You made reservations… at a diner?"

"Just get in, smartass."

We headed straight for the booth. After we got situated, a waitress, no one I knew, placed water on the table and handed us our menus.

"Do we go for the usual, or go all out tonight?"

"Let's keep the momentum going and get crazy. I'm going to get the lemon-and-herb Alaskan salmon."

"For maximum insanity, I'll take the rib eye," Marcus said, upon skimming the choices.

The place was busy tonight, almost filled to capacity. Calling ahead to reserve the booth wasn't as crazy as I'd thought. I looked to my right and noticed a man sitting alone. I knew I recognized him, and his large protruding nose, but couldn't place where from.

"What's got your attention?" Marcus asked.

"Oh, nothing… was just thinking."

"Of?"

"What else? Work."

"One-track mind…"

"I've been accused of that repeatedly this week. Mainly by you." Through the corner of my eye, I saw the lone man watching us openly. The waitress showed up with our drinks, and Marcus placed our food orders. It gave me a moment try to and figure things out… but the moment wasn't long enough.

"Old high-school chum?" Marcus asked, stealing a glance.

"No, but I recognize him from somewhere. And he obviously recognizes me."

Marcus grinned. "Maybe he can't take his eyes off your radiating beauty."

I couldn't stop my mouth from dropping open. Closing it, I squinted at him while cocking my head slightly to the side. "Tell me, Marcus. Does that corny crap actually work?"

"What are you talking about—crap? It's one of my best lines."

"Well, seeing what usually catches *your* eye, I can see why," I said with a wink.

"I love your winks… and I love you."

That took me so off guard. I didn't know what to say. I loved him, but I didn't know if I was in love with him. The night we spent together meant everything to me, but I wasn't that kind of person…

"Marcus… you mean the world to me…"

"But you don't love me?"

"No, I do. It's just all so fast… but I do love you." I blushed. "But let's talk about something else. Michael O'Reilly said—"

"The whole idea of getting you out tonight was to help you put work aside. You have to meet me halfway here."

"You're right. I'm sorry. Honestly, I'm not good with any of this."

"I know. That's why I'm here to keep you on track."

He smiled warmly.

"So far you're doing an excellent job. Thank you."

"My pleasure."

When the waitress returned with our salads, she handed Marcus a folded piece of paper. His face quickly changed from easygoing to angry in a snap second. He grabbed the waitress by her arm, and forced her back to our table.

"Who gave you this?" Marcus asked her.

She pointed in the direction where the man used to be. He was gone. "He was sitting right over there, but it looks like he left. I'm sorry," she said, and walked away.

"What does it say?" I asked him.

Was the note folded in the same way as the one in my house? Was it the same size?

"Get your coat. We have to go." Without waiting for my response, he dropped some cash on the table and got up to put on his coat.

"Marcus?"

"Now, Isabella," he said, throwing my coat at me.

He didn't wait until I had it on before making his way through the maze of tables and out the door. Once outside, Marcus walked toward a man halfway down the street. Once the man had spotted us, he started running. Marcus followed suit. I yelled after him, but he ignored me.

I tried to run, but the heels hindered my progress. Those female detectives in heels who run after perps and catch up to them without breaking a sweat? Unequivocal bullshit. I debated whether to take them off and run in my stockings, but decided against it. The rain had begun to accumulate and was quickly flooding the street. I hurried behind as fast as I could.

When I rounded the corner, just as Marcus had moments before, I tried to look for him. Once I spotted him again, he was nearly at the end of the street chasing the man into the road. I'm sure I saw it coming before he did: a car, a silver sedan, headlights lighting up his pants.

"Marcus, watch out!" I yelled… but it was too late.

I watched in slow motion as the car slid sideways toward him. He must have heard me, because he turned around and stood there watching as it approached. He should have had enough time to get out of the way, but he seemed paralyzed where he stood.

The car slammed into him, rendering him unconscious.

The perp doubled back to help the driver shove one of my only friends into the car. Then they disappeared. I tried to dial 911, but my hands were shaking.

I ran forward as the shock of it all took over. My meddling did this… My ego.

The rain fell on the spot where Marcus once stood. I couldn't possibly have seen it, but I imagined I saw it wash away the blood.

***

It was minutes before the cruisers arrived. With simple words, I explained what happened, but there wasn't much they could do. The rain had washed away any traces of tire tracks. Apart from myself, there were no witnesses. I didn't get the license plate, and there were no security cameras nearby. All the officers could do was take my statement then head to the diner to speak with the waitress. I went with them.

"I don't know what I can tell you," she said, wringing a cloth in her hand. "He seemed normal. He gave me the note and asked me to give it to the man sitting with this young lady."

"Did you read it?" one of the officers asked.

"No."

"Have you ever seen him before?"

She shook her head. "I would have recognized him if he was a regular, and he wasn't."

"Did he pay cash or by credit card?"

"Cash. And I hope you catch him. He's a lousy tipper."

"I see… would you be able to describe him to a sketch artist?" he asked.

She now appeared frustrated. "I can try, but please understand that it's been pretty busy, and I've seen a lot of faces tonight."

"I can do it," I chimed in, and the officer nodded.

When I made my way out of the diner, it had just stopped raining. The sky too was beginning to clear. I looked down as the accumulated water rushed toward a sewer grate—that's when I saw it. At the last moment, I snatched up the piece of paper before it was lost forever.

It was mostly illegible. It warned us to back off before we regretted it.

I crumpled the paper in my tightly closed fist.

Suddenly, it was as if my younger life were flashing before my eyes: the abuse, the torture, how Anna and I had been passed around like flyers on the Berkeley campus.

Jonathan had to have been behind this. He was the one who had taken Anna's young life, stolen from me the only other person I've ever loved. Jonathan had dug deep in my chest and ripped out my soul. Jonathan… It had always been him, but now he was mine.

The urge to make him suffer was pulling me inside out, snatching every fragment and bringing it all together. A new layer formed above the old. No longer did I have to follow the instructions of the voices. The voices had merged into one—AND I WAS THAT VOICE. For once, I knew what needed to be done. To find Marcus and avenge the deaths of the girls and of my childhood, I had to do this alone, without using the recording or involving the police.

Every single one of them was within my sights, and I would save the best for last. He would watch everyone around him disappear… and then it would be his turn. I would savor the moment, draw it out, make him beg for the same death he'd given my sister.

The rushing water beneath my feet had taken my fear with it. It was time for the masks to come off.

***

Heading home in the front seat of a cop car, my cell phone rang. It was Melanie.

"I've been trying to get in touch with Marcus," she said. "Can you give him a message from me?"

"I can't. I'm sorry. Marcus was taken tonight. I have no idea if he's even still alive."

"Holy shit. My God. What happened?"

"I'm sorry. I just can't right now."

"Okay… Isabella, I called because I couldn't get in touch with Detective Matthews either. There's something you two should know."

"What's that?" I asked, trying to sound concerned. In truth, I was desperate to get off the phone. I wasn't sure I could deal with anything else that night.

"We were able to identify one of the girls through dental records: the brunette. Brittany Simons. Last seen walking home from school three years ago. She was eight years old."

"Where was she from? Hello? Mel, where was she from?"

"Oh, Austin, Texas. Her family is on their way now."

"Thanks for letting me know."

"Please let me know if you hear anything about Marcus."

"I definitely will. I have to go now. Talk to you soon."

Texas, three years ago...

Sounded like something I'd heard recently. And where the hell was Matthews?

"I'm so sorry. Could you bring me to the Newark precinct instead?"

The officer stared me down. My stare was stronger.

CHAPTER TWENTY-SIX

BODY COUNT

AS SOON AS I walked into the precinct, I could tell word had gotten around that Marcus had been abducted. Almost everyone was there. I went to Matthews's desk then checked around the building; he was nowhere to be found. I saw another detective I knew and headed straight for him.

"Detective Sanders, have you seen Matthews?"

"I saw him earlier this afternoon. Are you sure he's not here?"

"No, but I doubt it… thanks…"

I pulled out my cell phone and punched in his number, but it immediately went to voicemail. His phone was off. All officers, regardless of rank, on duty or off, were supposed to be reachable at all times. Why would he turn off his phone? What had happened to him?

After I quickly gathered my thoughts, I called a cab.

***

I went to the Jersey Tavern, which, while a favorite of mine, was also an old hangout of Matthews's. After a quick scan around the bar, I took a seat. Eric had my drink in front of me within minutes.

"No stir stick," he said with a warm smile.

"Thanks, Eric."

"They'll find him," he said in a reassuring voice.

I guess I shouldn't have been surprised that word had spread so quickly. "Have you seen Matthews here tonight?"

"Nope. But if I spot him, I'll let you know."

"Thank you," I said, shifting my concentration to the drink in front of me.

As I drank, I went over things in my head.

Michael was Jonathan, which meant my father was still alive. He seemed to be connected to some sort of group that referred to themselves as "The Brotherhood." Their common interest was prepubescent girls, which they had a habit of killing once their use had been exhausted. Michael was linked to all four girls, along with Anna and myself, by our specific branding. But whoever killed them felt something for these girls. To them, they were more than mere objects: dressed and placed so they could be found instead of being hidden or buried. When they couldn't get me, they took Marcus instead. Did I miss something?

Where did Matthews fit in? He was nowhere to be found the night Marcus was taken. He had worked on the doll murders and Ember's case—though Marcus took him off the latter. Ember didn't trust him enough to talk, and he had no opinion about her family aside from Cody, which was extremely suspicious.

Another drink appeared in front of me. I offered Eric a weak smile. I could probably finish off a whole bottle if I wasn't careful. But I didn't care. I downed it and signaled for another.

I felt someone slide in beside me, and with a hopeful glance, I turned to see Melanie. I tried my best to hide my disappointment that it wasn't Marcus.

"Thought I'd find you here. I've been trying to call you, but you weren't answering." "What's going on?" I asked.

"I'm on my way to a crime scene and want you to come along. It's bad."

"What is it? Mel… You didn't come find me for a robbery. What's going on?"

"Three new girls were found in Weequahic Park."

***

The crime scene was identical, save one detail. Instead of a post, the three young girls were positioned around a tree. Not much difference as far as I was concerned.

"Sick bastard," Melanie muttered.

I couldn't agree more.

How many girls did they have in their possession? Were they cleaning house now that Michael knew I was on to them.

Was this my fault?

"Killed the same way, it would appear. And I'm sure the autopsies will be precisely like the last three I completed," Melanie said pensively, squatting beside the bodies. I joined her.

"Maybe this time there'll be trace evidence left behind," I said, though I knew it was unlikely. They'd picked the perfect time. It had just rained. Anything there would have washed away.

I scanned the faces of the people surrounding us. Still no Matthews. This was part of the ongoing investigation, so he should've been there.

I called him. Once again, it went to voice mail. Either he had gone missing as well, or there was more to this.

Either way, it was something I needed to check out.

CHAPTER TWENTY-SEVEN

THE INTERROGATOR

THE NEXT MORNING, walking into the precinct was like walking onto a trading floor. With no leads on Marcus, and the discovery of the new set of girls, all this commotion was to be expected. As I made my way through the floor, I was surprised to see Matthews heading toward me.

"Where the hell have you been?" I asked. He had the sketch artist in tow.

"Okay, okay—but before all that, we need to get a composite of the man you saw at diner last night."

"I agree. But then we need to talk," I told him.

I followed the sketch artist into one of the rooms.

"This shouldn't take too long. You'll be back in the drama shortly," he said, readying his things. "I'm Daniel."

"Nice to meet you, Daniel." I'd seen him around a few times but we'd never been formally introduced.

I watched as he fired up the computer. Technology… I'm not saying the old way of doing sketches isn't good, but this was even better and was quicker to complete.

"What can you tell me?" he asked.

"He was Caucasian, tall, heavyset, with a round face," I began. "His eyes were a bit farther apart than what you'd normally see. He had a large protruding nose and a small mouth. Overall his features looked disproportionate. He was—"

"Okay. Great. Can we take it just a little slower though?"

He brought up a couple of photographs as examples, each with a feature I'd mentioned. Pointing to the screen, I picked the ones that matched best.

"What color was his hair?"

"Dark brown, maybe black, and it was neatly cut, short."

"Eye color? Skin tone?"

"Don't know about the eyes but he was pale. Almost as pale as I am."

"Okay, one sec." I sat silently watching him pull it all together. Within ten minutes he was done.

"Would this be him?" he asked.

"Raise the eyebrows slightly, make them a bit thicker." He made the slight corrections then looked back at me. "That's him."

***

Arriving in front of Matthew's desk, I couldn't miss his deep sigh. He stood up.

"Let's go to one of the rooms."

"To be honest, Dean, I'm getting a little tired of rooms," I said.

"Look, I know you're pissed off—"

"Pissed off? No, that's what I was last night. Today is a whole new monster."

"Which is why I'd rather take this to a room."

Why? So no one could hear us talking? So our eavesdroppers wouldn't view Matthews the way I did then? I didn't want to, but if I didn't comply, I wouldn't get very far.

"Fine. Lead the way."

Once inside the meeting room, we sat down on opposite sides.

"So tell me, Dean, where were you last night?"

He sat calm and collected in his chair. "As I've already told my superiors, I was out of range for cell service when all this happened."

"That's not particularly specific is it? You were supposed to be working last night. You weren't." In here I wasn't a psychiatrist; I was an interrogator.

He squirmed in his seat slightly. "I was. I was looking into... well, what I thought was a lead."

"What you *thought*?"

"Turned out to be a dead end."

Looking at him now, through a psychiatrist's eyes, I noticed his tension: a slight bead of sweat had formed and was making its way down his forehead. It wasn't hot in the room. He couldn't look at me when answering my questions—first having to raise his eyes to the right as if to recall what he had done last night—was a telltale sign. They were simple questions that required simple answers, but the way he reacted told me he was lying. For a detective, he wasn't hiding his tells very well.

"Do you want me to tell you what I've been thinking?" I asked him.

He hesitated for a moment. "What's that?"

"You weren't out of cell range... Why'd you turn your phone off, Dean?" I asked, studying him closely. "Were you pissed that Marcus took you off Ember's case? Maybe his disappearing wasn't such a bad thing for you in the end?"

"I don't have to listen to this you know." He was again shifting in his seat.

"Why won't you tell me?"

He shook his head. "I had nothing to do with Marcus's disappearance. Nothing!"

"Then why do I think you're involved in all this?"

Confusion now masked his face, feigned or otherwise. "All this?"

"You really want me to say it?"

"You have no idea how far off you are," he responded, clenching his fists.

"I don't think I am… and now I just have to prove it."

"I'm a good guy, but you better be careful, Isabella…"

"I've been hearing that a lot lately, and now from you," I said calmly. "Where is this threat coming from?"

He tried to laugh it off. "It wasn't a threat."

"Then what would you call it?"

"You threatened me. You're also intimidating me against my will. I told you to stop. That's what that was."

"Different words, but they still have the same meaning behind them."

"I'm not threatening you, Isabella!" He was becoming frustrated, angry. "Do you have any idea what your careless assumptions could do to my career?"

"Do you honestly think I give a shit?" I shot back, raising my voice slightly. "I have six dead girls and a missing lieutenant. If you were in my place, what would you do?"

This time he looked me straight in the eyes. "Look at it from all angles before I started pointing fingers."

"Isn't it 'guilty until proven innocent' with you guys?"

He released a sigh before wiping at the hair now sticking to his forehead. "That's not how it works…"

"Here it does. I'm just playing along."

"You couldn't be more wrong."

"Prove it."

***

Whatever was going on, I had to follow my ritual. I'd made a promise to Anna the day I came back to New Jersey, and I couldn't break it. More than that, I needed to be with her.

I stood in front of Anna's headstone, but instead of positioning myself as I usually would, I sat down alongside it, resting my head against the cool marble. I closed my eyes for a moment and pictured her sitting beside me.

"If there ever was a time when I really needed to hear your voice, it's now," I said, allowing the tears to finally escape.

I wasn't a crier; I'd lost the ability to do so a long time ago… but the tears had been brought back to life, and I didn't try to stop them.

"He's here, Anna. He's putting other girls through what we went through," I said. "There's this little girl, Ember, who reminds me of you. You would have liked, Ember."

I hated the silence; I needed to hear something besides my own voice… but that's all I had.

"I couldn't protect you, but please help me make sure that Ember and the other girls within their grasp will be safe."

Head flat on the gravestone, I closed my eyes and allowed the tranquility of the place to envelop me.

CHAPTER TWENTY-EIGHT

A STROLL IN THE WOODS

FIVE DAYS HAD PASSED since Marcus's disappearance. After speaking with the police chief to confirm that Marcus had no living relatives or loved ones—besides myself—I needed to keep myself busy so as not to be reminded of that fact. To distract myself, I'd gotten Drew O'Reilly's schedule down to the second. I knew where he was at every moment; I knew what he would do even before he did. I set up a nice little place for him, and waited for the right opportunity to put everything into motion.

Tonight was the night.

The moon was full, each star was in attendance, and the sky had never been blacker. I watched as he left the Rusty Nail in Brooklyn at 2:00a.m. He locked his car after getting in. Every movement he made screamed caution. He was aware and afraid... as he should be.

I'd found a beat up car on Craigslist, just for this occasion—a brown 1985 Chevy Citation. I didn't register it. I went as far as grabbing someone else's plates, an easy task to accomplish, one that would ensure the car couldn't be traced back to me.

I drove ahead as Drew made his nightly trip back to his home in Newark, periodically checking my rearview to make sure he was still behind me. He didn't disappoint. Halfway through Branch Brook Park, I slammed on the brakes and braced for the impact.

Screeching tires. Burnt rubber. He followed as I parked on the side of the road. The damage to his car would be minimal… just enough to piss him off. He got out, inspected the damage, and made his way to me.

Before rolling down my window, I made sure the hoodie was still in place. Everything else was ready too.

"I'm so sorry, sir," I told him when he reached my window, keeping my head tilted downward. He was livid.

"Sorry? Did you learn to drive at golf n' stuff? The fuck are you doing?"

"Everything right. I needed to get your attention."

"You want my fucking attention?"

Drew leaned down to glare at me. "You stupid c—"

He didn't get the chance to finish.

Like a coiled snake, striking with perfect precision, I injected my cocktail—diazepam and propofol—into the artery in his neck. He hit the ground hard. Being a psychiatrist has its perks. I stepped out, smacking Drew with the door, and made for the other car. As I turned off his engine in the darkness, I knew no one would see a thing. By the time his car was found, it wouldn't matter. The only thing left was lugging a sicko a few measly feet. It was all too easy.

***

Branch Brook Park is the biggest public park in Newark—notable for its large collection of cherry blossom trees. It boasts fourteen different varieties, approximately 4,300 in total, spread throughout 360 acres. The Old Blue Jay Swamp had been transformed into a wonderful lake... but I doubt Drew appreciated the scenery.

I sat on the ground a few feet away from him, utilizing the tree coverage to the fullest. I'd just kidnapped a man, but I found myself playing with a twig. It was taking longer than expected for him to wake up, and I was becoming impatient.

I'd taken off his clothes. With stakes and ropes, secured him to the ground by the wrists and ankles. I even covered him with a tarp... he wouldn't be going anywhere. With the ground starting to freeze, it was a hard task, but I managed it. I always managed it.

Finally, he stirred. He was moaning, moving his head from side to side, his eyes still closed.

"Drew? Open your eyes, Drew," I said, seductively.

He did, and I was delighted when he realized he couldn't move. I watched with a smile as the panic set in. He struggled, but the stakes were in the ground as far as they would go. His thrashing was soon replaced with shivering as the cold set in.

"You bitch," he growled.

"Has my name changed? I've been called that quite a few times in the last few weeks," I said teasingly.

"You won't get away with this," he said through clenched teeth.

"Oh, Drew. Silly boy. Do you think this is the first time I've done this?" I asked, looking down as I walked a full circle around him. "Guess again."

He allowed a laugh to escape. "Why me? Do you really think I'm the mastermind behind this?"

"Nah, that would be giving you too much credit."

"FUCK YOU," he roared. But the rain kept his voice from traveling.

"I have to start somewhere, and it might as well be with the lowest scum on the totem pole."

He didn't like that remark. The thrashing began again. I pressed the tip of my boot into his forehead.

"If you don't stop, I'll bash your head in," I said, calmly. "Drew? Buddy? Are you done with your fit?"

He stopped. The anger dissipated. "Found Marcus yet?"

"I'm sorry?"

His grin widened. "You deaf, bitch? I asked if you found Marcus."

"That doesn't concern you."

"Lowest rung my ass. Who do you think orchestrated that?"

I raised an eyebrow. "Are you sure you want to take credit for that?"

"Credit where credit is due."

I knelt and put my mouth close to his ear. "I know it wasn't you," I whispered. "You'd only go after little girls."

"You think you're so smart?" Drew asked with a laugh.

"I do. How would Michael feel about that?"

"About what?"

"How does it feel to live in his shadow... having to take orders from him, obeying everything he says? I wonder how he'd feel if he knew you were taking credit for his work."

His voice became as rigid as his body. "I don't take orders from no one. I do what I want, to who I want."

"Then let me ask you another question: how did it feel when he told you I was off limits?"

That question obviously surprised him. "You bugged us?"

"See, that's why you're stuck to the ground with your legs and arms spread… tied up like the girls you raped. You underestimated who you went up against. Admit it. You have to obey everything Michael tells you. It's okay, Drew. You can tell me."

"I'm going to kill you."

"I'll take that to mean I'm correct in my statement."

"What's the plan? What are you going to do to me?"

"Think hard," I said. "I'm sure even you're smart enough to figure it out."

"Then do it," he said flatly, turning his head away.

"Don't want to talk anymore?" I asked, digging a knee into either leg. He winced. "You want to join Brittany?"

"Who?" His smile quickly disappeared.

"Oh, I see. The names don't matter, only what they can provide you… she was the little girl you took with you when you left Texas. The one you killed when you were done with her."

He shook his head. "I didn't kill her, not my thing."

"Then who did?"

"Do you seriously think I'm going to tell you that?"

"No, but I thought it was worth a try."

I took the Bowie knife and put all my weight behind it, plunging it into his chest. The life drained from his eyes as quickly as his blood rushed from the wound.

***

Drew safely in the car, I rolled down the window just enough so I could get out. I revved the engine and let go of the brake, carefully veering the car toward Old Blue Jay lake.

It didn't make as much noise as I'd thought it would. The water entered through the open window. Its coldness, like little daggers, sent a chill throughout my body. Swimming through the window, I quickly swam my way up to the surface, taking in a huge gulp of air. I'd gotten the car out far enough so it wouldn't be noticed. I hoped Drew would remain submerged for the duration of winter; just need the lake to freeze over.

I made my way to the bag I'd stashed earlier and changed clothes. I hurried out of the park to where I'd parked my car earlier that day— two blocks away at an abandoned factory. After tossing my bag, full of wet clothes onto the passenger seat, I headed home.

I turned up the heat as far as it could go.

***

I arrived home at 4:00a.m., armed the alarm, and headed upstairs to the shower. The heat cleared away the chill of the cold lake water.

Once finished, I put on a bathrobe and called the precinct for an update on Marcus. Zero leads. The rest of the night was filled with sighs.

Marcus, where are you?

CHAPTER TWENTY-NINE

THE SETUP

KATHERINE WOULD BE EASY. I needed her out of the way to keep Ember safe. It was early evening, and she was at the grocery store, where I planned to "accidentally" bump into her. I rounded the corner with my cart and lightly crashed into hers. I made a show of apologizing, but watched carefully as she realized who I was.

Surprise glued her to where she stood. "Dr. Porter, what are you doing here?"

"Same as everyone else: shopping," I replied. "How are you?"

"I'm not supposed to talk to you," she said, coming back to her senses, quickly trying to maneuver her cart around mine. I didn't make it easy.

"I'd like to apologize for the way I've been with you," I said, working to simulate remorse in my voice. "I realize how difficult everything must be for you."

She narrowed her eyes, looking at me skeptically. "It's been very difficult. And you haven't made it any better."

"I know. I was going to call you actually. To try to make amends, I've set up an appointment so you can see Ember."

"According to you, I don't want to see her. I just want to hurt her."

"You do want to see her... because she's your daughter, and you're concerned about her," I said, coaching her. "I know you haven't attempted to contact her since I put those restrictions in place."

Her body was starting to relax a bit; she was obviously taking the bait. "No, I haven't. You've made it really hard for me to be her mother."

I put on my most sympathetic face, showing her I was taking the blame for her predicament. "I know I have. How about if I pick you up tomorrow morning, and bring you over to see her? Unfortunately, I can't lift the restrictions yet, but if I'm with you, you can have some time with your daughter."

She was mulling it over, the skepticism never leaving her face. "You'd have to come after Michael left."

"Here's my cell number," I said as I wrote it down on a sheet from my memo pad. "Give me a call when he's gone, and then I'll come by and pick you up."

She hesitantly took it and slipped it into her purse. "You'll really give me time alone with her?"

"I will. But only if you want it."

I almost felt bad for her. Katherine didn't look like she had any clue what she wanted.

CHAPTER THIRTY

MOTHER DEAREST

I WAS ALREADY in position when the call came. As I watched Michael's car shrink in my rearview mirror, I told Katherine I'd be there within the hour, depending on traffic of course. When I was sure no one was around, I left my car and made for the house. I carefully unhitched the gate, walked to a back window, and peered inside.

Katherine was in the kitchen, coffee cup in hand, flipping through the newspaper. She scratched at her bathrobe, finished her coffee, and walked toward the stairs that led to the upper level. Once I was sure she wouldn't be making a reappearance, I pulled open the window and slipped inside.

I heard the water running upstairs and quickly checked the house for unwanted visitors. With her younger son in school, and Cody in juvenile detention, I didn't expect to find any. It was 9:17a.m., when I finished looking. I couldn't count on Michael staying away. I had to be quick and meticulous.

Carefully, I made my way up the stairs. A quiet creak of the floorboards told me she was in her bedroom, probably undressing for her bath. I pondered the best place to take up position; I chose the bathroom. There was an enclosed shower in one corner, and a running bath the shape of a semicircle in the other. Between the two was a window. I closed the blinds, and waited behind the door... She would notice me when she closed it. I'd have to be quick.

She entered the bathroom humming a tune, pinning her hair to the back of her head. She turned off the water. As she walked back toward the door, she let the bathrobe drop from her body to the floor. With a single hand, she pushed the door until it came to rest, but she noticed me through the crack.

She screamed, falling backward, clutching at the counter. I leapt into action, rushing toward her neck with the needle. She raised her hands to shield her face, and caught her in the arm. I'd have preferred the skin below the nape of her neck, but within seconds of pressing down on the plunger, I held her limp body in my arms. I dragged her to the bathtub and positioned her so she sat leaning against a curved sides.

"I'd ask if you were comfortable, but right now you shouldn't feel a thing. I just injected you with bupivacaine," I told her, closing the toilet lid and taking a seat.

Her anxiety was rising, which was evident in her eyes. "I don't understand."

"What don't you understand?"

"Why you're doing this," she said, as a single tear made its way down her cheek.

"Those were the exact words my mother said to me ... that she didn't understand."

"And what did you tell her?"

"I told her I was the one who couldn't understand—couldn't grasp how she sat idly by and watched while Michael raped my sister and me..."

"I don't have a choice." She pleaded with me, willing me to understand. "I prayed I'd never have a girl. I tried to abort her when I knew..."

"There's always a choice. The two of you made the most selfish ones you could. You're weak. Self-preservation is all you care about."

"That's not true—"

"No? It had nothing to do with the fact that you'd never be left alone, be safe?" Katherine lay there like a broken doll, her head leaning slightly to the left. "You had a choice, just like my mother did, to end the silence and stop him."

"If I could've pushed a button I would have!" she shot back. "It's not that simple. Think! If I die, who'll be there to protect Ember?"

"Who was there to protect Ember when you kept your mouth shut?" I was becoming angry. "Who asked her to take her own life?"

She was moaning now. Wailing. "You didn't hear him. The way he raged... I wanted... I though, at least she wouldn't have to suffer anymore... please..." she muttered. The tears were overflowing. "Tell me what to do and I'll do it. I'll work with you. I'll help you."

"You're a puppet, Katherine. It's time to sever the strings."

I shoved her body under the water. There was no thrashing. No final bolts of lightning before her storm ended. I climbed in the tub with her and watched her eyes. Open. Staring in horror as she knew she was going to die. They whipped around in every direction, before they settled on my face, looking down at her through the water: the last thing she would ever see.

When I was satisfied, I changed my clothes, grabbed my bag, left the bathroom. I hurried downstairs ready to leave through the back when I heard a knock on the door, stopping me in my tracks. I headed to the front window, but peeking out, I didn't recognize the man standing on the front porch. He was a medium-sized, well-dressed, African-American with a shaved head. As the pounding began, I made my way through the patio doors in the kitchen.

One of Michael's men. He had to be.

I exited through the back gate and ran toward my car. I sat low in the seat and waited. The man rushed out the front door and onto the porch, quickly scanning the area before retreating back into the house. That was my cue to leave.

***

I'd just parked my car at the precinct when I saw Michael walking toward me. I fully intended on walking right by him, but he had a different idea. He stopped a few feet in front of me, blocking my path.

"We have a meeting tomorrow morning," I said. "We can talk then." He didn't budge.

"You're seriously going to confront me here?" I asked, motioning to the area around us.

"Watch me."

"Come on, Michael. I pegged you as being a lot more controlled than that."

"I thought the same of you. Haven't you learned anything?"

"How do you mean?"

He was trying hard to keep his temper in check. His body was rigid, and his face twitched as he tried to maintain control. "You've started

something you won't be able to finish. First with Drew, now Katherine... and I liked her. She was nice."

Bringing forth my best mask of empathy, I said, "I just heard about
that. I'm sorry for your loss."

"You can stop with the act, Isabella," he said through gritted teeth.
"I know it was you."

"It's normal to want to place blame anywhere except where it be-
longs," I told him in my most sympathetic voice. "We can speak more
about this tomorrow morning."

I started to walk away, and as I was passing him, he grabbed my
arm and tightly squeezed it. I grimaced as his nails dug into my skin,
forcing me to stop.

"You know what kind of man I am, and you still test me." He
yanked on my arm, dropping me to my knees. "I like you there. Maybe
I'll have you suck on my cock before I kill you."

I jerked my arm away and stood up.

"I could kill you right here, and no one would bat an eyelash," I
told him. "Take a look around. There are cameras everywhere, and after that little display, do you really think the courts wouldn't rule self-
defense?"

He backed away, the fire in his eyes taking a brief respite. He
smiled. "You're right. There's no rush. I'll see you tomorrow morning,
Dr. Porter."

I forced myself not to look back. If he was starting to lose control,
it would force my hand, and I'd have to complete my work that much
faster.

CHAPTER THIRTY-ONE

QUIET NIGHT AT HOME

I RETURNED TO the townhouse to curl up with a bottle of wine. I locked up as normal and cracked a book. It was all beginning to its toll on me. Since Marcus's disappearance, I hadn't had a moment to myself, and I refused to let it go to waste.

I was a few chapters in when I heard it: the soft beep of my alarm being deactivated. I flung my book on the bed and made for the kitchen. Opening a low cupboard to not draw attention, I took out a pan—unfortunately, not without sound. I readied myself as best I could, and hid just behind the double doors of my wooden pantry.

My mind raced. I knew something was coming—that was clear. What I didn't know was that Michael employed someone skilled enough to bypass the security... In moments, the sex trafficking theory replaced the pedophile ring in my mind. The Brotherhood had connections. It was all too obvious.

As I heard the soft creak of steps on the wood floor, I slowed my breath. Every step brought me closer to sheer panic. The darkness of the pantry didn't help anything. He stopped for a moment outside its wooden doors. I knew then that he would open them, and I would be discovered and killed; when panic had taken my name from my memory, I still knew that. But somehow, he walked on—the sound of his creaking steps finally moved beyond the slit in the doors.

I sprang out, suddenly swinging wildly with my pan. I batted the gun away before I even saw it, but before I could do any real damage, he knocked the pan to floor and tackled me to the ground. Sprawled on the kitchen floor, he clenched a strong hand around my ankle, and I struggled desperately to get free. For a moment, I felt like the little girl under the bed again. Helpless.

And then I got an arm free and broke his nose. Or I hoped I did. His face was covered in a mask, and I didn't stop to measure the blood. In moments, I had a kitchen knife in my hand. When I turned, I saw my assailant reaching for his gun. I charged forward, not knowing if a bullet would go through my head, or my heart. I charged with the knife, blindly, losing myself in the fight for my life. He grabbed the gun at the same time I sank the blade into his arm.

He rolled backward in shock, leaving the gun in its place. I went to stab at him again, but he leapt up suddenly and I prepared to defend myself. Surprisingly, he didn't run toward me, but through the living room, and out the door.

***

I armed the alarm again—not that it would do me any good—then I called the chief of police.

"Leo, it's Dr. Isabella Porter. I'm sorry to disturb you so late... I could be better. How about you? That's good... Because I received a threat on my life... Just a phone call, nothing yet, but he sounded serious. I'm really worried. I need police protection tonight... and from now on as far as I know." It went on like that for a while.

When I was off the phone, I briefly mourned the loss of my quiet night. And then I wet the mop.

CHAPTER THIRTY-TWO

FINAL LINE CROSSED

THE POLICE PROTECTION was only valid when I was at the house. When I returned after giving Ember her book the next day, I found it raided—the gun I'd hidden behind last week's pad thai was missing... Fortunately, the raid justified the police protection, and I was given a number to call whenever I needed it.

Despite the recent drama, today would be a good day. It was the day I would finally get to see Michael crack. He'd been consistent up until then, but his unraveling edges were beginning to show. The man in my home was par for the course, but he must have been falling apart a little, or he would never have confronted me at the precinct. I was just about to leave my house when my cell phone rang. "Hello?"

"It's Ember. She's gone," Dale said.

"She can't be! I saw her yesterday."

"She is. I went into her room this morning. She was gone."

"Wasn't Bonnie with her last night?"

"We decided to give it a try—you know, her being on her own. Bonnie was with me. We checked in on her before we turned in for the night, and she was sound asleep."

"What about the officer?"

"That's how we found out she was missing."

"What do you mean?"

"His morning replacement found him in the squad car, shot in the head."

Suddenly, I felt a lot less safe.

"When he came in," he continued, "we rushed up to Ember's room together. That's when we found her gone."

"That's quite a window of time… Well, I have a meeting with Michael this morning that I can't miss, but I'll be there as soon as I can."

"You tell that bastard if he harms one hair on her head, he's dead."

"Dale, I promise you we'll find her safe," I assured him.

"You promised she'd be safe from the start," he shot back. "I'll believe what you have to say when she's back home."

He hung up.

Dale was angry and rightfully so. I'd promised him I would protect Ember no matter what, and I'd failed—again. I had to find her, and quickly, otherwise she wouldn't be alive when I did.

***

I slammed my bag on the interview room table.

Michael looked up at me with a smile. "Bad morning?"

"Bad life. Where is she?"

He raised an eyebrow. "Who?"

"You know exactly who I'm talking about."

"The death of my wife has been very hard on me. I suggest you be more respectful." I heard feigned innocence in his voice but saw true evil in his eyes.

I roughly grabbed his collar in my hands. "Ember! Where's Ember, Michael?"

He hit me right in the jaw. I fell to the floor in a heap. He rose, casting his shadow over me.

"That was self-defense. You know it. The cameras show it. If you have a problem with that, I might let the others in on your little secret, Bella."

I lay silent in shame. Against the will of my soul, I'd been forced to relent.

"Now as to the whereabouts of my daughter… I thought that was under your control?"

I stood, returning to sit at the other side of the table.

"You may not have done it personally," I said, "but you're involved, and we both know it."

Disgust covered every crevice of his face. "What part of your tiny brain can't grasp this? I told you before—you started something you can't possibly finish."

"So another young girl has to die to prove your point?" I was trying to hide what Ember actually meant to me, but I was failing.

Suddenly the most evil of smiles appeared on his face. "Another? Do you mean Anna?"

"You don't have the right to speak her name. Do it again, and the first thing I cut off will be your tongue," I warned him.

"Is that any way to speak to your father?" he asked, the smirk deepening as the last word left his lips.

"I don't have a father."

"You really don't see it?"

"See what?"

"We're one and the same, you and I, cut from the same cloth — literally and figuratively. Faked any emotions lately? You can do all you want for the sake of outward appearances, but inside we both know who you truly are."

I hoped he was wrong, but had no argument to refute his claim. Whatever the truth, how we used our inescapable natures were galaxies apart; perhaps it was that alone that made us different.

"Do you want to hear me agree with you? Would that satisfy the need you so obviously have?" I asked. "What then? I join you and we rule the galaxy together? Father and daughter?"

"Do you have to fake your humor as well?" he asked. "Should I pretend to laugh for you, or have some dramatic revelation? Bella, you are my daughter!"

I remained in my seat, holding onto its edges so hard, I thought it might break. "Sarcasm comes easily to me, especially with people like you. Don't pretend to know who I am."

"Do you think I forgot you when you left to live with your aunt and uncle in Rhode Island? Even though I no longer existed to *you*, perhaps there was a remote possibility I didn't follow suit?"

"What's your point old man?"

He raised a finger for emphasis. "My point is simple. I've kept tabs on you for the past twenty-three years. I knew you were coming back here before you did."

"You're a lying sack—"

"Am I? You think you're so smart? Put your anger aside for a moment. Maybe you'll find out how I did it… If not, you can always focus on what matters."

"You're right. Where's Ember?"

"She's safe. That's all you need to know for now."

"As long as she's with you, she's anything but safe. I'm what you'd call an expert on the topic."

"Then, being the expert you are, you know I won't give in that easily," he said, pausing just long enough to fill the room with tension. "Leave New Jersey. Permanently move away, and she'll be brought back to Dale and Bonnie unharmed."

"I trust you as much as a pack of starving wolves. You'd never let her go."

"Are you really ready to put that theory to the test?" he asked in the most serious tone he'd used yet.

"You know what, Michael? You're right. I've wasted enough time as it is. I know what needs to be done." I got up and slung my bag over my shoulder. "We're done for now."

He stood suddenly, knocking the chair to the ground behind him. I froze.

"One more thing before you go. This is strictly between you and I—a choice you made and a consequence to your actions."

"What's that supposed to mean?"

"No outside authorities. If you decide to involve the police, I'll pass her around one last time before I kill the brat, my daughter or not."

I nodded and made for the door.

"Tick tock, Bella! Better get a move on! Who knows how much time is left."

I stormed down the hall, fuming. I was just turning my first corner when I bumped into someone—Dean. *He was near the door... had he been listening the whole time?*

"I'm sorry. I wasn't paying attention," I said.

"Were you talking to my suspect?"

If he'd been in the viewing room, he wasn't letting on. "I had a meeting scheduled with him this morning," I said, eyeing him suspiciously.

"That meeting was cancelled. Don't you ever check your phone?" I stared him down. "Well, now that Marcus isn't here, I'm back on the O'Reilly case," he said, exuding his newfound authority. "With Ember now missing, Michael O'Reilly has to go through me before any further assessments are done."

"Understood," I said. "I'm on my way over to Ember's aunt and uncle's house to give them some support, if that's okay with you."

He nodded. "Sure. I think you're more needed there for now anyway. I'll let you know when it's okay to start assessments again."

I wondered as I walked away, listening to the interview door open and close behind me, how long he'd been waiting to put me in my place.

***

Rather than a single squad car there were at least half a dozen in front of the Donnelly home, along with news crews and inquisitive neighbors. I showed my ID to a uniformed officer, and made my way to Bonnie and Dale.

"This is a circus," he said.

"But it has the potential to work for us," I told him. "If anyone sees Ember, you can rest assured it'll be reported."

"Oh, please. If Michael has her, he'll keep her out of sight."

"He hasn't won this. I'll find her and bring her back."

"First," Bonnie said, "my niece is repeatedly raped, then Marcus goes missing, my sister-in-law kills herself, the officer sworn to protect her gets shot in the head, and now, after everything, she's gone. How can you think this'll ever take a positive turn?"

Her face told me she'd been crying since that morning. The tears threatened to start again. Dale put his arm around her and whispered something in her ear. She nodded before heading into the house.

Dale turned his own moist eyes toward me. "She isn't holding up very well..."

"And how about you? Your sister just died," I gently asked.

He let out a weak laugh. "She was my sister, and I loved her, faults and all. But her death was only a matter of time. Even when we were children, she was always putting herself in one bad situation or another. When I found out about Michael... I'm in no way saying she deserved to be killed..." He trailed off, unable to finish his thought.

He was talking about her death as if it weren't an accident; I decided to leave it be. "I understand what you're saying, but losing her, along with everything else—well, it's got to be a lot to take in."

"All I want is Ember. That's all that matters."

"And I assure you, our complete focus is on finding her... but I think it's best we go inside, away from all this commotion."

He nodded. When we went inside, there were as many people inside as there were outside. Family members and police officers intermingled throughout the house, showing moral support for one another.

Dale sighed. "You know, it's hard to believe Ember had all these people behind her, and he was still able to get to her."

I looked at him, then back at the crowd, and realized he was right. Suddenly, I needed to see her bedroom.

"Is forensics done upstairs?" I asked.

"They are. Feel free to take a look around. Maybe you'll catch something they missed."

I nodded and made my way to the stairs. Entering her room was like walking into a town after a tornado hit. Her most secret possessions were carelessly strewn about for all to see. The only place that seemed relatively untouched was her bed. The covers were still pulled back from when she was lying in it, but her pillow and stuffed animals remained as they always were. I sat on the edge of the bed and looked around to see if anything spoke to me. Nothing but silence. Until I heard it.

I stopped where I was and listened intently. Then I heard it again... The whispers... Reaching under her pillow, I found the book I'd given her the day before. Sitting back down, I examined it, willing it to speak to me. I opened it to the page where she'd finished last. I smiled when I saw she was using my card as a bookmark, but there was nothing there that gave me any clue as to her location. The only thing left was to check the lake house. I didn't think she'd be there, but it was the only lead I had.

CHAPTER THIRTY-THREE

1993

IT WAS 6:00p.m., but I wasn't waiting for morning before heading to the cabin. I stopped by my place with a police escort, to grab a few things, and was back on the road within minutes. It would take around five hours to get there, and even though I wished I could shorten the drive, it would give me the opportunity to think through various scenarios.

There could be no one there at all, or the cabin could be full of brothers. Ember could be hidden anywhere, whether in the cabin itself or in the vicinity, and that could be the real challenge—figuring out exactly where. The cabin would be the easiest to check, but the surrounding woods? That could take me days, if not longer. And there was no way of knowing if I was off the mark. Of all the questions I asked myself, one rang out above the others—

If she's not there, do I leave?

I thought back on how the situation had progressed, and how, if I'd done things differently, maybe Ember would be asleep in bed. Once the pieces started falling into place, I ignored my true job and got too personally involved—something I'd never done before. It wasn't just

Ember... Three more girls were dead. I'd let myself get boxed in with Michael. There were few choices left.

***

It was coming up on nine-thirty, and my car was whining for gas. I pulled into a service station, prepaid, and waited for my tank to fill. Growing impatient, I walked inside.

At the coffee station, I poured myself the largest cup they had. After adding sugar and milk, I took a sip... it tasted like shit. On my way to the cashier, I grabbed a bag of chips and placed them both on the counter.

"More gas with that?"

It was the same guy as the last time—lanky and probably in his late teens, with a rash of red pimples on the sides of his face. "No, I'm good," I told him. "Listen, do you remember me? I was here about a week ago."

He shook his head. "That'll be three fifty-three."

Why was he lying? When I handed him the money, his hands were sweaty; he didn't look me in the eye; he kept changing the foot he was leaning on... Either he did know me, or he desperately had to go to the bathroom. My money was on the first.

Instead of leaving right after I received my change, I stuck around to see him go into the back room. Then I headed toward it.

"Long brown hair. Yeah, same one." The kid was talking to someone on the phone, a photograph in his hand.

"I thought you said you didn't recognize me?" I said.

Startled, he hung up the phone and quickly turned around.

"You can't be back here."

"Then call the police!" I yelled, taking him off guard.

I grabbed at the photograph in his hand, taking half of it back with me.

"Can't say this is my better half," I said with a smirk, looking down at it. "Where did you get it?"

It was a recent photograph. I knew exactly where and when it was taken: just outside my townhouse the morning I drove to Queens to meet Ember for the first time. I knew this because the only time I usually tie my hair up is when I'm heading to a crime scene. That morning I'd gone out of my routine.

"Miss, you're gonna get me in a lot of trouble."

"Where did you get this picture of me?"

"I'm going to have to ask you to leave," he said, trying to sound tough. He failed.

"And I'm going to have to insist you tell me."

"If you don't leave, I'm going to call—"

I squatted to the floor and, using my right leg, sideswiped his feet from under him. Before he had the chance to move, I spun myself back up to a standing position and placed my left foot on his chest.

"This is your last chance," I warned him. "Where did you get this picture of me?"

"My boss," he said. "I was told that if you entered the station again, I should call him."

"Did he tell you why?"

He shook his head. "No."

"What's your boss's name?" I asked, but he didn't answer. "Okay, nod if I get it right. Michael O'Reilly?"

It was hesitant and barely noticeable, but he nodded. Son of a bitch owned this town. I threw my half down at him and removed my foot. A wet patch had formed in the crotch of his khakis.

"You may want to clean yourself up before you head back out there," I said casually before making my way out.

***

So now there were only two scenarios: either he would call up all of his men, or he would move Ember. Seeing as the element of surprised had been eliminated, I drove straight to the cabin and parked beside it. There were no other cars. The cabin was dark. I'd probably been wrong this whole time, and she was never there... but I'd come too far. If she was here, and I left now, I might never find her again.

I put on latex gloves and made the perimeter. Nothing seemed out of the ordinary. I crept up the few steps and tried the front door, but it was locked. Looking around, I checked the typical places where a key could be hidden but found nothing.

It was all crazy. I really didn't want to resort to breaking windows to get in. However, when you had no other choice...

After searching the ground, I found a large rock, and struck a pane of glass in the window next to the door. It didn't break—it just popped out of place and landed with a clatter on the floor. I reached in and turned the deadbolt until I heard its satisfying click. Keeping hold of the rock, I walked inside.

It was quiet... maybe a little too quiet. Save the sound of crickets coming in through the broken window, I heard nothing. Soundproofed? Would make sense. Even though the cabins were few and far between, sound traveled well here. I guessed there was a reason the noise level was kept to a minimum.

I found the flashlight app in my phone before leaving the door. I activated it hesitantly, not wanting to draw attention to myself... but it was better than turning on the lights, and I needed to see. There was nothing on the first floor, so I made my way to the second level.

When I arrived, I noticed five rooms—six if I counted the bathroom. Holding my rock close, I began checking each one. They were all the same: the same furniture, the same bedding, the same lack of decor. The only thing that stood out was that the shutters were on the wrong side of the windows. Examining the shutter in the third bedroom, I found a latch where a padlock could be placed. The windows couldn't be opened. All that could be seen were gray plastic strips hanging an inch away on the other side. Even the doors locked from outside of the room.

At first glance, the furniture seemed rudimentary, but on examining it closer, I found otherwise. Instead of a bed frame, the mattresses were on platforms. It reminded me of those captain beds children sometimes have, the ones with a drawer built into the side. I tried to pull the drawer open, but it wouldn't budge... that's when I noticed a small square padlock on either side. Using the rock in my hands, I easily popped them open.

I pulled at the drawer again, but instead of the small space I expected, I found an area nearly as large as the platform itself. It had a cover on top of it with a small window blanketed in mesh on one of the ends.

They kept people in there.

Without warning, the door to the room slammed shut. I bolted upright as I heard the sickening click as it was locked. I scrambled to open it, but I knew it was futile. Standing still, I listened for any kind of noise but heard nothing. I did, however, smell something—something burning. Someone had lit a fire. I was never meant to leave this room.

The smoke entered beneath the crack of the door and slowly filled the room. I rushed to the bed, and yanked off a pillowcase. I folded the pillowcase into a triangle and tied it around my mouth. When it was wrapped tight, I shoved the naked pillow under the cracks under the door.

I jogged to the window and tried to break it with my rock, but it was laminated glass—sturdy and perfect for sound proofing. The window won. I couldn't think straight. I kept bashing until I was beating it with only my fist. My eyes watered and I couldn't see. I needed something bigger... stronger. I groped in the smoke until my hands wrapped around the leg of an aluminum chair. In a fit of coughs, I turned to see flames licking at the doorframe, burning their way inside. My knees were weak, and I was filled with an overwhelming Déjà vu. I was back in the lake house, in more ways than one. I wouldn't last much longer.

I dragged the chair over to the window, but it was too heavy to lift... or I was too weak. I raised it a couple feet from the floor, but it crashed repeatedly. Suddenly, fear took me and I knew I was going to die... and that was okay. What wasn't okay was the satisfaction my death would bring to Michael. Thinking of Ember, once again one of his many playthings, I grabbed the chair in a rage and hurled it at the glass. The window started to crack, making a spider-web pattern on the pane. This time, I raised it above my head, and put all my remaining life into it. The glass shattered and a burst of rushing flames set my hair on fire.

I dove through the window. The rushing air put out the fire. I was high up, and as I fell, I prayed the fall wouldn't kill me.

***

I stumbled to my car, covered in cuts and bruises. As I drove away from the cabin in a daze, I briefly stopped to look back. My vision was filled with flames. The whole of the cabin was engulfed... And I couldn't help but laugh. Michael had tried to end my life the same way I did his, and we both failed.

We really were one and the same.

CHAPTER THIRTY-FOUR

LIKE FATHER,
LIKE DAUGHTER

I NEEDED A DOCTOR, but not knowing the length of Michael's reach, I decided to wait until I returned to the city. Only an hour in, I struggled to remember a time when I hadn't been driving. The pain in my head and arm was excruciating. I felt myself blacking out at the wheel so many times. I hadn't so much as buckled my seatbelt for the first half hour… for someone who'd been driving their entire life, I was quite bad at it. "You can't park there," a security guard called out to me. I'd just stopped in the ambulance bay.

"Then tow it. See if I give a shit." I lost my step and was on my knees. I didn't remember opening the door.

"Miss… You're bleeding," he said, rushing up to me. "Are you okay?"

"I'd have to say no." I looked up at him. "I'm not driving. Did I crash?"

I was on my back, watching a tall Caucasian guard push an invisible man in a wheelchair. And then the darkness finally won.

***

My God did my head hurt! I wanted to open my eyes, but the lids had merged into one. I kept trying, and finally pried it to a slit. Looking down at myself, I realized I was in a hospital gown, my lap covered by a blanket, my left arm in a full elbow cast, my right one hosting an IV. I knew I was looking at my own body, but it definitely didn't feel like it was mine. I felt intense pain, but also a numbness. I tried to move but I couldn't.

"Please, remain still. You suffered quite a bit of damage," a male voice said.

I recognized the voice, but the name escaped me. I tried to follow where the voice was coming from. On my left sat Dean Matthews. Behind him, the early morning sunlight streamed in through a window and threatened to force my eyes closed again.

"What happened?" a voice asked. It took a moment for me to realize it was mine.

"That's what we were hoping you could tell us." His voice was soft, almost comforting. "All you told the security guard was that you'd driven for a long time. That was it."

It was all coming back to me, albeit in pieces. I tried to shift my body but gave up as quickly as I'd started.

"It feels like a semi ran me over... a dozen times."

He shifted to lean in closer, supporting himself with the arms of the chair. "Arm fractured in a couple of places, a few bruised ribs, and a concussion. Maybe you were."

"Dean, why are you here? Better yet, how did you know where I was?"

I was surprised to see concern appear on his face. "We got a call from the hospital. I wanted to make sure you were okay."

"I'm fine."

He raised an eyebrow inquisitively. "Iz… What were you up to?"

I remembered what Michael told me—that my suspicions might be correct. Well, here I was, with Dean right beside me.

"Let's trade then. Where were you last night?"

"Working. And yes, it can be confirmed," he said with a sigh. "Why do you hate me so much? You really think I did this to you? I don't even know where you were."

"I'm pretty sure if you don't already know, you'll find out shortly."

He raised his voice slightly in irritation. "From who? My best buddy, Michael O'Reilly?"

"Sure, let's stop pretending. I know you're linked to Michael, whatever you say."

Surrendering, Dean got up from the chair quickly. "Fine. Fuck off then. Probably best we're not friends anyway or I'll wind up disappearing like everyone else."

"Well that's just—"

"Enjoy your stay, princess."

He moved toward the door.

"You can follow your 'leads' or whatever you're doing, but there's not a chance in hell I'm staying here!" I said, following my words with a laugh.

I pulled out the IV and looked around for something to stop the blood that gushed from the puncture wound. In utter silence, Dean grabbed a few tissues and handed them to me.

"I'll be here less than a day, tops," I said, embarrassed.

***

Despite the nurse who scolded me for ripping out my IV, and the doctor who went on record that he didn't agree with my leaving, all in all my discharge went quite smoothly.

Melanie insisted I stay at her place, as she didn't feel comfortable with my being alone. I couldn't argue. I didn't have the strength.

Once we arrived at her loft, she brought me upstairs and set me up in her room. I argued halfheartedly as I'd done before, but decided I was tired and took a short nap instead. A few hours later, catching me heading down the stairs, she rushed to help.

"Seriously, Melanie, I'm fine."

She gave me a stern look. "You shouldn't even be here. You belong in the hospital!"

"And I shouldn't have taken a nap with a concussion, but that didn't stop me either. What can I say? I'm a rebel."

I walked over to the couch, unaided, and sat down.

"Can I get you anything?" she asked.

"Tea and Tylenol?"

I heard her moving around in the kitchen: filling a kettle with water, and setting it on the stove.

"Didn't I have court today?" I asked.

"That's on Monday."

"It's Sunday?"

She peeked her head out from the kitchen. "It's Saturday."

"Right. Oh, and once I finish my tea, I'll be heading back to my house."

She walked out entirely. The disapproving look she threw me was too strong to be done while leaning. "I thought we decided you'd be better off here?"

"No, you decided that. It's nothing personal; I'd just be more comfortable in my own home."

The kettle was whistling. Melanie disappeared for a moment and returned with the tea and Tylenol I'd asked for. I tried to open the bottle. The combination of a childproof cap and a cast didn't bode well for my chances. Melanie grabbed the bottle in a flash and slapped two pills onto my palm.

"Thanks, Mel."

"Care to talk about what happened to you?"

"I was out trying to find Ember."

Her face softened. "Yes, I heard she went missing."

"Not missing. Taken. Someone knows exactly where she is."

"Who did this?"

"All I'll say is that whoever has her doesn't want me finding her."

"Then leave it to the police."

"No," I said, not looking at her.

"Izzy! Why are *you* trying to find her?"

"It's not something I want to get into right now…"

Suddenly, her softness disappeared.

"So when would be a good time then?" she yelled. "When *you* go missing? When you're dead?"

"I love you, Mel," I said softly. I watched her eyes begin to water. "You've always been there for me… but believe me when I say this isn't something I can explain. Not just to you—to anyone."

She observed me in silence before saying, "I'll let it go—for now. But you're going to fill me in. When you're ready."

Melanie was the perfect friend. She knew when to push, and she sensed when to pull back. We both worked in forensics… perhaps that's why we thought the same way, noticed the little things other people usually miss.

"Can I ask you a question? It doesn't leave the room, okay?"

"Sure, anything."

"What are your thoughts on Dean Matthews?"

She sat silently for a long while. "Honestly," she said finally, "he's a bit hard to read. He definitely has rough edges—there's this arrogance about him… Why do you ask?"

"I wanted to see if you had the same perception about him as I do."

"And do I?"

"I don't know. Maybe."

"What are you thinking, Izzy?"

"I'd rather not involve you in this. Just look at me, and you'll understand why."

"I'm still here to help," she said. "Whether it's as a sounding board or simply to vent."

"Thank you. I appreciate that."

And I did. With Marcus gone, she was my only friend. She could say what she wanted, but without Michael dead and gone, I could never tell her a thing.

***

I convinced Melanie to let me go home, but not before I promised to call her if I needed anything. Once alone, I dialed Michael's number.

"I was wondering when I'd hear from you."

"Sorry about the delay," I said sarcastically. "I was in a bit of a situation. Couldn't be helped."

"Your resourcefulness took me by surprise."

"Like father, like daughter, right?"

"Exactly," he said.

The more I talked to him, the more his voice gained recognition within me. If I hadn't known what he'd done, I'd half expect a rough-sounding voice, with a nasty vocabulary to match. But he was the exact opposite. His voice was calm and soothing, articulate, giving off the impression that, no matter what happened, he would save you from the monster behind the closet doors. The problem was that he was the monster.

"I'd like to see you. I think it's time."

"I couldn't agree more," he said. "Where?"

"You know where."

"I'll give you some time to rest up. Let's say, Wednesday evening?"

"Wednesday. In the meantime, I want proof that Ember is still alive. Think you could do that?"

"Not an unreasonable request. Good-bye, Isabella."

"Good-bye."

About fifteen minutes later, a picture of Ember came through on my cell phone. She looked like she'd been through more of Michael's special treatment, but she was alive and holding today's newspaper in front of her.

CHAPTER THIRTY-FIVE

ABANDONED

CONSCIOUSNESS WAS RETURNING, yet Ember wasn't entirely sure if she was awake or still caught in the horrifying dreams. Tremors made their way through her body: a personal earthquake from deep within. Still, she was unable to move her body even a bit on her own.

She thought she managed to open her eyes, but she couldn't be sure—she could see only darkness.

Am I even awake? she wondered.

She was parched; her throat felt raw; her body ached. She still wasn't certain what had happened.

"Uncle Dale! Aunt Bonnie!" she was finally able to muster as a whisper, before it turned into screams that she couldn't stop. She suddenly realized why her throat was raw: she'd been screaming before. Something was wrong with her... Why couldn't she stop?

For what felt like hours, she hovered between consciousness and unconsciousness, repeating her initial reaction every time. The tremors left her body, replaced with feebleness; she was starting to regain some of her mobility. She reached out an arm, heavy as it felt, and it was met with a wall. She did the same on the other side. Same result. She kicked a foot up, only to hit another wall.

Her breathing quickened. Her eyes widened in the dark. With sickening realization, she recognized where she was. She was back there. In the box. Would anyone know where she was?

Ember started to cry, and she couldn't stop. Her thoughts raced uncontrollably; she couldn't get any of them straight.

"Isabella?" she whispered.

She had promised to protect her, to keep her safe from those who had been hurting her. Yet still she found herself where she'd been many times before. "You're a liar."

CHAPTER THIRTY-SIX

KARMA

"TELL THE COURT your role in the investigation," the ADA said.

"I was asked to assess and give my professional opinion regarding the O'Reilly family."

"And regarding Cody O'Reilly, what have you concluded?"

"Cody O'Reilly seems to be of sound mind and fully aware of the criminal charges against him," I began. "In the beginning, he denied any truth to the victim's claims, but later recanted his previous statement and took full responsibility for the abuse inflicted upon Ember O'Reilly."

"And in your professional opinion, would you say this is normal in these type of cases?"

"Normal in the sense that an accused has been known to later change his or her statements, for whatever reason, and take ownership of what he or she has done," I stated. "But in this case, the timing of Cody's confession was out of the ordinary."

"How so?"

"His confession followed a failed suicide attempt by Ember, who alleged that her mother told her to kill herself in order to save the family. When Cody made this confession, his responses suggested he had been coached—in terms of words, tone of voice and body language. I do believe he was, in some capacity, involved with what happened... but I'm nearly certain he's not entirely responsible, nor did he confess on his own."

"Nothing further, Your Honor."

"Does the defense wish to question Dr. Porter?" asked the judge.

"Mr. O'Reilly has confessed to the allegations against him. There's little need at this time, Your Honor."

"You may step down, Dr. Porter."

I stood up from the witness chair, left the courtroom and made my way over to the bench, where Melanie was waiting.

"How'd it go?"

"I don't know. This was the first time I tried to convince a jury that, regardless of a confession, the accused hadn't acted alone. I really don't know."

She gave me an optimistic look. "Well, then perhaps they'll keep the case open."

"Even without my testimony, using sound judgment, they'd have to know that his acting alone was impossible. The physical evidence doesn't add up."

"No arguments here."

"I just hope they don't take the easy way. It's too easy to put a bow on this case even if they know in their hearts it isn't right."

She checked her watch then looked up at me. "Want to grab some lunch?"

"Sure. Just give me a moment. I need to stop by the restroom first."

Melanie stood up and adjusted her skirt. "I'll get the car and meet you out front."

I didn't need to go to the restroom, but I did need a moment. I'd noticed Michael in the distance, and he'd signaled for me to come over to him.

"It isn't Wednesday yet," I reminded him as I approached.

He blended in well with his surroundings, sharply dressed in a gray suit and meticulously polished black leather wing tips, his white hair slicked back as always. He could easily be mistaken for a lawyer—briefcase and all.

"Oh, come now Isabella. That doesn't mean we can't speak in between."

"I have nothing to say to you, unless you want to tell me where Ember is."

"Good one, but no," he said, smiling. "But I am impressed by your ethics. You could have easily put an end to this all by allowing Cody to take full responsibility."

"And risk the pleasure of seeing your reputation disappear? I'm alright, thanks."

"Hey, it's your choice. You'd better rest up to help that body of yours. You're going to need it." He walked back to the courtroom he'd just left.

He was right; I needed to prepare for our next meeting… or else it could be my last.

***

Melanie and I decided on some Italian takeout and brought it back to her office to eat. She had some work she needed to catch up on, and I… well, I had some things of my own.

"Why didn't you just tell me you had to talk to Michael O'Reilly?" she asked.

"Were you spying on me?"

"I'm not a fool. It was pretty obvious."

"Are you trying to step in for Marcus while he's gone?" I asked, feeling a little ache at mentioning of his name.

"If you freak out every time a friend shows concern, you won't have very many friends."

"Well that explains that."

"And I don't appreciate the Marcus comment."

"I'm sorry… I just… miss him."

She stared at me for a moment.

"Did something happen," she asked. "With Marcus? Did you two… Can I ask that? Did you two do anything?"

"Yeah… I slept with him."

"Oh…"

"I thought things were going really well… I thought that he was someone I could love. For real. That was right before he was taken."

"I just wish you would tell me about things. This and before with Michael."

"And what would you have said if I had told you I needed a word with him?"

"Don't. Stay away. *Run!*"

"That's why I didn't tell you," I said with a soft laugh. "I know what I'm doing."

"I just wish you would let me in on it," she said dismally.

I had to give her credit; she was persistent. "I already told you I can't tell you too much."

"And what about you?" she asked.

"What about me? I'll be fine. Stop worrying."

She shook her head vigorously. "Nope. Can't do it."

"Seriously, Mel, is this how it's going to be until this case is finally over?"

"With all that's happened, can you blame me?"

***

Since I left Melanie's, I'd been spending my nights at my parents' old house, making sure it was both ready, and armed with a highly advanced security system. I also checked to make sure Ember wasn't there. She wasn't. Unfortunately, she wasn't in any of the obvious places, and I didn't know where else to look. Recon was all I could think to do.

I followed one of the members of the Brotherhood, hoping to get some sort of clue. It was boring business. We made stops at Michael's house, a restaurant, a bar, and a home—I'm assuming, his. I'd sat in front of the house for over an hour, and the little patience I had left was wearing thin.

With a syringe in my hoodie, and a pair of latex gloves, I left my car and made my way across the street. Looking around the different points of the home, I saw only two men inside. I had to separate them to take them both down… but I only had one syringe.

I rang the doorbell.

The man who answered recognized me immediately. His mouth hung open and his breath was heavy. I thought he'd stare at me forever.

"Seriously?" he asked, just when I was ready to grab a lawn chair.

"I can tell you're very wise… Yes, seriously. Now, can I come in?"

"Why would I let you to do that?"

"Well, either we can talk inside, or I CAN TALK TO YOU REALLY LOUDLY OUT HERE! Your choice."

"All right. All right… Geez, you've got some balls," he said, shaking his head.

"I'm told I take after my father. I'll follow, if it's all the same to you."

I followed behind him, closing the door with my elbow. The place was a mess. I'm not usually one for stereotyping, but no women lived here. It smelled like dirt and sex; I would have needed a ruler to measure the grime… but I could hardly touch the ground for all the clothing, dirty plates and bowls.

"The maid's on holiday?" I asked sarcastically.

"A smartass too. You get bored of following me around and waiting in your car?"

"You got the bored part right. Where's your buddy?"

He shrugged. "Maybe he's pointing a gun at you through the floorboards… Maybe he's asleep. What do you want?"

"I'm trying to find someone, and I was hoping you could help me."

"Yeah? Who?"

"Ember, Michael's other daughter."

"Don't know who she is."

"Oh, please. We all know you probably had your alone time with her at one time or another."

He scratched his head as if trying to recall.

"My mind's drawing a blank."

"Somehow that doesn't surprise me," I said, making my way closer to him.

He thought he was so damn smart.

"I—"

"So, nothing? Really?"

He backed up a bit, almost tripping over a pile of garbage. "You won't find her here."

"Do I make you nervous?"

"No… but I think it's time for you to leave."

"Not yet," I said, as I lunged forward and stuck him in the neck with the tranquilizer.

He would have hit the floor harder if it hadn't been for the trash he landed on.

I walked around him to search out the other brother, but he came to me instead. Instantly, I recognized him: his disproportionate facial features, his large protruding nose, his pale skin tone not dissimilar from my own.

"You fucker!" I said. "Where's Marcus?"

"It should have been you following me that night. You're a lucky bitch, I'll give you that."

"See your buddy? I think the odds are in my favor."

"Little girls like you need the element of surprise." He was only a foot away from me now.

"Hasn't Michael taught you anything?" I asked, a smile on my face.

"Why do you say that?"

"Never underestimate your opponent." With that, I swung my cast and hit him directly on the side of the head.

Before he knew what was going on, I held my Taser to his heart, and pumped him full of electricity. I held the button down until he fell the rest of the way to the floor, unconscious.

***

I sat at the cleanest spot in the house, and waited for the men to wake up. I'd found some BDSM equipment in one of the rooms: a few sets of fleece hog-tie systems, rubber-ball gags, and leather cat-o'-nine-tails. I used the hog-tie systems to bind their hands and feet behind them, and the balls to keep them silent. Stunner was the first one to come to. He looked up at me, his face red and furious. Fortunately, he couldn't voice his displeasure as the ball strapped in his mouth was doing its job.

"So between the two of you, who's the dominant, and who's the submissive?" I asked, leaning down closer to him. "If I had to guess, I'd say you're probably the bitch."

He rocked back and forth, growling, but couldn't get anywhere with the restraints. After a few moments, he finally calmed down.

"Okay, so I'll have to remove the ball so we can talk. If you go a decibel too high, I'll break my cast over your head this time. Understand?" I flipped the Taser on, sending sparks into the air. "Or would you prefer this?"

He nodded as best he could. I knelt and removed the ball. He took a long series of deep breaths, as if he'd had a hard time breathing.

"I'm sure you've noticed your numbers are decreasing. Any idea why that is?"

He merely nodded.

"It's okay. You can speak."

"Because you have some kind of vendetta against Michael, and you're going through us to get to him."

I raised an eyebrow. "Is that what he told you?"

"Yes."

"Did he tell you who I was?"

"Some pissed off girl," he muttered.

"You haven't been in the Brotherhood long, have you?"

He shook his head. "Just a few years."

"I'm not just some girl he pissed off. I'm the older version of Ember."

He gave me a confused look.

"I'm his daughter."

"Both his other daughters are dead."

"One of them is, but as the bruise on your chest, I'm very much alive."

"What do you want?"

"I want to know where Ember is."

He laughed. "You think he would tell us?"

I pulled back the sleeve of his right arm to reveal a deep gash.

"Well, he trusted you enough to try to off me—at least twice if I'm not mistaken. Maybe three times. The fire was you too, right? He wouldn't do that himself."

"And what do you think will happen once he finds out about this?"

I cracked him across the head with my free hand. His eyes widened.

"It's not Michael you have to be worried about right now," I whispered. "Now, tell me, what exactly is the Brotherhood?"

"Just a bunch of guys who get together. Like brothers."

I cracked him again, right in the temple. He started yelling, so I put the ball back on for a few minutes and tazed him once in the arm. When he was quiet, we began again.

"Okay, that's my fault," I said. "I should have made this clear from the start. There's no point in lying, because I'll be able to tell... I'm not big on the whole torturing thing, but I'll make an exception each time I think you're feeding me bullshit. I believe you don't know where Ember is. I don't believe you're just a bunch of men who hang out."

"You're right. We do share a common interest."

"And what would that interest be?" He was hesitating, and I couldn't blame him. I pulled up the sleeve of my hoodie to expose the skin beneath. "Is this what the Brotherhood's about?"

"Y-yes," he finally managed. "In a way."

"What's the criterion to become one of your victims?"

"I don't understand."

"Right. Simple language. I already know female... What else? Young? Old? Caucasian? Blonde hair? What? How do you choose your victims?"

"Young females."

"Young as in prepubescent?"

He nodded. "Yes."

"So far so good. Where's Marcus?"

"Look, I just grabbed him. Where Michael took him after that, I have no idea."

I was sensing he wasn't being totally forthcoming, but honestly it was hard to tell. He was under a lot of duress.

"Besides the cabin, where do you hide people you grab?"

He continued to try to break free from his restraints, gently rocking on his belly. "The only place we know of is at Lake Placid. That's the most you'll get out of me."

"Are you subtly trying to tell me to give up?" I asked with a smirk.

He smirked right back. "By all means, keep asking questions and expecting results."

Tranq-guy was coming around. I'd made sure the dose was smaller than I'd given Drew. I hated waiting.

"If you promise to keep quiet, I won't put the ball back in."

"I promise," he quickly replied, relief washing across his face.

"Thank you," I said, then made my way to the other man.

I repeated the same warning to him before removing the ball. "So I'll ask you again—where's Ember?"

"You'll never find her in time," he said through clenched teeth.

"So you do know more than you were letting on… In time for what?"

"If you don't find her soon, she'll be dead. Whatever anyone does. And it won't be by Michael's hand."

"Okay, well, I guess that's it then, if you have nothing else to tell me," I said, before reinserting the ball in his mouth. I acted as if I was going to walk away, but turned suddenly to taze his neck. I held it down. I watched him squirm and assumed it was his tongue he was biting down on.

"Stop it! You're killing him!" my other guest yelled.

I waited just long enough to let him know that I was still in control before releasing the trigger.

Returning to my conscious guest, I found him fighting against the restraints. I picked up the ball, and he bucked his head, making it hard to reinsert.

"I'll have to ask you to stay still."

"If you let me go, I'll help you find her. I'll get Michael to tell me where she is," he pleaded.

"I appreciate that, but honestly, if he hasn't told you guys yet, he won't. Now it'll be worse for you if you don't stay still." When he did, I finally put the ball back in his mouth.

Taking the whip I'd found, I walked behind him and positioned the handle across his throat. I placed the end against my cast, pulled back hard, and didn't stop until there no longer was any movement coming from him. I repeated the same process with the other man. Once I'd confirmed they were dead, I removed the balls and ties. Picking up a few papers from the floor, I went to the stove and lit them on fire. When they began smoking, I placed them on the floor. In no time at all, the other trash ignited, spreading quickly. Then I left.

Sitting in my car, I watched the house go up in flames. At least the visit hadn't been a total waste. Even though I didn't find Ember or Marcus, I was able to confirm what the Brotherhood was. As pretty as the fire was, the cops would be there soon. It was time to leave.

CHAPTER THIRTY-SEVEN

CONFESSIONS

BACK AT MY TOWNHOME, I stared at the picture Michael had sent me of Ember. I hoped to see something I'd missed the first time—something that might give me a clue as to where she might be. What the brother had told me kept echoing in my mind…

She was running out of time.

As I was regretting that my meeting with Michael wasn't sooner, my cell phone vibrated in my hand.

"I see you're still quite busy, even with what's coming up."

"Michael, buddy, how you been? It's been too long."

"I'm going to fucking kill you!" he roared.

"You tried that once," I said. "Can't we just get along?"

"Piss me off too much and I'll kill her. For real. No takebacks."

I froze. He had me.

"Okay, Michael. I'm sorry."

"That's a good girl…"

Someone else must know where she is if he's not going to kill her outright. Or he's just fucking with me.

"Michael… Can I have another picture?"

He sighed. "And what will that do, Isabella?"

"Just please send it," I said, and ended the call.

A few minutes later, far sooner than I expected, a new picture text came in. I screamed and dropped the phone, cracking it all across the top. A dead girl was hanging from a frayed rope. Her neck was broken. It was Anna. The bastard actually paused to take a picture before I found Anna's body all those years ago.

The phone vibrated on the floor. I could barely read the new text for all the cracks—

"I'll see you tomorrow."

He was fucking with me, trying to distract me from what I should be doing. It wasn't going to work. Michael was going to die, and I'd make damn sure Ember never shared Anna's fate.

***

I knocked on the door to Melanie's loft, but she didn't answer. I leaned against her door and allowed myself to slide to the floor in the hallway. Wrapping my arms around my legs, I decided to wait for her.

Some time later, I heard the elevator chime, and peered up. Melanie finally stepped off. When she saw me, she rushed up and knelt beside me, the worry masking her face.

"Are you okay? How long have you been here?"

"A few hours, I think."

"You should have called me. I was at work." She stood and helped me up. "I would've come straight home."

"I didn't want to bother you."

"Never a bother. Come on. Let's go inside."

I sat on the couch, and Melanie got us some drinks. She handed me an Irish coffee, and took a seat beside me.

"Tell me what's going on."

"I'm not sure I'll be able to find her. I've searched everywhere, and I always come up empty-handed."

"Izzy, this isn't your responsibility," she said softly, placing her hand on my shoulder. "This is for the police to figure out, and they *will* find her."

Could I tell her it was because of me that both Ember and Marcus were missing? She knew a portion of my past, but not nearly as much as she imagined.

"Mel, this is closer to me than you realize," I started, staring into the steam rising from my mug. "I know things no one else does."

"Really? Like what?"

I hesitated before I answered, choosing my words carefully. "She's on a time limit, Mel. Michael told me when I asked for a picture to prove she was still alive."

I could tell by her expression that she was confused. "Michael has her? How do you know that?"

"Because I've been digging around, and because Michael texted me and confirmed it."

"Izzy, you have to go to the police. Do you still have the messages? You have to show Dean! This isn't for you to solve, and if you know something—"

"I don't know who I can trust at the precinct anymore, especially Dean. You don't understand."

"You're right. I don't."

"I think Dean may be involved in all this. I'm just not sure how yet."

214

Melanie gave me a quizzical look, and then we sat in silence for a few moments before she finally spoke. "When you asked Michael for proof that Ember is still alive... Did he send you anything?"

"The first time, yes. The second time he sent me this."

I pulled out my phone and showed her the last picture. Melanie's face turned pale. "Who is this?"

"It's Anna. He sent me a picture of my dead sister."

She placed my phone on the coffee table. "How could he possibly get this?"

"Mel, don't ask me to go there." I pleaded with my eyes. "I know anyone looking in from outside would be saying the same thing: that I should go to the police. Hell, even I would. But believe me when I tell you that if I do, Ember will be just another body on your table."

She searched my face for the answers my mouth refused to give... She didn't find anything.

"I knew that man was sick. I just didn't realize how sick he was. What else did he tell you?"

"That he's the only one who knows where she is, and when she dies, it won't be by his own hand," I said. "What the hell does that even mean?"

"Did he send you the picture of Anna before or after he told you that?"

"After."

Her face was now pensive. "Maybe he's saying Ember will kill herself? ... I don't know. It's somehow connected."

"Yeah, I think so too, but I can't figure out how."

"Think it through—everything Michael O'Reilly has done and said up until this point... I think he was giving you a clue... but why would he do that? He's got a lot of leverage over you... too much not to use it."

I knew she was right, but I couldn't get past the frustration of not being able to figure it out. I knew Michael was playing a game, had been since the beginning... I had all the pieces. I just needed to figure out how they fit together.

"Thanks, for talking me through this. I'll figure this out—I have to."

"As a professional, I'm going to tell you to hand any information you have over to the authorities," she said in a serious tone.

"Mel—"

"I wasn't finished. As a friend, I can understand, up to a point, what you're doing. There's a connection between you and Michael that you can't tell me about."

I looked to the floor. "You're right..."

"Hey, look at me," she said, and I did. "I know you well enough that you wouldn't be doing this unless it was absolutely necessary. If there's anything I can do to help, just say the word."

***

When snooping around Marcus's office the other day, I was able to locate Dean's house; that's where I headed after leaving Melanie's. I wasn't sure what I was going to say—or if he was even there—but I had to try to get something from him. After parking my car, I walked up the driveway to the modest-size, gray, vinyl-covered bungalow.

I knocked on the door, and within a minute or two, he opened it.

As expected, he looked surprised to see me. "Isabella... what are you doing here?"

"I need to speak to you. Can I come in?"

216

"I thought you wanted nothing to do with me," he said, a worried look on his face.

"I'm going to be honest—I still don't trust you, but you're the last chance I have."

"For what?"

"To find Ember and Marcus."

"Come in."

He stepped aside to let me through.

I waited just inside the entranceway; once he closed the door, I followed him into the living room. He gestured for me to take a seat, and I took the one with the wall behind it. Taking a quick glance around, I was surprised at how neat it was for a bachelor pad. It made me think of my own home, as it was sparsely furnished, though everything he seemed to own was high-end—leather furniture and nothing that screamed IKEA. He did well on his salary.

"Can I get you a drink? Whiskey, right?"

"Yes, please."

He walked over to his liquor cabinet and produced two glasses. "I'm out of ice. Is that okay?"

"Sure."

After handing me my drink, he took a seat on one of the couches.

"I know where you were… The night you got hurt."

"How do you know?"

"Right now that's not important," he said flatly, gently swirling the liquid in his glass.

"Were you there?"

He leaned forward, resting his elbows on his knees, still concentrating on the drink between his hands. "No. Knock it off."

"Did you have something to do with Marcus's disappearance?"

"Again, no." He paused for a moment before continuing. "Why didn't you listen to me?"

"I'm sorry?"

He had me pretty confused.

He looked me straight in the eyes. "Why didn't you stay away, Izzy?"

Only four people ever had called me that: Anna, Marcus, Melanie, and...

"This might sound crazy... when I was fourteen... were you there? Did you help me get out?"

The numbness was starting to take over, first clouding my thoughts then distorting my vision. I almost lost hold of my glass but gripped it tighter to prevent it from falling to the floor. I was remembering. Dean would have been sixteen at the time, always trying to protect me when I was up at the cabin, when both Anna and I were up there. He wasn't Dean to me though.

"Was your name Lucas?"

"Yeah. I changed it when I was eighteen."

"Why haven't you told me before now?" I asked, trying to shake the memories into action within my mind.

"Because I couldn't. I still can't get into all the details," he explained.

"Do you know where Michael took her?"

"I wish I did. Then this would no longer be an issue."

I let everything simmer for a while. I couldn't think of a reason he would try to set me up now... why he originally would protect me only to later put me in danger.

218

"What was the reason, Dean? Why did you try to save us?"

"I'm sorry. That's not something I can say."

"Dean, tell me your involvement with Ember… tell me where Marcus is… tell me something! I'm at my wit's end here!"

His voice took on a serious tone. "I need you to take your focus off me for a second and concentrate on Michael. Don't underestimate him, and pay close attention to what he says."

I really had nothing to say to that because I already knew what he was telling me. I took a long drink from my glass then turned my head so I was looking off into the distance.

"Can I ask you something?" he said.

"I'm not sure that's fair… but go on."

His voice lightened, almost to a whisper. "It's tomorrow night, isn't it? When you're meeting with him?"

"Dean…"

"I'm not asking for details. I just want to know if it's tomorrow."

I moved my head back so I could look at him. "And what does it change if you know?"

He shrugged. "Nothing, I suppose. Whatever's going to happen will happen. But knowing this may be the last time I see you…"

Why would that matter?

"I can't think that way if I want to walk away from this," I said.

He nodded. "I know…"

CHAPTER THIRTY-EIGHT

TICK TOCK

I WOKE EARLY the next morning, and made my way to the bathroom. I took a shower, dressed, grabbed my bag and left my house.

I stopped at a café, grabbed a latte and a muffin, and headed to my family's old home. It was the first time in a while I'd spent the night away from it, and I had to make sure nothing had been done to it while I was away. It appeared as though, unlike me, Michael was keeping his distance until tonight. I still didn't know the exact time of our meeting, but it didn't matter. I was prepared.

The passing minutes were hours; forever had passed before night-fall arrived. On a chair I'd brought down to the basement, I sat and waited. It could be any time now... and it could be any time now for Ember as well. Should something happen to me, I'd prepared for the recording of Michael to be leaked upon my death. I was almost all-in already... pot-committed as the gamblers say. I'd come too far not to toss the rest of the chips in. The first thing I had to do was get her location out of him. Then I could kill him. I could only hope Michael would play nicely.

Then I remembered what Dean had told me the night before—I shouldn't underestimate Michael and needed to pay close attention to what he said to me. I kept that at the forefront of my mind as I continued to wait.

I almost missed it, but I heard the faint sound of the front door opening and closing—the alarm purposely deactivated. He was there. I listened as he walked across the living room, making his way to the basement door.

A singular set of footsteps.

From my chair, I watched as he made his way down the stairs, stopping at the bottom.

"Hello, Isabella."

"Michael."

"It's been years since the last time I was down here," he said, looking around the basement. "Good choice on your part."

"I felt it was fitting."

"Nothing's changed over the years. It's just missing a few of my personal belongings."

"Let's cut with the small talk… where are Ember and Marcus? Are they still alive?"

"I'm sorry to see that you haven't yet figured it out, but you know I can't tell you" he said, shaking his head. "I guess I gave you much more credit than you deserved. And Marcus, well, I'd be worried about Ember at the moment."

I shrugged. "It's not over yet. I could still surprise you."

He pointed to his wristwatch. "Tick tock, Isabella. Time doesn't stand still, and it's not going to wait until you get a clue."

I stood up and walked the short distance to where he stood. He backed up a bit when I got too close.

"Try it," he said in a voice barely above a whisper, "I'm not my innocent wife, or my murdered brothers."

"I hope your recent losses haven't been too difficult on you," I said with seething sarcasm.

"You mock me. Yes, the people who surround me are pawns and easily replaceable... But you stole from me. Difficult? No. Inconvenient. Yes."

"A true sociopath."

"Labels? I do love labels. What are you then?" he asked. "You decided to kill both my wives. Both innocent women. You don't look particularly remorseful."

"Who said I killed your first wife? That's an assumption on your part, I'd say." I took another step toward him, with him taking another back. "Do I frighten you?" I asked him.

"No, but I'm not stupid. I told you we were one and the same. I know what I'd do."

"Tell me why. Why are you the way you are? Why do you do the things you do?"

"I could ask you the same question."

"And I'd answer that I'm the byproduct of you."

He shook his head. "You can't blame your actions on me any more than I can blame my own parents. I do what I do because I can, because I enjoy it. A life without control isn't one worth living."

"What if my upbringing had been different? What part is genetics?"

"Ah, psychology… nature versus nurture," he said. "What school of thought do you follow, Isabella?"

"I like to think it's more nurture, otherwise I'd have to admit that I can't control some part of me… that I have no choice but to be like you."

He rubbed his chin, a pensive expression emerging. "Is that why you minored in genetics? Trying to find out if what you are had been bred into you?"

"Does it matter?"

Michael shrugged. "I guess not. I just don't get many opportunities to have an intelligent conversation with someone." Suddenly, it dawned on me; he was stalling for time—time I knew Ember didn't have. I had to move this forward if he wasn't going to. Once again I took a step toward him, but this time he stayed where he stood.

"Which will it be? Suicide? Death by fire? Perhaps a knife to my chest? Or do you have something worse planned for me?"

"Something far worse."

"So I guess the time has come."

"It has, Jonathan… It's time to finally end it."

I lunged forward, intending on knocking him out with my cast, but for an older man he was quick, and he easily dodged me. I made another run at him, but again he quickly moved away. I made the mistake of leaving my back toward him for too long, and he seized the opportunity, putting me into a chokehold.

I couldn't move. I struggled, reaching for my cast, but the pulsing in my neck and head consumed me. Within a minute, I'd lose consciousness. After that, I was dead. I tried to elbow him, but he held on tight. After a long moment of struggling, I slipped my fingers into my cast, and began to see red. Somehow, with two fingers, I managed to grab the syringe, removed the cap with my mouth, and jabbed it into his leg. Once I depressed the plunger, I almost passed out. When the red cleared from my vision, I was on my knees breathing frantically— Michael on the floor beside me.

It was going to be a long night.

***

Once again, I was waiting for someone to wake up. It took everything in me not to end his life here and now, but I had to find out where Ember was. Michael was now coming to, and I positioned myself beside him on the floor.

"I hear one of the side effects of Etorphine is a pretty bad migraine. How's yours?"

"It's there," he said. "Hope that's enough for you."

"Ember and Marcus."

He laughed hysterically. It was as if I were the one tied up on the floor. I put up with it for about a minute.

"Care to let me in on the joke?"

"I'm sorry. Did you actually think I'd just give you Ember's or Marcus's location?"

Melanie's words came back in a flood of realization… *too much leverage not to use it.*

"Well, it would save me from having to resort to your tactics and torture it out of you."

"Try it. You could cut my arm off and feed it to me. I won't say a fucking word."

"What do you want?"

"You take Ember—or don't, I don't really give a shit—and then you leave. You live no less than 500 miles away. If you come back, everybody you ever so much as look at again will die."

I nodded.

"Look at the photo I last sent you."

"I get the threat."

"No, you don't. Humor me."

I grabbed my cellphone from my bag. Sitting on the floor next to him, I pulled up Anna's photo.

"Here it is. What's your point?" I asked.

"Think back to what those idiots told you."

It felt like I'd swallowed sand.

"They said Ember was alive, but had a time limit. When she died, it wouldn't be by your hand."

"What else?"

"You're the only one who knows where she is."

"I'd like to make a small correction. As of tonight, one other person knows... in case of my untimely demise."

"You sadistic bastard."

"You're a fool! I asked you for one thing: to leave. I don't owe you a damn thing. You thought you won because you cheated in a fight?"

I got up and walked away from him, sitting back down on the chair.

"I'll do it... I'll leave."

"You're goddamned right you will... Now look at the photo."

I looked at Anna's photo and willed it to speak to me. Then it hit me.

"In the beds at the cabin, there were these miniature coffins," I said. "Obviously built by someone in the Brotherhood to keep outsiders from learning what was happening there."

"Close. But since your last visit, the cabin once again has been burned to the ground."

"I wasn't finished," I told him through gritted teeth. "What if one was made that was smaller but could still house a child—small enough to easily transport her without raising suspicion?"

I again looked at the picture of Anna. I'd had the answer in my phone since yesterday.

"Bingo."

"It would have been hard to accomplish but not impossible." I looked down at him. "And if I kill you, the orders will be to prematurely end Ember's life."

He nodded as best he could. "Right now a man is waiting down the street in a car. Once you leave, if he comes in and doesn't find me—or finds me dead—a simple call will be made, and it's done."

"And how do I know, once I leave, that simple call won't still be made?"

"How do you know she isn't dead already?" He smiled, looking quite powerful for someone on the floor. "Have I given you any reason not to trust me?"

***

Once outside, I called Melanie, the only person I trusted at this point. Everything went well. She agreed to what I asked of her. I ended the call and headed for my car. As much as it pained me, I'd left Michael behind back in the basement—still breathing. I located a parking spot, grabbed a shovel and flashlight from the trunk of my car, and made my way through the gates, toward where I thought Ember would be.

Every step in the darkness brought me closer to my sister's grave. I stuck to the trees until they melted into grass. I tried to silence my steps, but soon I was on an open field, feeling naked as can be. I looked all around me, but saw nothing. I could hardly hear a sound over my breath, until the crack of gunshot sent me sprawling on the ground, my flashlight and shovel abandoned.

Shit!

The area was too open. The ground wasn't an escape. I started to run toward Anna's grave.

Another gunshot rang in the distance. I fell over forward, as warm blood rushed down my shirt. It felt nice in the cool night.

I crawled toward the gravestone, and placed my back against it. I didn't hear another shot, but it wasn't long before I heard sirens. If I was right, Ember would need immediate medical attention. I silently thanked Melanie for making the call.

Taking the phone out of my pocket, I aimed the flashlight toward the ground. Protruding about a quarter of an inch from the ground was a small tube—one I'd have easily overlooked had I not been there to find it. I made sure I did nothing to disturb or obstruct it. I was grinning when the first police officer arrived.

"Are you okay? The medics are behind me... Just hold on."

"I'm fine. Don't worry about me."

"We were told there may be someone under there?" she said.

"Yes, Ember O'Reilly. She went missing last week," I said. "There's a shovel and a flashlight over there... can you send someone to grab it?"

She nodded and met up with the rest of the emergency team. One man ran up to me with a shovel. I explained the need for the tube and told him to avoid it at all costs. Soon more people arrived with more shovels. They tried to get me to leave, but I wouldn't. I forced a young man to sew up the scratch on my shoulder, all the while, I checked to make sure the tube remained unobstructed. After a long time digging, and a few near-disasters with the tube, we all heard the unmistakable sound of a shovel hitting something solid.

***

They proceeded very carefully so as not to break through the wooden box. Some removed soil from the top, while others tried to clear the dirt surrounding the perimeter.

"Just hang on, Ember. We're almost there," I called out to her. I was hoping to hear something back but heard nothing. I looked up at the men and women working. "Remember, she could have been in there for at least five days. She's had oxygen, but we don't know if they left any provisions for her inside."

Melanie finally showed up and knelt by my side. Once again conscious of the blood on my breasts and torso, I waited for the accusations. They never came.

"You did it," she said. "You found her."

I sighed. "Well, let's hope I didn't figure it out too late."

With Melanie's arm around me, I stood and watched as they replaced shovels for crowbars and tried to gain access from different sides. Finally, the lid popped open and everyone gathered around to pry it off. The smell of feces and urine permeated the air. One man was overtaken with a fit of coughing.

Inside lay Ember, curled up in a fetal position, surrounded by empty water bottles. Michael was right. Time had been running out. A few days without water and she'd be gone. A paramedic leaned down to make a quick assessment of her condition. We all waited with bated breath.

"Her pulse is weak, but she's alive," he said, to the relief of many. "Let's get her out of here."

As a group of them carefully removed her from the box, another paramedic made her way over with a gurney. As soon as they laid Ember on it, I was by her side.

"Everything's going to be fine, Ember. He'll never put his hands on you again, I promise." And with that, she was wheeled away to an ambulance.

"You should go in the ambulance," Melanie said.

"It's just a scratch… I'll meet you over there soon. I'm going to check up on Michael."

***

I returned to the house, made my way up the front steps and through the door. It was quiet. Too quiet. I headed straight for the basement. Once I reached the bottom step, I found exactly what I'd expected— nothing. He was gone.

After a moment, I saw a piece of paper on the floor where he once was: a message. I tried to absorb the words, but needed a long moment to decide what to do with the information Michael had provided.

CHAPTER THIRTY-NINE

ONE AND THE SAME

IN THE ELEVATOR at the hospital, I'd just pressed the button to Ember's floor when I got a text—

"Don't worry, Bella. We'll meet again soon."

I got off on the third floor, the pediatric intensive-care wing. I'd only walked a few feet when someone pulled me into their arms. It was Dale, with Bonnie standing close behind him.

"You found her alive," he said, not letting go. "You did it. We owe you everything."

"I promised I would, and I wasn't about to give up until I did," I said, returning Bonnie's smile. "Is there any update regarding Ember?"

Finally letting me go, Dale looked at me. His eyes more tired than before, but the relief more than made up for it... until he saw my wound.

"Nobody told me you were hurt. I shouldn't have—"

"It's fine. It's not a big deal."

He took me by the hands. "We should be hearing something soon," he said somberly.

"And Michael," Bonnie said, walking up beside us. "Did you catch him?"

"We need to talk. But not out here. Follow me."

They followed me down the hall and into a vacant waiting room.

"Please take a seat," I said, sitting down across from them.

"I think you should know who I am, and I'd rather you hear it from me."

They looked a bit perplexed; Dale was the one who answered: a simple, "Okay…"

"When I was a teenager, I took my aunt and uncle's last name. My original last name was Baldacci."

"I don't understand what this has to do with what happened to Ember," Bonnie said.

"Michael's last name—his *real* last name—is Baldacci as well."

Dale's eyes widened. "Oh, my God, he's related?"

"Yes, he was my father, which makes Ember my half-sister."

"Wait, wasn't she found buried beneath the grave site of Anna—"

"Baldacci," I said. "Anna was my sister. She died when she was Ember's age. That's why I was able to find her."

"Why are you telling us this?" Bonnie asked.

"Michael's still out there, and he'll want to continue his game where he left off," I explained. "Eventually the truth might come out, and when it does, I didn't want you thinking I was keeping anything from the two of you. I hope it also helps you understand why I'd give my life to make sure Ember is safe."

Bonnie seemed shocked, and Dale appeared to be looking right through me. "So in the end, you're one of them," he finally managed to say.

Suddenly, a sense of guilt cloaked me, and I wasn't sure if I could ever shake it off. After everything that had happened, if anything I'd become more like him than I was before. But right now, only Ember was important.

"In a sense, yes. If I could change my genetics I would—but I can't. Even so, I was able to walk away from that more than twenty years ago because I was raised by a loving aunt and uncle. Ember will have that opportunity as well, through both you and Bonnie. And, if you'll have me, I'll also be around to make sure of it."

Dale smiled warmly. "She couldn't ask for a better big sister."

"We don't have to tell her everything, not even who I am. But I'd like her to know I'll always be there for her."

"As a wise woman once told me, 'we'll take this very slowly and see how it goes,'" Dale said, smiling again. "You're not Michael. That much is clear at least."

"Thank you, Dale," I said.

But he was wrong. In a sense, I was exactly like my father—only I used my inescapable darkness to stop his. It wasn't going to be easy. Michael had gotten away; I was starting at square one again.

***

As Bonnie and Dale went to get an update, I found Melanie sitting in the waiting room and made my way to her. I sat beside her and gave her a little nudge with my shoulder.

"How are you doing?" she asked. "How's your shoulder?"

"The shoulder's fine…" I let out a long breath, thinking about how to answer the rest. "Have you ever felt every possible emotion at the same time?"

"Not exactly, but I can imagine."

232

"I'm happy I found Ember alive," I started. "But there still aren't any leads on Marcus. If I know Michael, I'm worried he might be dead."

"He'll be found too. Don't worry."

I gave her a false smile. "And I'm pissed because Michael is still out there, sad because there are five unidentified girls at your morgue, and mortified that there might be more out there."

"I think you've covered pretty much every emotion," she agreed. "So now what?"

I put my head between my hands. "Honestly? I don't know."

Melanie placed a hand on my knee. "But you do know that you don't have to do this alone, right?"

Dale turned the corner before I could answer. "Ember's awake and asking for you."

"Do you think that's wise?" I asked. "She must be exhausted. She should sleep." To be honest, a sudden nervousness had overtaken me. I didn't know why, but I couldn't ignore it.

"Ember made it clear that she wanted to see you, and I'm not going to deny her wish."

"I'll be waiting for you here," Melanie said.

I got up.

Taking a deep breath, I followed Dale to Ember's room. She seemed attached to every machine possible, but she looked as if she were regaining some of her natural color. I took a seat beside her bed.

"I'll give you some time to yourselves," Dale said.

I didn't know where to start, but Ember made that decision for me.

"I don't know how long I'll be awake. I had to see you before I passed out again," she said. "I wanted to say thank you."

I gave her a gentle smile. "Really, Ember, you don't have to thank me."

"My dad told me who you are—that you're my sister. And after all he did to you, you still tried to save me. You never gave up."

A tear began to form in her eyes.

Michael actually told her? Probably to spread the information, and get me off the case.

Ember's hair was greasy and slick against her head, and she appeared to have lost a bit of weight—not that she'd had much to lose. I had to stop the tears from welling up in my own eyes when I found the new markings on her uncovered arms.

"I kept a promise I made to you. Don't thank me. It was my obligation."

"You don't take gratitude very well, do you?"

"Are you sure you're eleven?" I asked with a wink.

"I'm turning twelve in a couple of months," she said, smiling.

"So you're okay with all this... me being your sister?"

"We're connected. I knew it before I saw the scars. I've never had a sister..."

"Well, you're stuck with me now."

"I'm glad...'" she said through a yawn. "I want to be stuck..."

Her eyes began to flutter as the medication took effect. That was my cue to leave.

I stood up and, leaning carefully over her, placed a soft kiss on her forehead. Dale was waiting for me outside.

"I'd have to say it's going well so far," he said, as he placed his hand on my arm, giving it a squeeze before he entered Ember's room.

***

I made my way back to Melanie; she stood when she saw me coming.

"Can I give you a ride anywhere?" she asked.

"Thanks, but I have my car. I need to tie up some loose ends."

"Do you need me to come with you?"

"It's something I have to do on my own." I leaned over and placed a hand on her shoulder. "But you can come with me tomorrow to my new house."

"You bought a house?"

"I did. It was something I just couldn't let get away."

CHAPTER FORTY

MICHAEL'S FINAL WORD

I PICKED THE LOCK to get inside. I was never really good at it, but given enough time, I could usually accomplish the task within fifteen minutes, give or take. Much better than breaking windows.

The house was dark, and I made my way through the kitchen to the living room. Before taking a seat in the same oversize chair, I poured myself a drink. As I sat in the dark, I wasn't entirely certain how this would unfold, but it needed to be done.

***

An hour later, the beams of headlights danced across the room as a car pull into the driveway. When he flicked on the ceiling light, he was startled to find me waiting for him.

"Isabella!" Dean yelled. "What the fuck?"

"I came to clarify a few things with you," I replied. "Hope you don't mind, but I fixed myself a drink."

"You can't just… I mean, couldn't you have talked to me at the hospital?"

"No. I had to give what you said—and what I've learned since then—some thought first."

"Okay," he said, taking a seat on the same couch as before. "But next time, wait outside."

"How long have you known Michael?"

He let out a long sigh. "I already told you—"

I stopped him before he could continue. "This will go a lot more smoothly if you just answer the questions and honestly."

Dean sat there for a moment, not saying anything. Playing with his fingers, he finally looked at me again. "My entire life... You know that. Why would a boy just randomly be out there by the cabin? You're too smart to know."

"How?"

"He knew my mother... I was around him a lot, but there was a period of time when I didn't see him."

"When was that?" I asked.

"When I went to college, and then the academy."

"But you never lost touch, did you?"

He sat back in the couch, pushing deeply into the back cushions. "We did for a time, and then I received a call from him after your mother's death."

"What was that about?" I decided it was better to keep calm, and I maintained that in my tone.

"I can't get into this."

"I'm not leaving you a choice, Dean. What was the conversation about?"

"He asked me to keep an eye on you, so to speak. He gave me all the information I needed to do so," he said. "I even transferred to the same college you attended."

"And you were the one who told him when I came back to New Jersey."

"Yes."

What Michael had hinted at was starting to make sense now that I heard it from Dean.

So Michael's note on the floor—was that true as well?

"Is Marcus still alive?" As I asked it, I was afraid of his answer.

"As far as I know, he is. But again, I have no idea where he is."

By his demeanor, he seemed to be telling the truth. "Do you know why he was taken?"

"They meant to take you. I'm guessing they settled for him to throw you off your game," Dean said. "You were connecting the dots a lot quicker than they thought you would."

"Well played… But I think I played better."

He offered a weak smile. "You definitely had them watching their backs—even I was watching my own."

"And now?"

"Are we talking about me?"

"Yes."

"I hope that if you wanted me dead, we wouldn't be having this conversation right now."

He was right. There were things I still needed from him: to find Marcus and Michael, to learn what the extent of his involvement—besides protecting some of us—truly was.

After a period of silence, I finally asked him, "What would you say if I told you Michael left a final note for me?"

"Wouldn't surprise me. What did it say?" He seemed to be tensing up now.

"You're not just a cop… you're also my brother."

CHAPTER FORTY-ONE

SHATTERING SILENCE

IT WAS COLD. It was dark. What he told me to do ricocheted like ammunition inside my head. All I wanted to do was stop, as my body was relentless in its protests, but the inner echoes were even more persistent in their commands to run. That's what kept driving me forward.

In the middle of the night, I was making my way through the maze of trees and knee-deep snow, not entirely certain where I was going or even if I was headed in the right direction. Regardless, I kept running.

Struggling for breath, trying to ignore my dwindling stamina, I pushed on until I emerged from the forest and onto the snow-covered gravel road. It was another hour or so before I spotted the first vehicle approaching. It stopped when I blocked the road, but by that point, I knew hypothermia was setting in. I'd been lucky. God only knew when another vehicle would arrive.

The faint sound of breaking glass startled me. I could still feel the cold surrounding me, my body screaming in pain. I was still partially dissociated. "My name is Isabella Porter. I'm thirty-seven. This is New Jersey. It's Wednesday, November 2, 2016..." I repeated the grounding speech out loud until the dissociated state had passed. I strained to

focus on my surroundings, the numbness being the most stubborn—
and the last—of the sensations to dissipate.

"Isabella?"

It was Dean, and I was at his house. I was remembering. I'd just
asked him to confirm what Michael had hinted at.

The corners of his eyes crinkled in concern. "Isabella, are you all
right?"

Still trying to get a firm grasp on the here and now, I could only
stare at him. I watched as he knelt and picked up the shards of glass at
my feet.

"I'm fine. Why does everyone keep asking me that?" I finally managed, looking down at my bleeding hand.

Was I fine? Ember was back and safe, but Marcus was still gone,
and Michael had gotten away again. And here was Dean, in front of
me, cleaning up the mess I'd just made... I was still facing so many
unanswered questions.

"I'm sorry. I'll be okay," I said. "Would you mind if I got another
drink? I promise to be more careful this time."

He gestured toward the bar behind him. "Of course, please."

After pouring myself another glass of whiskey, I sat down on the
couch, and made sure to keep the glass between my legs.

I looked up to find Dean staring at me.

"What just happened to you?"

"I dissociated. It's been happening a lot more with everything
that's been going on."

"Dissociated?" he said, his face skewed.

"It's a common defense or reaction to a stressful or traumatic situation," I said. "In laymen's terms, it impairs the normal state of

awareness and limits or alters one's sense of identity, memory, or con-sciousness."

"Those are laymen's terms?" He offered a weak smile.

"Trust me—I could have gotten a lot more technical than that."

He looked down at the floor. "I'm sorry."

"For what?" I asked, confused.

"I would've been straight with you from the beginning, but…"

I shook my head. "Honestly, it wouldn't have mattered. Dissociat-ing isn't something that's new to me."

"Well, then, I'm sorry about that."

"Don't be… so you're my half-brother?" I asked.

It explained why Dean had wanted to protect Anna and me. Even Ember. However, it didn't explain why he kept quiet as to the Brother-hood's activities—or whether he was also involved in it in any meaningful way.

"Yeah… Jonathan is our father…"

"First I want to thank you," I said.

"For what?"

"For what you did for Anna and me, your sisters…"

Dean looked at me sheepishly. "You don't have to thank me for that."

"I do—and I'll thank you for a lot more in a bit. You're going to tell me everything, including how you're involved in all this."

He just stared.

Usually I like silence. I bask in its infrequent appearance; I soak in every bit of tranquility it offers me. At this moment, however, the si-lence filled the space between us, gnawing at my insides: a gaping void, needing to be filled with sounds, words, anything. It clung to us like a poisonous cloud that at any moment could choke the life from us. I couldn't take it anymore. I was the first to break it.

"Dean… this needs to be done. Now."

He nodded then got up from his chair and made his way to the window, set in the wall between us. As he stared out into the blackness, I got the impression that the words he tried to find were eluding him.

"I knew what was going on within the Brotherhood," he finally said. "I grew up surrounded by it, saw what was happening to those girls…" He paused for a moment, lowering his head. "I did what I could, when I could… to help them escape. But I couldn't help them all."

My muscles softened as I began to look at him with empathy rather than suspicion. "You never should have been put in that position in the first place. None of us should have. What happened isn't your fault. I hope you know that."

"I do," Dean said, before turning back toward me. "But to keep my standing with my father, I had to look past so many things… I let girls die, Isabella. I know I couldn't save them, but I didn't even try. Whatever you thought of me before or after, that makes me a bad person."

"What I'm having a hard time understanding is, once you were older, and within the police force, why didn't you say anything to finally put an end to the Brotherhood?"

"There's more to it than you think." He turned back toward the window.

"Then tell me. Help me understand."

Even with the lights dimmed, I could make out what he was doing. He finished undoing his tie and began working at the buttons of his crisp white dress shirt. As he undressed, my body's automatic response was to freeze. My mind was racing for the motives behind this action. I shifted my weight onto my feet, should I have to defend myself. Once he'd taken off the button-up and thrown it onto the chair, he made his way to me. His torso was still covered by a white cotton T-shirt, but as he got closer, it was hard to miss what he wanted to show me. I stood up just as he reached the couch, and, for a moment, we stood face-to-face.

"Not all brothers liked little girls," he began, then pulled the T-shirt over his head and let it drop to the floor. His torso mimicked my own body—scars that were flushed and raised, differing in shades between iridescent red and deep purple. I took his left hand in mine. After turning it so I could see his inner wrist, I gently ran my fingers over the infinity symbol branded into his skin. "For some of them…" he continued, "I was their type."

"Dean… I had no idea."

He shrugged. "Why would you? You were in your own personal hell, trying to protect yourself and Anna. When the Brotherhood figured out I couldn't be groomed to be one of them, they groomed me *for* them."

"That night, when you helped me escape… you should have come with me."

"No." He shook his head. "I did the right thing. I knew I wouldn't be around for much longer because I'd be away at school, and I honestly thought Jonathan was dead. I knew I'd be okay. But you—you had to get as far away as possible."

"Of course, he wasn't dead. And you were left to keep enduring everything."

"That's true, but we can't go back and change things. We can only move forward and try to correct them." He took a seat on the couch next to me. "And believe me when I say this. I want him dead just as much as you do."

"Why now? You're finally agreeing that the Brotherhood has to end, but you've been silent all these years…"

His eyes were misting. "You know why Jonathan told you about me, right?"

"Mind games. That's all."

"No. I think he wanted you to kill me."

"Why?"

"You know the statistics, Izzy—the stigma that follows a man who's been sexually abused. But now I've got you, and I've seen that it's possible to fight back and save others from a similar fate—something I should've done a long time ago. He knows which side I'm on. You should too."

Dean had suffered the same fate as the rest of us…

"If you mean that, and are willing to put your career—your life—on the line, help me find Michael, and we'll do this together."

"So does that mean you trust me now?" he asked, his eyes hopeful.

"More than before… But we'll have to take this slowly… one step at a time."

CHAPTER FORTY-TWO

X MARKS THE SPOT

THE NEXT MORNING, I sat at the desk in my home office, sipping coffee, mulling over the information I'd just learned from Dean. I desperately tried to poke holes in it, analyzing every word he'd said. I remembered every detail of his composure and voice, and analyzed it to make sure what his disclosures were, in fact, true. How could I possibly not have known?

But once he'd exposed his scars to me, the same as I did with survivors, it was impossible to ignore the evidence.

The ringing of my cell phone stole me from my thoughts, and I sighed. I would have to purge my thoughts for a moment. I still had work to do.

"Hey, Mel."

"Hey. Do you have time to stop by the morgue today?"

"Is everything okay?"

"Yes, well, I think so… I just need to go over something with you."

"Can you give me a hint what it's about?"

She lowered her voice, as if an uninvited guest were listening. "I'd rather speak to you in person."

"I can be there in under an hour."

"Perfect. See you then."

Something wasn't right. Melanie's usual cheerful tone was missing. And her hesitation at talking over the phone was out of character.

***

I was there in forty-five minutes. I didn't even poke my head in first. Melanie was sitting at her desk as I walked over to her, two coffees in hand.

"Thank you," she said, grabbing one. "I've been swamped since last night. Haven't had time to grab one yet."

"You're welcome. Too much to hope that explains your cryptic request this morning?"

She put the coffee on her desk then got up and walked over to the other desk and grabbed the chair by the arm, bringing it back with her. "Far too much. Please sit down, Isabella."

I sat down. Melanie did the same before handing me a dark brown folder. "This is the autopsy report for Katherine O'Reilly."

"Okay…" I looked at the file then back at her. "And this is what you couldn't talk about over the phone?"

"I want you to read it and tell me what you think."

I opened the file. "It was an accident, Mel. I don't understand—"

"Just humor me, okay?" she said in a soft but stern voice.

I nodded and began reading. Everything seemed standard for an accident, up until I got to the diagram of Katherine's injuries, followed by the full toxicology report. COD was suffocation due to water inhalation… drowning. But the diagram of her body showed a mark on her arm, noted as a possible puncture wound. The toxicology report showed a high dose of bupivacaine in her system. I closed the file and handed it back to her. She placed it on her desk and picked up her coffee, taking a sip without taking her eyes off me.

"So it might not have been an accident?" I asked, keeping my voice even. "Is this what you wanted to let me know?"

Melanie nodded. "The evidence collected by Detective Matthews's team at the scene included a scrap of paper containing the number of a prepaid phone. It was found on the island in the kitchen."

I'd forgotten that Dean had taken over the two cases Marcus and I had been working on before his disappearance. It would only be natural that he'd be investigating any deaths of those involved as well. "It could have been hers. Or Michael's."

"It might have been, Izzy." Melanie looked queasy. "I'm not accusing—I'm just stating facts… there was a strand of your hair on Katherine's body."

"What are you trying to say?"

Melanie looked me straight in the eyes. "I'm not saying anything. I'm just asking."

"I ran into her at the grocery store the day before. If she bathed in the morning, which it seems like she did, any hair I'd gotten on her would have remained until her bath."

"Why wasn't this reported?"

"How? There's not exactly a 'ran into a suspect' form. And I resent the implication."

"You're right. I'm sorry. It's just… Michael couldn't have killed Katherine; his whereabouts at the time of her death have been confirmed. But I'm not sure… the toxicology report."

"Yes, I know," I said. "But if I went around killing people, I'd have started with Michael. You know that."

"I'm sorry. Again, you're right."

I hated lying to Melanie, but I was never going to disclose that particular truth to her. I was stewing in my guilt when my cell phone came to life. I put my index finger up to indicate I had to take it—and then I did. As I continued to listen, I couldn't stop smiling. After five full minutes, I ended the call.

"So you won the lottery?"

"It was Dean Matthews! He's at the precinct. Marcus just showed up!"

She immediately got up and grabbed her coat. "I'm coming with you."

"Alright, let's go."

CHAPTER FORTY-THREE

THE REUNION

WHEN WE ENTERED the precinct, I scanned the room, trying to see if I could locate Marcus. Dean spotted us and immediately made his way over. The whole bullpen was abuzz: police officers whizzed by; a paramedic team headed for the door that Mel and I had just left. I suddenly became very nervous.

"Where is he?" I asked, gently moving Dean off my path. "Is he all right? I need to see him."

"Calm down, Isabella. He's safe and sound. He was just checked out by the paramedics. He's talking to the Feds."

"What are the Feds doing here?"

"After everything that's gone on, and then with the new set of girls being found, the chief thought it was a good idea."

That's the last thing we need right now.

I could easily work around the Newark PD, but the Feds? There was no working history between us. "Where are they from? They're not local are they?"

Dean shook his head. "Direct from Quantico."

I looked at Melanie. "Did you know about this?"

She nodded. "It's why I wanted to talk to you this morning. I had to turn my findings over to them."

A tingling awakened the surface of my skin. I shook my head, trying to get out the anger threatening to overtake me. I turned back to Dean. "Do you know who they sent?"

"There's Special Agent Wes Richford. He handles crimes against adults, kidnappings, murders, et cetera," he explained. "There's Special Agent Angela—"

"De Luca, specializing in crimes against children—same as me."

"Do you know her?" Melanie asked.

"She and I attended Brown university together. After graduation, I went into private practice after declining a job with the FBI. She accepted. We were at the top of our class and highly sought after."

"Why didn't you take it?" Mel asked.

Because I couldn't afford to have them learn about my past.

I shrugged. "I felt I could reach more people in private practice."

"Speaking of your classmate..." Dean interrupted, bringing us to silence as Angela approached.

I would've recognized her without knowing she was here. In school, she'd always been in the habit of dressing like she was on her way to a business meeting... now was no exception.

Angela wore a sophisticated black skirt suit, and a form-flattering, long-sleeved jacket, complete with an asymmetrical button closure. Her black patent leather heels, which added a good three inches to her five-foot-eight frame, gave her the extra boost of authority she had always seemed to crave. When she finally reached our group, she towered over all of us.

"Nice to see you again, Melanie," she started, before cutting off her response by turning toward me. "And Isabella, it's been a while. How are you?"

I had to stop myself from rolling my eyes at her. She had no real interest in me except to dissect the work I'd done on these cases.

"Nice to see you, Angela. And busy."

"Yes, I can see that. I've been going over the reports. When you do have the time, I'd like to pick your brain about these two cases."

I nodded. "Whenever's convenient for you. But before I do that, I want to see Marcus."

"I understand the two of you are close. I can't imagine how hard it's been since he disappeared. It shouldn't be much longer."

I didn't like the tone, or the body language she was emitting. She seemed suspicious about something. Whether it was Marcus, me, or both, I was sure to find out soon. Like me, she wasn't one to mince words.

I gave her my warmest smile. "Thank you, and you're right. Marcus and I *are* close, and I'm anxious to finally see him. I need to see for myself that he's okay."

"Wait here. I'll see if I can move things along," she said, before turning and walking away.

"Breathe, Izzy," Melanie told me. "You're tensing up, and it's not going to help the situation."

If it was obvious to her, it was even more so to Angela. I'd have to be more careful.

"Melanie's right, Isabella," Dean said. "They're going to try to pick apart our whole investigation. If you let Agent De Luca get under your skin, she'll just dig that much more."

They both were right.

"I know," I said, "Thankfully, I'm over the initial meeting with her. It won't happen again."

Melanie placed a hand on my shoulder. "As much as I'd like to stay and see Marcus, I have to get back to the morgue. I've got a male hit-and-run victim to examine. Call me later. I want to know how things go."

"I will. And thanks for coming, Melanie."

"Anytime," she said with a smile, before heading for the door.

"Do you recognize her from Brown University?" I asked Dean when we were alone.

He nodded. "I do, but I don't think she recognizes me. Part of my job was to be inconspicuous while I kept an eye on you—and I was good at it. Hell, you didn't even know I was there."

"True. But it wouldn't take much for her to find out your background."

"Same for you... that's the real reason you didn't take the job with the FBI."

"Precisely..."

I trailed off. The person I wanted to see most in the world was heading straight for me. I had to stop myself from running across the room to him. Once we were standing in front of each other, I couldn't hold back anymore. I put my arms around his neck and hugged him, hoping that I'd never have to let him go.

"So I take it you missed me, Porter?" he asked.

I pulled away, and there it was: that trademark smirk. The same one that, countless times, I'd wanted to slap from his face... but now I wanted it to be permanent.

"No, I just rush up and hug everyone I see, smartass!"

Marcus brought me back in for another hug. "And you'd want me no other way."

"Never," I whispered.

As we continued our embrace, Angela, along with Special Agent Richford, stood by and watched. I caught a glance of her as my cast gently bumped Marcus's neck; the suspicion never left her face. I'd have to figure out what it was and fix it fast.

CHAPTER FORTY-FOUR

WRONG SIDE OF THE TABLE

IN HIS OFFICE, Marcus closed the door and started kissing me. It was all too sudden.

"Marcus…"

He nibbled on my neck, and gently pressed my back to the wall.

"Marcus… Marcus stop. Marcus, stop!"

I shoved him off. He didn't look too pleased about it.

"I'm sorry," I said. "It's just you can't come back and start kissing me like that. My mind doesn't understand… I love you, but not like that right now.

He sat in the chair behind the desk.

"It's like I never left," he said, bitterly.

I took a seat across from him. "But you did, Marcus. You've been gone for quite some time."

His face dropped a little. "Always straight to business with you, Izzy. Can't I savor the moment?"

"You'll have time for that later. Right now, you need to get caught up with what's going on. More importantly, I need to know what happened to you."

He let out a long sigh. "Well, if I didn't believe I was back before, I sure do now."

"I'm sorry, but things haven't stopped around here while you were gone," I reminded him. "And now that the Feds are here, it's about to get worse. You know that, right?"

"Yeah. I wasn't too impressed to see that the chief brought them in. I thought you had figured things out and that's why I was released."

"Released by whom?"

"Your guess is as good as mine."

I was confused. "You mean it wasn't Michael O'Reilly?"

"If it was, he never made himself known to me," he said. "Once I was put in the car, I was drugged and woke up in a dark, empty room. There wasn't a single window, so I couldn't get a feel for where I might have been."

"Well, I can assure you it wasn't up at Lake Placid."

"Really?" He sounded surprised.

"Really. The Brotherhood burned it down while I was in it," I said, showing him my cast.

"How bad is it? Was it a full break or just fractured?"

"Fracture."

"At least that's a bit of good news." Marcus sighed. "Wonder how long it'll take them to rebuild the cabin this time."

"We have worse problems… Michael is still out there. I almost had him, but I had to make a choice. It was either I let him go, or let Ember die."

"What were you doing going after him in the first place?" He raised his voice slightly. "That's not your job. Leave it to the police next time."

My defenses rose, but I reminded myself that Marcus didn't know what was going on at the time. No one did.

"During our last interview, Michael told me this was now between him and me. He said if I went to the police with what I knew, he would kill Ember. You would have done the same in my shoes."

He took a moment to think. "Probably... but I wasn't exactly in a position to do much of anything."

"Marcus... What happened to you?" I asked.

"You know, you could always wait until Special Agent Richford's report is completed, saving me from repeating myself..."

"Marcus..."

He put his head between his hands, rubbing his temples. I could practically sense his headache as he looked back up at me. "Fine, here's what I can tell you. I was in that room the whole time. They gave me enough provisions to live, and I had to shit and piss in a bucket—which they at least had the decency to empty every day. So besides being a bit dehydrated and losing some weight, I came away relatively unscathed."

"Who released you? Did they actually bring you here?"

"No idea. They had me blindfolded and tied; dropped me off in an alley downtown. Not sure if they or a passerby called the police, but they came to get me. I refused to go to the hospital, so they brought me here and called the paramedics instead."

"And they never told you why they took you? You had no interaction at all with anyone—besides what you just mentioned?"

I trusted Marcus, but his story seemed a little off.

"As far as I knew, they wanted you. I figured they took me instead because I'm the one who chased the man at the diner."

I'd been thinking a lot about the note since then. It never made sense.

"Uh-oh," Marcus said, interrupting my thoughts. "That look is never a good sign. What are you thinking?"

I smiled. "It's nothing. Just thinking about the note you got at Andros Diner."

"You've seen it?"

"I did. Caught it right before it was washed down the sewer."

"And?" he pressed.

"Why did the waitress give it to you when it was meant for me?"

"Because I intercepted it before she had the chance to," he said matter-of-factly.

"That's not what the waitress said…"

Either his memory was distorted, or mine was. Before I could finish my thought, there was a knock at the door.

"Come in," Marcus said loudly.

The door opened, and Agent Richford poked his head through. "Dr. Porter, Agent De Luca wants to know if you could meet with her. I also have a few more questions for Lieutenant Hudson here."

I looked back at Marcus, who looked particularly unhappy.

"I guess we'll talk later," he said.

"We will," I assured him, as I got up from my chair. "Where can I find her?"

"Interrogation room four."

I thanked him and took my leave.

***

I hated the interrogation rooms, but I was grateful Angela's invitation somewhat hinted at her hand before we started to play. I walked down the hallway to the partially open door. I saw her sitting on the side the interrogated usually sat, facing the one-way mirror. I smiled; her tactics hadn't changed a bit.

I lightly knocked on the door to make myself known. "Special Agent De Luca?"

She looked up from the file she'd been reading. "Isabella, come in. And really, there's no need for formalities. We go too far back for that. Don't you agree?"

Tactics two and three. Even though being questioned in an interrogation room was meant to put me on edge, she sat on the opposite side to put me at ease, making it seem like it was nothing formal, and the mention of our history was meant to confuse me. That's okay. I could play too.

She didn't say anything else until I was seated across from her. "I hope your visit with Marcus went well," she began.

"It did. Thanks for speeding everything up," I said, putting forth my best smile.

Angela smiled back. "You're very welcome. And don't worry... I don't plan on keeping you too long. I know you probably want to get back to him."

"If it's useful for the investigation, please, take all the time you need."

"Perfect." She closed the file in her hands and grabbed the one below it, opening it to the first page. "So. You were among the first called in when the Meadowland bodies were discovered. Is that correct?"

"It is, yes. It's routine for the Newark PD to call me to the scene, especially in scenarios such as that."

"And why would you say it's routine?"

"Well, like you, my specialty is crimes against children. And as you know, someone like us can gather a lot of information just by viewing a crime scene."

Angela nodded. "In total agreement." She flipped through a few pages. "It says here that at that time you didn't think it was the work of a serial killer."

"Correct."

"What brought you to that conclusion?"

"As it's written in the report," I explained, "I agreed that it was the work of an experienced killer, but we were unable to find any similar cases that would suggest serial at the moment. Saying so at that time would have been premature."

She closed the file and went back to the previous one. "The case of Ember O'Reilly. You were given that file the same day, yes?"

"That's right. Marcus gave it to me later that evening." That was quite a jump for her. I did my best to figure out her train of thought as we went along. "He was supposed to give it to me earlier, but the Meadowlands girls were discovered before he had the chance to."

"I see," she said without looking up from the pages, then abruptly closed the file and finally made eye contact. "When did you realize the two cases were linked?"

That caught me off guard, but at least I understood where she was headed. "I was beginning to explore the theory once the autopsies were completed, and after I'd met with Ember O'Reilly."

"By that time, you should have been suspecting a possible pedophile ring, as well as a serial killer."

"Pedophile ring, yes, but a serial killer was still questionable."

"Could you please explain? First, how you came to that conclusion, and second, why you never entered the possibility of a pedophile ring into your reports."

I took a moment to calm the voices whispering in the back of my mind. "All we had were the three young girls, whom, I should mention, were killed at the same time. There was no cooling-off period in between and still, nothing found remotely similar in New Jersey or anywhere else across the country. As for why I didn't mention the possibility of a pedophile ring: it was nothing more than a working theory. We had one young girl who'd been sexually, physically, and psychologically tortured by the men on the paternal side of her family. The three girls were sexually and physically abused, but, unfortunately, that is not remotely uncommon in murder cases involving young girls."

Angela gently tapped the tip of her finger to her lips before continuing. "At any time did you mention your theories to Lieutenant Hudson?"

"As the investigation was progressing, I kept him informed about what I was thinking, yes."

"So why not mention it in your reports?" she asked again.

"Is this really what the interview's about? My record keeping? I just said that I suspected a possible pedophile ring. In a small town, illegal institutions can carry a lot of power. How would you have proceeded?" My patience was wearing thin. "Or is it really about the FBI not being called in sooner?"

"Is that what you think?" Throughout our discussion, Angela kept the same expressionless tone of voice.

She wasn't going to shrink me. I took my own tone down a few notches. "You tell me. You're the one who's asking the questions."

"Is it possible, Isabella, had either theory been mentioned in the reports—which were being forwarded to the DA—that we might have been called in sooner? That perhaps a second group of three young girls wouldn't have been found dead, almost exactly in the same way as the first three? That Ember O'Reilly wouldn't have been abducted?"

I leaned into the table, crossing my arms in front of me, looking her straight in the eyes. "No, Angela. I don't believe it would have prevented anything."

"Okay. I think that's it for now." She closed the file. "Would you mind picking this back up tomorrow morning, say nine o'clock?" Short interviews designed to prolong the stress... A page right out of my book... and yet, she sounded as if we were two old friends who'd just caught up on old times over cups of coffee.

"Sure. I'll bring coffee," I said with a weak smile.

CHAPTER FORTY-FIVE

TO NEW FRIENDS

IT WAS EARLY EVENING, and I'd made my way to the Jersey Tavern. Instead of taking my usual seat at the bar, I grabbed a booth. Besides Eric bringing me my drink, no one bothered me—which was just how I wanted it.

Marcus was resting at home after our lunch that afternoon, and Melanie was exhausted after being caught up to speed on Marcus and the Feds. She told me she was going to spend the night inside, just after she disclosed how she'd decided to rule the death of Katherine O'Reilly an accident—both of which were huge burdens lifted off my shoulders. It seemed I could finally get a night off.

Until Special Agent Richford walked in. Unfortunately, because of where I was sitting, I could be spotted from the entrance. I finished my drink moments before he found his way to my booth.

"Dr. Porter. How are you this evening?" he asked.

"Special Agent—"

"Please, call me Wes."

"Very well. Wes. What brings you here?"

"Decided to take a look around town," he said. "A couple of offic-ers at the precinct told me this was a good place to grab a drink and something to eat."

"You heard right," I said, then took my first real look at him.

He was dressed in a dark-gray suit, his red tie loosened just enough for him to leave the first two buttons open. Probably in his late thirties, he was around five foot nine and looked to be in good shape, his suit fitting his body well. His hair was black, slightly graying at the sides, and neatly cut, and I was surprised to find myself a bit attracted to him. His blue eyes seemed to peer right into me.

A male version of his partner?

I brought my attention back to his face. "So where's your counter-part?"

He shrugged as a smile took over. "Actually, Agent De Luca isn't my partner. In fact, I'd only seen her a few times before we were both asked to come here," he explained. "So… what will it take to be invited to sit with you?"

I couldn't help but let a laugh escape. I still wasn't in the mood to be social, but I might be able to use this opportunity to my advantage. I gestured toward the bench across from me. "Please sit with me, Wes."

"I'd be honored, Dr. Porter." He removed his jacket, neatly folded and placed it on the bench before sitting down.

"You can call me Isabella."

"Isabella… pretty name." he said. Immediately, his face reddened.

I found this somewhat amusing. Compared to Marcus—with his horrible pickup lines and endless flirting—this man gave me the small-est compliment and instantly blushed. It was refreshing. Before long, Eric was at our table.

"Visitor?" he asked, always curious when a new face arrived.

"This is Wes Richford. He will be working with the NPD for the next few weeks or so. Wes, this is Eric, my favorite bartender in all of Jersey."

"I see. I heard a couple officers say Marcus was found, but I haven't seen him yet." He put his arms up as if they were his exclamation marks.

"He went home to rest this afternoon," I told him. "He said he'll try to drop by tomorrow."

"Excellent." He took a quick look at my empty glass. "Now I know what *you* want, but what about Wes?" he asked, looking at him.

"I'll start with a Scotch, neat. And if I could have a food menu too, that would be great."

"I'll be right back with that," Eric said, before heading toward the bar.

"So I heard you were given a bit of a hard time this afternoon," Wes said.

He took me a bit by surprise. "Oh? Who told you that?"

"The police chief. Let's just say he reminded us that we were invited and that the invitation can be revoked at any time."

"Huh, I wasn't expecting that. But Angela's questions weren't anything I couldn't handle. I'm sure she told you we went to school together."

"Heard all about it—all the way here. What exactly did you do to piss her off anyway? Get slightly higher grades?"

"Well, that and I turned down the position she accepted."

"Why did you?" he asked curiously.

Eric returned with our drinks and a menu for Wes. I thanked him and delved right into my whiskey.

"Will you be eating?" Wes asked, offering to share the menu with me.

"I had something earlier."

"Okay. So why'd you turn down the job."

"Are you nonchalantly interrogating me, Special Agent Richford?"

"Not in the slightest. I'm genuinely curious," he said quickly. "If it's something you don't want to discuss, I can respect that."

I could tell he was being genuine. Despite being someone who doesn't trust easily, I could see being friends with him under different circumstances; I usually can pick up on that pretty quickly.

"It's not that I thought being with the Bureau wouldn't fulfill what I wanted to do with my life... I just didn't think it would give me the freedom I needed to fulfill it all. I wanted to help people in a more personal way, and I didn't want to get caught in the bureaucracy of things... Does that make sense?"

"Completely. Consider the subject closed." He smiled warmly. "In fact, let's consider work as a whole off limits. How does that sound?"

So much for trying to gauge what was truly going on, though I still welcomed the idea. "That fulfills my wants for tonight. Complete and utter nothingness."

He nodded. "We could sit here in silence, and I would still be content with your company."

"Let's not... but I believe I can return the compliment."

He grinned. "As long as you believe so..."

"I'm sorry, that sounded horrible. I'm not really good with this." I looked into the glass between my hands.

"Hey. I never asked for you to be someone you're not. I planned on having dinner, a couple of drinks, and now maybe get to know the woman who saved that little girl's life. Trust me, I'm not complaining."

"You're sweet, Wes. Thank you."

He raised his glass. "To new friends."

Again I couldn't help smiling at him. What had started as a roller coaster of a day was definitely ending on a good note. I'll take what I can get.

"To new friends," I repeated, and our glasses met.

***

I arrived back at my townhome before midnight, reset the alarm, made my usual rounds, and headed upstairs to the bedroom. I let myself drop onto the bed, still fully clothed and not caring. I was exhausted. My heavy eyelids immediately began to close.

And then my phone rang.

"You've got to be kidding me," I mumbled into the mattress willing myself to ignore it… but I'd ignored it too many times before.

"Thought you might have been sleeping," said the voice on the other end.

"So you decided to give me a call?" I asked, annoyed. "But I guess I should be more astonished that you're calling in the first place, and so soon."

"I wanted to see how you're doing with the new developments. Happy that Marcus is back?"

"You're so close to pulling off the caring act—but you're not quite there, I'm afraid," I said sarcastically. "What do you want? Here to tell me how bad I am for staying in Newark?"

"To feed my curiosity."

"About?"

"I've been informed that the Feds have finally made their appearance," he said. I could practically hear the smile in his voice. "What are you going to do now, Isabella? Another obstacle in the way."

I wondered how he'd gotten that information. He was either having me followed, or someone had told him… *Dean?* "Don't concern yourself about that. My advice? Worry about yourself."

"That would be a waste of my time, as I've repeatedly proven to you… Good night, Isabella. We'll catch up soon."

He ended the call.

Before my brain could stop me, I threw the phone across the room, watching as it hit the wall, the already cracked screen shattering completely, littering the floor with little beads of glass.

"Shit," I muttered.

I had to pull myself together. Now definitely wasn't the time to start unraveling.

CHAPTER FORTY-SIX

A CHANGE IN DIRECTION

AT FIVE O'CLOCK the next morning, I made my way to Dean's house. After I knocked four times and rang the doorbell twice, the door opened to a groggy, annoyed Dean.

"What the hell, Isabella? Do you know what time it is?" He was dressed in just a T-shirt and boxers.

"Do you even own a robe?" I asked, pushing my way past him. "And I really need to talk to you. Honestly, you're lucky I didn't show up when I originally wanted to."

"Then obviously it's something that couldn't wait until a half-decent hour." He closed the door and followed me into the living room. "The least you can do is make coffee. Everything's in the cupboard above the percolator."

"Fine, sit. Back in a moment." I went into the kitchen. As the coffee was brewing, I made my way back. "When did you last talk to Michael?"

Raising his head off the back of the couch, he opened his eyes. "Can't I at least have coffee in hand? I don't know... last week?"

"When did you know the Feds were being called in?" I asked, the urgency plain in my voice.

"What's this about?" he asked, now sitting at full attention.

"Answer the question, Dean."

"Late last week the chief mentioned they might be called in. Now do you want to tell me what this is about?"

"I received a call from Michael last night. He knows about the Feds."

"Is that supposed to surprise me? This is Michael we're talking about," he said. "He's not going to back away from you, and he's always in the know about nearly everything that's going on."

"I never said either surprised me. What I need to know is how he found out."

"Yeah, yeah, I get the hint." He got up and made his way past me and into the kitchen; I followed him, watching closely as he poured coffee into two mugs. "You think I told him."

He went to hand me a mug, but my arms were crossed in suspicion.

"Seriously? Haven't we done this shit before?" he asked, clearly exasperated. "Am I alright or am I Satan himself? Pick a position and stick with it."

"It's not an overnight thing, Dean..."

He sighed. "No. I didn't tell him anything."

I finally took the mug from him. "I believe you... which means I'm being followed." I returned to the living room and sat down in an armchair. Dean retook his place on the couch, slouching forward.

"You can't be surprised by that either..."

"I'm not. But now, not only do I have Michael and God only knows how many brothers following me, but also the Feds. That doesn't leave me much room for maneuvering."

"You know you're not alone to figure this out, right? Assuming you don't knock me off or something."

"Sounds to me like you forgive me for barging in the way I did," I said with a wry smile.

He raised his mug in the air. "Now that I have my coffee, all is forgiven." He took a sip. "Ah, I feel sunshine, even though it's not out yet. Can you come over every morning?" he asked with a wink.

"Before dawn? Absolutely," I teased.

He shook his head. "Just to be clear, that was sarcasm. If there's any chance for confusion, I'll say right now: I actually like to sleep."

"Okay… so this morning at nine, I have another interview with Angela. Then I have to pick up a new cell phone and pay a visit to Ember. I'm starting to realize there's not enough time in a day."

"What happened to your phone? Or should I ask?"

"It broke. Just know that I'll be unreachable until I pick up the new one."

"You should change your number as well," he suggested.

"No, Michael needs to be able to reach me. He called from an unknown number last night. He probably ditched his last phone."

"So he's unreachable. Untraceable if he's now using a burner cell… smart move."

"It won't save him," I said, mostly to myself.

"Got any plans on how that'll proceed?"

"I do, but before I can put everything in place, I have to get the Feds off my back and off this case. With Marcus's return and Michael gone, I need to play nice until they realize there's nothing for them to do—which means no more dead girls."

"Yeah…" Dean trailed off.

"Do you know anything more about that? Who's behind those killings?"

He put his mug on the table and twisted his fingers, individually. "I assumed it was Michael."

There it was again—he was holding back, and he wasn't hiding it very well.

"Dean, we both know it doesn't fit his profile. He would make the killings as sadistic as possible. The person behind those deaths has some kind of connection to those girls."

"There's also Marcus," he casually proposed.

The silence was palpable.

"I can't believe you're suggesting that." I got up from the chair and headed to the window. The sun was just starting to come up, and I hadn't even realized how much time had already passed.

Dean remained where he was, picking his mug up and taking another sip of coffee. "Don't you find it strange that the day of Marcus's disappearance, three new girls showed up? Have you checked on his whereabouts before the first three girls were found? For the length of time they were there before being discovered, it's quite possible—"

"Stop!" I turned to face him. "Not a word. I trust Marcus a lot more than I trust you."

He stood up and made his way to me. "You asked me if I knew who's behind this. I'm giving you options since you shot Michael down."

I was already having doubts about what Marcus had recalled; I didn't need someone else to feed into that. "Marcus is off the table until you have a good reason to suspect him."

"Fine. All I'm saying is don't close yourself off to possibilities because of your relationship with him."

"No one is off the list of suspects," I shot back. "But first there has to be proof."

"Then find it, and you'll get your answers."

***

I arrived at the precinct at a quarter to nine, coffees in hand, and headed straight to Marcus's office. When I didn't find him there, the familiar feeling of anxiety set it.

"Don't worry. He's speaking with the chief," said a voice from behind, startling me. I turned around to find Wes, a smile swiftly disappearing from his face.

"Sorry," he said. "I really should stop doing that."

"Stealth skills can come in handy but definitely not when I'm holding three cups of steaming hot coffee," I said, regaining my composure and returning his fading smile. I removed one of the cups from the tray. "Seeing as Marcus is MIA, coffee?"

"I'd love some. Black?"

"Are we being picky when offered a free beverage?" I asked.

"Sarcasm… love it… it's black though?"

I laughed.

"Yes. It's black."

"Thanks." He took the cup from me. "Ready for round two with Special Agent De Luca?"

"It's not a boxing match! Unless you know something that I don't…" I eyed him curiously.

"Not a thing. In fact, we see each other so rarely, I can't even remember her first name," he said, returning the sarcasm.

I laughed again. "I see we share a common language. Funny how it didn't show last night."

He blushed. "The idea was to give a nonthreatening, good first impression," he said. "Had I known you spoke it, we could have abandoned English all together."

"To paraphrase you, don't hide who you are from me—it isn't necessary. Besides, I can read you like a book, regardless of how hard you try to hide it," I said, grinning.

"It's your job, after all. Consider me aptly warned… You can find Agent De Luca in the same room as before."

"Thanks, Wes. We'll talk later," I said, making my way through the door.

"I hope so. Just remember to keep your head down and sides protected. All bets are on you," he called after me. Again I couldn't help smile at the boxing reference.

The door slightly ajar, I saw Angela sitting on the appropriate side of the table. She might have been done with her tactics, but I decided to keep my guard up.

I walked into the room and closed the door behind me, placing her coffee beside her.

"If I remember correctly, two creamers and a Splenda," I said as I took my seat.

"As usual, your memory is immaculate." She took a long sip before continuing. "So is your penchant for being on time."

I registered the fact that people in our profession tended to talk more formally than most.

I nodded. "I like to be consistent. I don't see that changing anytime soon."

"Nothing wrong with that... Now I don't want to keep you long, as I know you have a job to do. Let's get started."

"Thank you."

"Do you have a connection to Ember O'Reilly and her family?"

There was the Angela I knew—straight to the point. She went for the jugular, but I refused to let it affect me. "How do you mean?"

She now had a pen in hand, poised to write. "Well, as you know, we have access to information that wouldn't normally be available to others."

More specifically, sealed juvenile files. "I know where you're going with this, and as a professional courtesy, I'll forewarn you: my past is exactly that—*my* past—and I'm very protective of it. What does it have to do with these cases? You'll have to give me a very good reason to discuss it."

Angela slowly nodded. "You're originally from Brooklyn and moved to Rhode Island when you were fourteen. Is that right?"

"Yes."

"Did your family move out there as well?" she asked, keeping her eyes on the file in front of her.

I felt the numbness begin in the tips of my fingers. "You heard my warning. You already know the answer to that. Next question."

"Okay... you changed your last name to 'Porter' to match your aunt and uncle."

"That's not a question. And please, if you want to ask me something, let it be without an answer already written in your little file" I warned her again. The numbness reached my shoulders, and tried to force its way further up my body.

Angela looked up at me. "Isabella, I know why you moved in with your aunt and uncle and why you changed your last name. I also know why you first met Lieutenant Hudson."

"I'm still waiting for the question…" This was now the second time today Marcus had been brought up—first by Dean and now her.

She softened her tone, which was unusual for her. "After reading the files of the cases you've worked in the past, this is the only one where you went above and beyond for one of the victims. So here's my question: why would you get so personally involved in this case?"

The numbness now encased most of my body, and I knew my head was next.

"*Survivors*," I corrected. "Besides her maternal aunt and uncle, Ember had no one. I gave her extra support because she was up against her entire immediate family, many of whom participated in organized rape. Hardly a typical case."

"But like you, she has her aunt and uncle. And like you, she suffered extreme torture at the hands of her family."

"Please make your point, Agent De Luca…" I said, my voice low.

"Here's what I'm having difficulties with," she started. "It was under similar circumstances that you first met Lieutenant Hudson—just before you were sent to live with your mother's family in Rhode Island."

"At my request," I interjected.

"Yes, I know. Now, not long after you started your private practice, Lieutenant Hudson convinced you to come back to New Jersey and work cases with similar undertones—"

This was bordering on ridiculous. "These cases are my specialty. That's not unusual."

"—Then you're handed a case, again by Lieutenant Hudson that's strikingly parallel to your own, for which you go out of your normal, *consistent* procedures and actually put yourself at risk to save the life of the victim... excuse me—survivor."

It finally clicked. She wasn't trying to attack me; she was after Marcus. Thinking back to our initial interview, when Angela was questioning my reports, she asked if I'd kept Marcus abreast regarding my working theories. I was totally safe... but Marcus wasn't.

"What are you asking me, Angela?" I said. "Yes, I'll admit that Ember O'Reilly and I come from very similar backgrounds. She also reminded me of someone, and I took an exceptional interest in her personally."

"Your sister... Anna?" she asked cautiously.

Her name said out loud sent a chill up my spine. "You can't... Yes. That's the connection you're seeking... But I fail to see where you're going with all of this."

"Let me ask you something."

"Finally, an actual question!" I said, raising my arms in an exaggerated gesture before letting them fall back to the table with a thump.

Angela let out a lighthearted laugh. "Yes, an actual question. In your expert opinion, and trying to remove yourself from the situation you're personally invested in, don't you find it odd that Lieutenant

Hudson up and disappears, and in his absence—the exact day he goes missing—three new girls are found?"

Once again, Dean's suggestion was echoing through her. They were trying to pin the murders on Marcus, and I was no longer certain if I could look at this objectively. I remained silent.

"Look, I know the two of you are close," she said. "Lieutenant Hudson took you away from the hell that was your life. That said, a professional, ethical person would never have put you on a case that was so close to your own past. The reason for that can be seen in how you reacted to it."

"I asked him to! He said—"

"I'm not saying you did anything wrong, and to be perfectly honest, I'm not sure I would have acted any differently if I'd been in your situation," she said, her voice softening further. "Let me run a theory by you, and then you can tell me if it's even a remote possibility."

I nodded and continued listening.

CHAPTER FORTY-SEVEN

EMBER'S SILENCE

AS PAINFUL AS picking up a new cell phone was, thankfully, I'd been tech savvy enough to back up my data and contacts, not only to my laptop, but also to the Cloud. Using one of the computers at the cell-phone shop, I was able to restore almost everything on my previous phone, save the items lost in the few weeks since I last backed everything up.

Now, as I was on my way to see Ember, Angela's comment kept resonating in my mind: *Let me run a theory by you, then you can tell me if it's even a remote possibility.*

After she told me her theory, I said I'd have to think it through and get back to her. I wasn't trying to stall, I needed to step back and review everything... try to look at the situation from the outside in—like Angela.

Her theory was that Marcus could have killed all six girls—in fact, that he was a member of the Brotherhood. Knowing beforehand that the two cases were connected, and knowing my past, Marcus had put me on the case, not because he thought I would be the best person to work it, but because he knew I would react the way I did—ultimately doing everything I could to protect Ember—which would allow him to distract me when I started piecing things together. Once I started making the connection, he conveniently disappeared and started cleaning up the evidence by killing a new set of young girls. Now that Ember had been saved and Michael had disappeared, Marcus was safe to come back as a victim of a kidnapping, which supposedly was to throw me off because I was getting too close to confirming my suspicions of the Brotherhood and its connection to the six girls and Ember.

I couldn't in good conscience disagree that Angela's theory was a possibility. I had only one major issue—she didn't know the whole backstory of the two cases. Michael was the one who connected Ember's case and the case of the six girls together: the branding, the torture, and the girls who were chosen. He admitted to it—that he did what he did because he could and would continue to do so until he was dead. Of course, even with his confession, it didn't blow Angela's theory out of the water. All it did was force me to think outside the box. I found myself going back to "What if?"

***

I pulled onto Dale and Bonnie's street, parked my car, and made my way to the house. True to form, Dale was sitting on the front steps, but this time, he wasn't alone. Once Ember spotted me, she stood up and ran over. Her natural color had returned and she seemed full of energy—and she proved it when she threw her arms around my waist, almost knocking me over. Then I placed a kiss atop her head.

She looked up at me and smiled. "Where did you go?! It's been forever!"

"Everything feels like forever at your age," I said, putting my arm around her shoulder and continuing my journey to the house. "How have you've been?"

"I'm doing good."

"Well, you definitely seem to be doing better. Still reading?"

"Of course! Does that mean…" She trailed off.

From my bag I pulled out *Shapeless Angels,* the next and final book in the series.

"Thank you! Thank you!" She gave me a quick squeeze then ran to show her uncle the gift.

When I caught up to her, Dale rose from the stairs. "Nice to see you, Isabella. I was wondering when you'd swing by next."

"I told you I'd be checking in regularly. I keep my word," I said, smiling.

Dale turned to Ember. "Why don't you see if your aunt Bonnie needs help with lunch? I need to speak to Isabella for a moment."

"Okay." Ember bounded up the stairs, disappearing from sight.

"Everything okay?" I asked, concerned.

"There's just a few things I'd like to discuss without interruption." He gestured to the porch and followed me under the enclosure.

Taking our seats, I tried to read his face to see what was going on. He seemed calm, but there was definite worry in his eyes.

"Michael hasn't been around, has he?" I asked.

"No, nothing like that. If he was, you'd have a dead man out on the front lawn," he said, his eyes dark. "Though I had two unexpected visits yesterday."

"Oh, who?" I kind of knew but waited for him to confirm it.

"The first was from the FBI, a female agent. She pressured Bonnie and me about why you'd taken a special interest in Ember. The other agent, a man, stayed quiet… But don't worry. We didn't let on about Michael. We didn't think it was necessary."

As much as I appreciated what they'd done, the last thing I wanted was for Dale and Bonnie to find themselves in an awkward position with the Feds. "I really appreciate it, but please don't feel you need to lie. That could turn out badly for the two of you."

"We didn't lie. And we had every bit of plausible deniability… We just didn't fully elaborate." He winked at me. "The woman wanted to speak to Ember, but Ember outright refused, saying she'd only talk to you."

That's probably when Angela decided to pull my file, though I thought I'd satiated her curiosity today, and hoped she wouldn't look into my past any further. "I'm assuming the agents were each one unexpected visit?"

"Actually, no. Marcus stopped by and took me by surprise," he said. "I thought he was still missing."

It surprised me too. "He returned yesterday morning," I said, feeling the last of our love drain away. "When did he stop by?"

"Marcus came by last night after the agents took off."

I'd left Marcus after lunch. He'd claimed to be exhausted, saying he planned to catch up on the sleep he'd lost while he was gone… He didn't have to stick to that plan, but why would he visit the Donnellys?

"And what was his visit concerning?" I asked.

"I'm not entirely certain. He was very… I don't know how to explain it… obscure?" I could tell Dale was trying to straighten out everything in his head. "He wanted to speak to Ember alone, but she again refused and stayed in her room. Then he just… it felt like he was trying to gauge what she had disclosed about her time away without directly coming out and asking."

That wasn't the Marcus I knew. He was straightforward and to the point—what would make him act that way? What was he trying to hide?

"And what did you say?" I asked.

"The same as what I told the FBI… not much. With Ember's reaction, and the way he was acting, I became suspicious. Bonnie and I both did."

I stood up from my chair. "Would it be okay if I spoke to Ember about it for a moment? I promise not to upset her, and I won't force her to talk if she doesn't want to."

"Please. It'll quell my curiosity as well. She hasn't spoken about it at all." He got up to direct me into the house.

Bonnie was in the kitchen, still preparing lunch. Ember was sitting on the living-room couch, reading her new book. I said 'hello' to Bonnie, then sat next to Ember on the couch. Dale hovered nearby. "So I heard you had a few visitors yesterday," I began cautiously. "Wasn't in the mood to talk to them?"

"No," Ember said simply, giving me a quick side-glance, her entire demeanor different from earlier.

"Okay, the FBI agents I can understand. They can be a little intimidating. But why didn't you want to talk to Marcus? I thought you two were friends."

She was still staring into her book. "Because Daddy told me not to."

I looked back at Dale. Bonnie was now standing beside her husband, worry evident on their faces.

"And when did he tell you that?"

"When he took me," she whispered, fear evident in her voice.

I placed my hand on her knee and gave her an encouraging squeeze. "You're safe, Ember. You don't have to worry about Michael anymore. Did he tell you why you're not supposed to talk to Marcus?"

"Because he isn't my friend anymore."

She got up and silently made her way up to her room.

CHAPTER FORTY-EIGHT

A GLIMPSE OF DARKNESS

BACK AT THE PRECINCT, I immediately found who I was looking for. When I entered the office, he looked up from his desk and smiled.

"Special Agent Richford, can I speak to you for a moment?"

His smiled transformed into a puzzled expression. "Professional titles... Okay, Dr. Porter, yes, I have a few minutes."

"Why are you here?"

"Hasn't that been established?"

"No, actually it hasn't. Agent De Luca I understand. You, I don't, nor have you told me why you're here. You've remained fairly quiet, besides having the odd meeting with Lieutenant Hudson and the chief. More of an observer, I'd say."

He looked me squarely in the eyes. "Isabella, where's this coming from?"

"I just came back from seeing the Donnellys and Ember O'Reilly," I said, and watched him run his fingers through his hair. "Agent De Luca was apparently doing all the talking, which makes sense—she's with crimes against children. But why were you there, silent, with no clear purpose?"

"She asked me to come along…"

"But just this morning you said you two haven't been working together closely. And then I learned this afternoon that you went with her to see one of my survivors." I was trying to stay calm but didn't know how much longer I could. "Why are you here?"

"Because of Lieutenant Hudson," he said, lowering his voice slightly and moving to sit on the side of the desk. "I work cases involving crimes against adults—murders, disappearances, assaults—but that's a small piece of what I do. I mainly handle cases involving sociopaths."

"So we're back to the serial killer theory."

"I'm sorry you didn't see it, but it's not a theory. I've been following Michael O'Reilly's actions long before you became involved."

I stood there stunned, unable to produce a word. The mention of his name had frozen me, and all I could do was blink… but my mind was still hard at work, question after question emerging.

If Wes had been keeping watch this whole time, just how much did he know? How long had he actually been in Newark, and what did he know about my origins and what I'd done? Is that why he wanted to have a drink with me last night—to study me?

"Isabella?" Still unable to speak, I heard his voice as though it was coming from a distance. "Dr. Porter, are you okay?"

I shook my head, finally breaking free. "Yes, I'm fine."

"Are you sure? It's like you saw a ghost."

I laughed softly, remembering Marcus saying essentially the same thing when I first saw Michael through the hospital window.

He raised a brow. "Care to let me in on the joke?"

I covered my face up to my nose with my hands and shook my head again. "If only it were a joke…" I put my hands on the table and took on a more serious tone. "What does Marcus have to do with any of this?"

"He was allegedly kidnapped by the Brotherhood, so I had to get as much information as I could. Michael O'Reilly still needs to be tracked down."

"Well, your partner seems to have a different point of view when it comes to who's been doing the killing."

"Honestly, we're not in total disagreement about that, but we already have Marcus within reach. He isn't going anywhere."

"So tell me, Wes. Last night at Jersey Tavern, were you trying to get a reading of me?"

"Actually I was there because I know Marcus frequents the place. The fact that you were there was a bonus," he said, relaxing his posture. "Yes, I should have been more forthcoming with you, but you have to understand—"

I finished for him. "My relationship with Marcus couldn't allow you to do that. I understand. So it's official then. While you're still in search of Michael O'Reilly, Marcus is a suspect as well."

He nodded.

"Well, then, I guess you answered my question. Thanks for your time, Agent Richford." I started to get up, but he gently placed a hand on my arm.

"Do you want to help your friend?" he asked.

I wasn't sure what I wanted to do anymore, even what I knew for that matter. "What are you suggesting?"

"Speak to him, as a *friend*, and then study him, as an unbiased *psychiatrist*."

"I can't believe you put those two words in the same sentence… Could *you* do it?"

Wes removed his hand and tucked it under his elbow as he crossed his arms. "I'm not sure. But if you truly believe we're on the wrong path, prove us wrong, and do it without letting on that he's a suspect. Either way, we'll get to the bottom of this."

***

I was starting to have my doubts: about Marcus, my abilities, whether I could actually separate the two… How could I secretly study the man who'd practically raised me? The man I was just starting to love. But if he were somehow involved, I had to put an end to it. I couldn't allow another threat to Ember.

Once I reached Marcus's office, I knocked lightly on the doorframe. He looked up at me and smiled. I didn't share his pleasure.

"Was wondering when I'd see you today," he said.

After closing the door, I took a seat.

"Busy morning. This is the first chance I've had. Kind of surprised to see you back to work so soon, though."

"The chief wanted to put me on leave, but I think I've had a long enough vacation."

I cocked my head at him. "Odd choice of words—'vacation.'"

He sat back in his chair. "Would you rather I use 'time in a dark room?' Perhaps 'kidnapping?'"

"You mean use the appropriate word for what it was? Yes. And I also think you should see the police psychologist or the therapist. You went through a traumatic event. You're not as immune to its effects as you might think."

"I have *you* for that," he pointed out. "And seriously, I don't need to see anyone—it's part of the job."

I shook my head. "No, it's not, Marcus. Part of the job is taking the leave that was suggested—and speaking to someone who specializes in this kind of thing." I couldn't understand why he was so against either one.

"I'm not taking leave, and I'm not seeing anyone about it. They're both unnecessary. End of discussion!" he said angrily, before pausing to give me a particular look. "You seem a little more on edge than usual. Anything to do with your meeting with Agent Richford?"

He'd apparently seen me walking into Wes's office.

"Actually, no. It has to do with another meeting I had, earlier this afternoon."

"Care to share?"

I nodded. "It's partially the reason I'm here. I met with the Donnellys and Ember."

I thought I glimpsed a twitch in his facial features, though I might have been trying too hard to catch a reaction.

"Why did you visit them yesterday?"

He sighed. "I know I declined dinner with you last night, but I felt cooped up and—"

"It has nothing to do with that. What you do on your own time is none of my concern."

"Then why are you asking me about it?" he said, obviously trying to keep his voice even.

"If you have to ask me that, we have a serious problem, Marcus. You've just returned, and you go to visit them, Ember being your focus. But she wouldn't talk to you, would she?"

"No. She went straight to her room and stayed there."

At least he was being honest... so far.

"Why do you think she reacted that way? As far as I can see, she's always been willing to talk to you."

He got up and turned his back to me. "Maybe because the Feds were there before me, and she was done speaking to cops?"

Did Dale and Bonnie mention the Feds?

"Marcus," I said, "I'd prefer to speak to your face, not your back."

He briskly turned on his heel. "Why? So you can observe my reactions? I'm tired of being interrogated, and the last person I expected it from was you."

"Is that how you're perceiving this? An interrogation? Marcus, after speaking with Dale, Bonnie, and Ember, I'm trying to understand the purpose of your visit last night."

"Through interrogation!" He paused, before sitting back down, propping his elbows on the desk. "Why? What did they say?"

I proceeded cautiously. "That they couldn't determine why you were there, that they were surprised by Ember's reaction toward you. That's why I'm here—trying to figure it out for them."

"I wanted to see how she was, knowing she'd been kidnapped as well."

My heart dropped. The Donnellys said he was pushing to find out what she revealed when she'd come back. At the least, he wasn't being fully truthful... I had to be careful with how I responded, or else I could put Ember and the Donnellys in danger.

"One thing Ember said stood out, and it's something I can't ignore."

"And what's that?" Marcus asked, his eyes darkening.

"She said she couldn't talk to you last night because Michael told her you were no longer her friend."

I felt the anger emanating from him, saw the coldness within his eyes shooting back at me. A chill was climbing my spine. I was seeing a glimpse of Marcus I'd never seen before.

***

I went straight to Wes, but I didn't stop. As I walked by him, without making eye contact, I softly said, "Watch that family," before making my way out of the precinct.

CHAPTER FORTY-NINE

SAINT ANDREW'S CROSS

IT WAS FIVE O'CLOCK, and I knew I should have called first, but I didn't. I knocked on the door for five whole minutes before, defeated, I turned to make my way back down the hallway.

"Izzy?"

I started to cry upon hearing Mel's voice. I turned to face her. "Isabella, come here," she said, soothingly. "How long have you been standing out here? I was upstairs… I'm sorry."

"It wasn't too long. I hope I'm not disturbing you. I know I should have called first."

She coaxed me to her with her arms. "You can come any time you want, announced or not. What's wrong?"

"You're all I have left…" I said between light sobs, walking toward her.

She put her arm around me and brought me inside the loft. Once she had me seated next to her on the sofa, her face painted with worry.

"Can I get you something to drink? Tea maybe?"

Nodding, I grabbed a tissue from the box on the coffee table as she headed for the kitchen. Kettle on the stove, she returned to her spot.

"What's going on? I don't think I've ever seen you like this."

"Everything I thought I knew isn't real. Everyone I thought I could trust… I've focused so much on my past, and Ember, that I was oblivious to everything happening around me."

"Am I one of those people?" she said, after a long pause, putting her hand on my knee. "The other morning, at the morgue—"

"If you were one of those people, I wouldn't be here," I told her. "You were just doing your job, and I can't blame you for that."

"Then who's the one putting doubts in your head? It's Angela, isn't it?" A defensive tone emerged in her voice. "You should know better than to listen to anything she has to say."

"But Mel, she isn't wrong. Actually, I've had time to think about it, and she's right. As hard as it is to say it, she's right about all of it."

The kettle whistled, and Melanie put her hand up. "Give me a minute to get our tea, and we'll get right back to this!"

She swiftly made tea and brought everything over on a tray. Picking up my cup, I inhaled its spicy scent and took a careful sip.

"Thank you, Mel."

"You're very welcome. Now, I want you to start from the beginning. We'll work through this together. Okay?"

I told her everything. I started on the first meeting with Angela, and moved on to the second. I told her about my conversation with Wes earlier that day. I admitted that even before Angela and Wes told me their theories, I'd started having doubts about Marcus's disappearance. Marcus's visit to the Donnellys put things into perspective. When I finally finished, I sat unable to look at her.

"Mel, please say something… even if I'm just overreacting."

"You need to calm down... but I wouldn't say you're overreacting," she said. "The woman I know is calm and collected—maybe a little too apathetic—but it's always worked to her advantage. You need to find the woman I know, or this could destroy you."

"How do I do that? Every time I turn around, I discover something new I should have known."

"So what? You're human! Things will be missed. But once you've caught it, take that information and use it. Don't let it beat you into submission."

I inhaled deeply. "Human... I think that's the first time anyone's ever called me that."

"You're unusual in your ways—I'm not going to lie—but you're still human, Izzy." Nudging my arm, she gave me a warm smile.

I gave her a hint of a smile back. "So after what I've just told you, what do you think?"

She was silent for few moments. "Honestly, Izzy," she said, "I'm having a hard time imagining Marcus being involved in something like that—the Brotherhood."

"So do I..."

"But now?"

"Even if I forget everything Angela said, it's hard to ignore the little things. If there's one thing I've learned through experience: the little things speak the loudest."

She nodded. "I wish I could disagree with that... My advice? Going forward, remember the man you know, compare it to the man who's returned, and try to determine whether the changes in his personality are the result of his being kidnapped."

"Thanks, Mel. You have no idea how much I needed that after all the bullshit I've been sifting through."

"If you need an extra hand sifting, let me know."

"You'll be the first person I come to."

She laughed. "Just so we're clear, I meant metaphorically. You work in manure—that's on you!"

I laughed with her.

In all honesty, Melanie was the only person I could trust and depend on to set me back in the right direction.

**

Nine-thirty that evening, I pulled onto N. 14th Street in Kenilworth, New Jersey, for the fifth time, to make sure I wasn't being followed. The area was a mix of industrial and residential buildings, so there wasn't much traffic; that, coupled with the darkness, meant it wouldn't be hard to figure out if I was being tailed. I wasn't.

I turned onto a residential street, parked, and walked back toward N. 14th Street. After sprinting across the 16th Street Park, I scaled the fence and maneuvered my way around a maze of transport containers. Once in the shipping yard, the only thing I had to worry about was the lone security guard, who usually slept in his booth by the front gate. I'd been surveilling the yard not long after my last encounter with Michael; it was fairly isolated—a great place to finally put this to an end.

The loading dock at the back of the yard. That was my spot. After climbing onto the platform, I shimmied backwards through the crack left by an ajar roll-up door. Nearly choking on the dust that rose from my clothing, I found the lantern I'd pre-placed. It gave off enough light to see, but not enough to be discovered. I made my way across the concrete when I heard a noise. I stood still, slowing my breathing.

"Took you long enough."

I shifted my lantern, ready to strike… Dean materialized from the shadows.

"Y-you asshole!"

I tried to catch my breath.

"What? Had to make sure it was you," he said, his grin wicked, but his voice low enough for funeral work.

"Really? You had to wait until I was halfway across the room?"

"Consider it payback for coming over so early this morning," he replied with a chuckle.

"I wouldn't be laughing right now if I were you. As you know, my payback is a bitch!" That shut him up quickly. "You get everything I asked for?"

"Not only did I get it," he said, walking to a canvas-covered object. "I set it up." He pulled off the canvas to reveal what was beneath. He looked at it, beaming.

I'd asked for two wooden planks larger than a fully grown man, both horizontally and vertically. They were to be attached to each other diagonally, at their centers, like a Saint Andrew's cross. Dean had taken it a step further by putting it on a makeshift stand.

"You do realize it will be harder to hide with it already set up?"

His excitement worried me a bit. As much as I wanted the same thing, he seemed to be taking a bit too much pleasure in the thought of killing someone, and I didn't like it.

"But at least this way, it's done, and ready for nailing," he said, grinning.

He was talking like an excited child. "Take it down, Dean."

"But Izzy—"

"Now! I'm not going to let you screw this up because you have a different idea than I do. Michael will be attached—not nailed—to it, while it's still on the floor… and then I'll hoist up."

Through the dim light, I saw the displeasure wash across his face—saw his blue eyes darken. "He deserves to die horribly for what he did to us—to them," he said through gritted teeth. "Don't go soft on him."

I took a couple of steps forward, making sure he could see my face clearly. "Soft? Is that what you think? It has nothing to do with softness. I'm not him, and I won't take the same steps he would to hurt someone." I took a few steps closer. Dean took a step back. "Don't misunderstand me… I get the anger you're feeling, and the thoughts running through your head… but we're not going to stoop to his level, no matter how much he deserves it. Understand?"

He turned his lowered head away from me.

I waited a few seconds before speaking again. "I need to hear that you understand what I'm telling you."

With his back still toward me, he answered softly but with a hint of anger. "I understand." And then he began to detach the cross from the stand.

I questioned my decision to include him, but it was too late to turn back now. He was involved whether I liked it or not—no matter the consequences.

CHAPTER FIFTY

SACRED GROUND

REGARDLESS OF GOINGS-ON, I didn't ignore my obligations—and the next morning was no exception. When I arrived at Anna's gravesite, a little blood still caked the tombstone, and the ground had been freshly re-filled after Ember's rescue. A new patch of grass had replaced the old, but with the weather turning colder, it was already almost dead.

Even Anna's death didn't stop Michael. He defiled her memory—desecrated her resting place... and it made me despise him that much more. My thoughts had turned dark, but I fought my way back. This was the place where I surrendered and pushed all other thoughts aside. I wouldn't let Michael to take that from me as well.

The cemetery hadn't been well maintained. Dead leaves were scattered all about. I'd started clearing them from Anna's headstone when, in the distance, I saw a woman watching me. When she realized I'd spotted her, she made her way over.

"If you'd paid closer attention, you would have known not to bother me on a Saturday," I fumed. "Especially not here."

"I meant no disrespect," Angela said, her hands neatly tucked away in the pockets of her black trench coat. She was now standing in front of me. "I wanted to see where Ember O'Reilly was found."

I was having a hard time containing my rage. "It was in the report. There was no need for you to come."

"I disagree, though I wish I could have dropped by when you weren't here... Though I suppose I want to speak to you as well," she said, moving slightly so she could read what was on the gravestone. "This is your sister, yes?"

I couldn't believe her boldness. "Leave, Angela. If you want to talk, we can do it after I'm done here and not a moment sooner. If you don't like that, then it can wait until next week. It's your choice." My stance was now defensive, protective of the person beneath our feet.

She started to back away. "Should I wait for your call or—"

"Meet me at Andros Diner. It's in the Dumbo neighborhood. I'll be there when I'm done."

Angela nodded and headed toward the cemetery gates... but I couldn't get my body to relax until she walked through them and out of view.

I sighed. *Just one day*, I thought. *One day to be with my sister. That's all I ask.* I sat on the ground, placing my head against the stone, and gently caressing it.

"I'm sorry, Anna."

***

I arrived at Andros Diner. I took longer than usual at the cemetery, partly because I wanted to spend more time with Anna, but also to make Angela wait.

I headed inside and noticed her, sitting at the counter, talking to Alex. I walked up to them.

"Isabella! Nice to see you again," Alex said. "Can I get you a menu too?"

"Just a latte, please." I turned to Angela. "We'll take one of the booths in the back," I told her, then walked away.

I removed my coat and sat down. Soon after, coffee mug in hand, she took the seat across from me. She smiled, but all I could do was stare back at her, without expression.

"Okay, fine. That was out of line, and I apologize," she said, breaking the silence, though her supposed sincerity wasn't convincing.

I looked at her in disbelief. "Out of line? You could have chosen any other day, at any other location, to speak with me. Pick up a phone even! Instead, you chose the day I set aside for my sister, sauntered up to her grave and insisted on questioning me!" I said, failing to keep my voice low. "That was more than out of line: it was complete and utter disrespect to me, and especially to Anna."

Our conversation was put on hold by the appearance of my latte. Alex set down the mug and quickly walked away without saying a word.

"I was being honest when I said I wanted to see where Ember O'Reilly was found," Angela said, keeping her voice low as well. "I had questions I wanted answered, and as you know, the scene of the crime is the best place to go."

"Please don't use that term again when referring to my sister's grave," I warned. "You have questions? Ask me. Leave Anna and Ember alone."

"You don't have to worry about Ember. She made it pretty clear she'd only speak to you," she said, slightly louder, before taking a sip of her coffee.

Was I detecting a hint of frustration? Was she finding herself in the same predicament as me, hitting walls when answers were preferred?

"I already know Ember refused to speak to you, and when you felt you weren't getting anywhere with the Donnellys, you decided to pull my sealed files." I waited for Angela to say something. When she remained quiet, I continued. "I'm now assuming you didn't get what you wanted from me either."

"No, I didn't," she said after a long pause. "What I'm having a hard time wrapping my head around is why Michael O'Reilly, Ember's father, decided to bury her with your sister. Your explanation of your connection to this child, I believe, is only part of it. You're holding something back."

So much for satiating her need for a connection.

"As you know, there's never an easy explanation for what a sociopath does, and Michael O'Reilly is no different. If you don't believe me, ask your partner," I said. "I was the one tasked with interviewing Michael and his family, trying to prove what they did to his daughter. So you're really surprised he decided to get rid of Ember and go after me indirectly?"

"And how did he know about your sister. You had a name change, so how did he know it used to be Baldacci? See, that's what's not clicking."

I laughed at her ignorance. "You think the FBI is the only organization that can access my file? If he has the right connections, it wouldn't be hard for him to find out. Hell, he could have simply followed me on one of my weekly visits to the cemetery—not unlike yourself."

She paused to think.

"So stop trying to find something that isn't there," I went on, "and ask me about the things that are. Did you know Lieutenant Hudson paid the Donnellys a visit the same day you did—that evening to be precise?"

"No," she said, clearly trying to hide her embarrassment.

"So much for keeping an eye on the man you suspect is involved— a supposed serial killer. *I* had to be the one to tell you about it. And after speaking to Lieutenant Hudson about it, I went directly to Agent Richford and asked that the family be watched."

Angela looked at me with curiosity. "So my working theory… you're ready to tell me what you think of it?"

"I can't discount your hypothesis, Angela. After speaking with Lieutenant Hudson yesterday, I'm starting to have questions myself. But don't take that as a fact. Until there's definite proof, I'll try to remain as neutral as possible… but with my eyes wide open from now on."

"And you'll keep Agent Richford and me informed regarding any new information you obtain?"

I sighed. "The people I hold close, I'll protect them with my life. But I won't stand by and do nothing if I think they're doing something wrong. I think I just proved that to you."

"We have no problems then," she said, bringing her mug back to her lips.

Until the next crisis arises…

CHAPTER FIFTY-ONE

FISHING EXPEDITION

MARCUS ASKED ME to meet him at the Jersey Tavern later that evening, hoping to make amends for how he'd acted the day before—at least that was his reasoning. I sat in our spot at the bar when a vaguely familiar cologne surrounded me. I turned to see Wes standing next to me. I laughed lightly. He frowned.

"Not exactly the greeting I was expecting. Is it something I'm wearing?" He looked down at himself.

"I'm starting to feel as though you and your partner are following me," I said, turning back around. He took the seat beside me.

"Again, Angela's not my partner. And I'm not sure what you're talking about."

"Then maybe you should start communicating with her; I can assure you, she doesn't seem to be aware of what you're doing either."

"What happened to bring this on?"

"Didn't you tell her about our conversation? Or that after I spoke with Lieutenant Hudson, I asked that the family be watched?"

"No, I haven't had the chance yet."

"Half a day and not a chance? Did you at least do what I asked?" My anger was returning, and I couldn't contain it. "Look, I didn't sign up to be the liaison between the two of you."

"Okay, you're obviously pissed off—I'm still not entirely certain why—but I don't believe this really has anything to do with me," he said defensively. "Yes, I've increased surveillance on the family. And I've been nothing but straight with you since the beginning. I even let you in on my true intentions, disregarding your relationship with the lieutenant."

I shrugged. "And?"

"Your turn. I want to know what happened between you and Agent De Luca."

Sometimes I have to learn when to shut up.

"I don't know if you're aware that I'm unavailable on Saturdays unless something comes up that needs my immediate attention." I was hoping that would be enough, without further explanation needed.

"I am. It's when you visit your sister's grave," he said without hesitation.

Should I be worried that he knew that?

"Well, Angela showed up at Holy Cross Cemetery today. Apparently, that was an appropriate place to hold another one of her interviews."

Wes shook his head. "She's good at her job, but I don't always agree with how she goes about it. I'm sorry."

His response surprised me. "Why would you be sorry?"

He shifted his body so that he was facing me. "Because you're right. It's not your job to pass on communications between the two of us. I'm also sorry that Angela took your personal, private time to ask you questions."

I sighed. "You make it hard to dislike you."

He smiled. "Well, I'll be sure to communicate better with Angela, so hopefully this will be the last time we start a conversation with aggression."

I smirked at him. "You considered that aggression? Really?"

"If it's not, I'd hate to be on the receiving end when you do get angry."

You have no idea...

"Now go. Marcus should be here soon, which is why I'm suspecting you're here."

"Yes, and with the same bonus as last night," he said slyly. "Talk to you soon." He walked over to a booth, and took a seat.

Eric was handing me a glass of Pappy Van Winkle when Marcus took the seat previously occupied by Wes.

"Since when did the two of you become close?" he asked, a slight annoyance in his voice.

"What's wrong? Are you jealous?"

"Of course I am. You know how I feel about you."

Strangely, it hurt to hear him say that.

"Well, I wouldn't say we're close, but we're all supposed to be working together, collaborating."

Eric, with a glass of gin and soda and a glass of simple soda water in hand for Marcus, interrupted us. "Marcus, finally I see you! You look well."

"I am. Thank you. Happy to be back." Despite his words, he shot Eric a look that wiped the smile from his face.

"Glad to have you back… If you need anything, let me know, yes?"

Marcus immediately turned his attention back to me. "Seemed non-work-related to me." Without missing a beat, he began sipping his drink.

"If it makes you feel any better, the part you apparently missed was me chewing him out. So it was work related."

"Oh?" His interest clearly piqued, he finally looked at me.

Now was the time for me to regain his trust. "I had an unexpected visitor this morning when I went to see Anna. Let's just say I immediately put her in her place, and I put Richford on notice as well."

"Huh… Agent De Luca has more balls than I thought," he said into his glass. "What did she want?"

"To ask why Ember was buried in the same grave as my sister. Probably trying to catch me off guard to get the answer she wanted."

"And did she?"

"I told her the truth: Michael is a sociopath, and to kill two birds with one stone, he tried to get rid of his daughter in a way that was also an attack against me."

"Speaking of our friend, have you heard from him again?"

"The same night of your return."

His reaction didn't disappoint; he shifted around on his seat, as though suddenly it were growing lumps.

"What did he say?"

"He asked if I was happy that you'd been returned, mentioned that the Feds were involved, then said he'd be in touch soon."

"That's it?"

I manufactured a strange look. "Should there have been more?"

"You never know with him." He returned his stare to the bottles of alcohol on the shelves in front of him.

"Marcus, why do I have a feeling you're not telling me something that happened while you were gone?"

"Because that's what the Feds want you to think," he said, keeping his voice low and nodding discreetly in Wes's general direction.

"Oh, right. I forgot. I can't think for myself anymore."

"That's not what I said, Izzy."

I kept my eye on him as I answered. "Ultimately that *is* what you said. If it helps, they've primarily been scrutinizing my reports and speaking about Michael. They've barely mentioned you."

His mood seemed to instantaneously lighten.

"Well, here's to them making a hasty exit." Marcus raised his glass. We clinked glasses, and both took a sip.

"So is this your idea of making amends for the way you acted yesterday?" I asked. "Because if it is, you're doing a horrible job."

He lowered his head. "I'm sorry. I'm a little on edge... obviously. I had no right to react that way, and I want to apologize for that too. You had every right to ask me what you did."

"Okay, that's a start. Ready to answer why Michael told Ember you're no longer her friend?" I'd confirmed with the Donnellys: they hadn't mentioned to Marcus that the Feds had just left.

"I'm guessing, for the same reason he let me go. What Michael does benefits Michael. Up and letting me go? That brings about a lot of suspicion on me. Making sure I couldn't get any information from Ember? Well that could make things a lot harder moving forward... I'm beginning to think it's all an effort to neutralize me... Thankfully, it proves that I'm not working with him—whatever these apes think. If I were, he wouldn't want to take that away from me."

He was actually making sense.

"Then wouldn't he do the same for me? Try to turn her away from me?"

"How is he going to do that, Isabella? Jesus... I'm thinking no matter what I say, you'll have something to try and debunk my reasons." He let out a sigh. "Can we just drop this and enjoy a drink together? Have you eaten?"

I wasn't going to get any further with him than I did, so I decided to drop it. "Actually I haven't."

"Why don't you grab a couple of menus? I have to step out for a moment to make a call—it's too loud in here," he said, pointing to his ear.

"Sure." I raised my arm to get Eric's attention.

Marcus got up from the stool and started to walk away, then immediately came back. "I left my cell phone at the precinct. Can I borrow yours?"

I really didn't want to do it, but I pulled it from my bag and handed it to him.

"New phone?"

"Don't ask."

He smiled and headed out of the bar.

Though I knew it by heart, I was still skimming the menu when he returned about ten minutes later. He handed me my phone, and dropped a couple of bills on the bar.

"Sorry, Izzy. I know I asked you to meet me here, but I have to go. There's something I need to do."

"Anything I can help with?" I wasn't about to let him escape that easily.

"No, it's personal. I'll talk to you tomorrow. The precinct in the morning?"

He wasn't giving me a choice. "Sure, Marcus, but—"

Before I could finish, he was heading toward the door. Not long after he left, Wes was back by my side.

"Any idea what that was about?" he asked.

My eyes on the door, I finally turned and looked at him. "He borrowed my phone, made a call, and left. You saw that right?"

"Yeah."

"To be clear, I take no responsibility for whatever that was. I let him use it to maintain appearances."

"Right."

I checked my phone to see the last number dialed: the precinct. Funny thing was, he was gone for ten minutes, but the call lasted less than one—and it was to his own phone number.

Our meeting wasn't to make amends; it was a fishing expedition.

CHAPTER FIFTY-TWO

WITHIN THE BRICKS

MY CELLPHONE RANG. I was driving, so I put it on speaker.

"Hello?"

"Hey. I thought you were coming in this morning." It was Marcus.

"I'll be in a little later. I have some things to do first," I said, turning onto the street.

"What things?" he asked, his inquisitiveness coming through.

"They're personal. I'll see you in a couple of hours. Bye, Marcus." I ended the call before he had the chance to press further. To be fair, I was no less forthcoming than he had been.

I parked in the driveway and made my way up the front steps, and through the door. Once inside, I raised my arms to the ceiling.

"Honey! I'm home!" I called out mockingly, half expecting someone to answer or suddenly appear. I needed to keep it light if I was to do this.

I knew I'd eventually make my way back to the family house; I needed that box… it was a little voice calling out to me—faint, but impossible to disregard. I vowed that once I'd found the box, I'd bulldoze the place to the ground and rebuild.

After making my way down to the basement, I pulled the cord that dangled from its rafter in the middle of the room—though it didn't make much of a difference. Thankfully, I'd brought a flashlight.

Looking around, I saw the chair I'd sat in that night, the lashing rings in the floor, and the ropes that had been cut to free him. I was so close, but he'd had an advantage over me, one that I'd ensured he wouldn't have this time. When I made my move, I would have my own backup. The ball was in my court; Ember's family was being watched, and most importantly, he didn't know a date had been set.

I walked to the first wall to my right, starting from the top and making my way down, checking every brick for weakness or movement.

This is going to take forever, I thought. Unfortunately for me, there really wasn't a better way to do it. Taking the wall horizontally, approximately a foot at a time, painstakingly pushing at each brick, I began to resign to the idea that the owners had fixed the loose stone, and I'd never find the box. An hour and a half after that, I was finished with the second wall.

Feeling like Quasimodo on a hot day. I walked back to the center of the room and took a good long look at what I had left. How the hell was I going to find what Anna and I had hidden twenty-three years ago? As much as I hated doing it, I closed my eyes and tried to bring myself back to that time—to when I was fourteen and Anna was alive. Immediately, I saw my sister hanging by the neck, and I quickly opened my eyes. After taking a deep, relaxing breath, and feeling my body go numb, I closed my eyes and tried again.

"Do you think we have enough?" Anna asked, *trying to hide her worry as best she could.*

"More than enough. It'll get us out of here," I told her. I didn't *know if that was true, but it wasn't her job to worry; it was mine—as well as getting her out and away from here.*

"But what happens if he finds out? What will happen to us?" Her *hazel eyes, which had many more flecks of green than mine, were now shimmering. She was close to breaking down. I'd seen it too many times before.*

I knelt in front of her. "Anna, he won't find out. We'll hide it where no one will find it; we'll be the only ones who know where it is." I took her into my arms. "Everything will be okay. I promise."

As I opened my eyes, streams of tears made their way down my cheeks. That was the first time I broke a promise to her, and it ended up costing her life. From then on, I made certain never to break a promise made with someone I care about. Hesitantly, I plunged deeper.

"No one will think of looking for it here! You're so smart, Izzy." *She was beaming.*

"Now remember, Anna. This is life or death—our lives and our deaths... You can't tell anyone, not a soul. This is between you and me. Understand?" *Looking her directly in the eyes, I held her hands in mine.*

She nodded, her expression now serious. "No one but you and me."

I suddenly realized a significant difference between the two memories: they didn't take place in the same location. After Anna's death, I'd suppressed the memory so well, I'd inadvertently blocked it completely. I went up the stairs, two at a time, and made my way to the back door. After unlocking the dead bolt, I stepped outside.

Hardly surprising, due to the condition of the house, the backyard hadn't been tended to in what seemed like years. The grass, which consisted mostly of weeds, was almost knee-high, and old furniture and garbage littered the small space. The one and only tree, an oak, should have been cut down, as it was dead; it reminded me of a decrepit old hand with thin fingers for branches. Trying not to get tangled in the jungle around my feet, I searched amongst the rubble. Moving things around, and then moving them again, I finally found it, and smiled in victory.

Though almost destroyed, it was still recognizable: a fire pit, built of bricks. I cleared them one at a time. Once I reached the bottom bricks, my focus was on the four in the center. After all this time, and with the weight piled onto it, they were well planted into the soil beneath. With much prying, however, they all came out. I quickly dug with my hands until my fingertips scraped something hard. More carefully now, I continued to clear the soil until the metal box appeared. I dug around its perimeter until I was finally able to pull it up and out. Holding the box tightly, I went around the side of the house and let myself out through the gate. I opened the trunk of my car and put it inside. I took my cell phone from my coat pocket and punched in Marcus's number. When he answered, I told him I wouldn't be making it in to the precinct—I wasn't feeling well, I said—but I wanted to meet him for breakfast tomorrow morning, his choice of place. He sounded disappointed, but said he'd see me the next day and to feel better. I was prepared to drive away when my cell phone went off in my hand. Number *unknown*.

"Michael?"

"Did you find what you were looking for?"

"I have a feeling it's unnecessary to answer that," I said evenly. "How long have you been following me?"

"Who said I'm following you?"

"I'm not interested in games right now. Maybe later."

"I'm looking forward to it," he said, the amusement evident in his voice.

I ended the call. I couldn't wait until it was all finally over.

Soon.

***

Before a quick visit with Ember, I scheduled police surveillance on the townhouse. They were there when I arrived at eight o'clock that evening. Once inside, I locked the door, armed the alarm, and made my rounds before heading to the basement where I tried my best to find a place to hide the box.

I still wasn't sure what I was going to do with it, but I knew for certain that this small metal box could destroy many lives—innocent or not—and that I'd have to guard it with my life.

Once it was in a safe place, I went upstairs to my bedroom, changed, and climbed into bed. For once. I was going to try to get a good night's sleep... but found it impossible with Marcus continuously running through my mind. I propped the pillows up against the head-board then leaned into them. Then I remembered what Melanie had told me—to compare the two versions of Marcus, the before and after—so I did exactly that.

Before his disappearance, he was the one who held me together, starting from such an early age. Throughout my youth, he had kept in touch to ensure that my new life was nothing but positive—and even visited on occasion. When I finished school and had a good practice set up, even though I never wanted to return to the area, the thought of being able to see Marcus whenever I wanted was what won me over. We were getting to know each other under different circumstances, as colleagues and friends, and that bond that first glued us together only got stronger with the passing years. Even including my aunt and uncle, he was the first person, save Anna, I was able to trust without reservation.

But now that he was back, everything had shifted, and I couldn't ignore the red flags that popped into each new interaction. I felt uncomfortable when I was around him—continuously analyzing, questioning, wondering which formerly unknown side of his personality might show itself next. He treated his kidnapping like time off, and questioned Ember as though something might have been said that would hurt him or his career. The most painful part was that we were growing further apart.

I reached up to my cheek, realizing I was crying. That had been happening a lot since Marcus's return, a reaction I'd thought I wasn't even capable of anymore. This was killing me inside more than I'd realized. I placed the pillows back in their original positions and, lying down, hugged one of them hard.

Please let me be wrong.

CHAPTER FIFTY-THREE

MENTAL SNAPSHOTS

MARCUS AND I MET for brunch at ten the next morning at an IHOP in Brooklyn. It was nothing fancy, but it was special. It was the same restaurant where he'd taken me the morning after my neighbor reported my mother's death.

After what seemed like a long, awkward silence, he finally spoke. "Have you come back here since that morning?" he asked.

"Never. Even though it was kind of you to bring me here before the train, it was a day I wanted to forget," I said, twisting my fingers.

"Neither have I," he admitted. "My life changed that day…" He trailed off. I wondered what he meant, but didn't have the heart to question him.

"I think both of ours did, though maybe not exactly how we'd planned, huh?"

"Probably not. I want you to know that I meant what I said that night, that I think of you as family—whatever else we are… and that I love you."

"Are you going soft on me, Marcus Hudson?" I asked him, smirking.

Surprisingly, he kept a serious tone. "Since my return, things haven't quite been the same between us," he said, rubbing the back of his neck, "and I needed to make sure you knew that."

"Thank you, Marcus. I do. I'll never forget what you've done for me."

He produced a sad smile as he put his hands on the table in front of him. "Do you think things will ever get back to normal?"

"How do you mean?"

"You and me, work... the normalcy that once was."

"I don't know." I reached over and put my hands on his. "So many things are up in the air right now. It all depends on where they land."

"You're talking about Michael, the Feds, and your diminishing trust in me."

I saw the inner battle in his eyes as he looked at me, and I wasn't sure how to decipher it. But right now, I didn't want to discuss any of it—what might or might not be, how things would turn out in the end. I just wanted one morning with the smartass, smirking, cheesy man I'd always known.

"Can you do me one favor, please? Just one?" I asked.

"What would you like?"

"Just for today, can we take a huge leap back, before all this started, and just enjoy each other's company?" I asked, my eyes beginning to mist. "Do you think we can do that?"

Marcus's smile warmed. "For you, anything."

I grabbed the menus and handed him one. "Are you hungry? What am I saying? You're always hungry!" I said, winking at him.

"Shut up... but yes, I am," he said, looking over the menu.

His head safely lowered, I allowed a single tear to roll down my cheek.

***

We spent most of the day together, taking in a movie and walking along the waterfront at Brooklyn Bridge Park. Before parting ways, we hugged like we did the first day I'd seen him at the precinct after he returned.

I made my way back to New Jersey at seven o'clock that evening. The lockbox was on my mind. I didn't want to open it, but I knew I was being foolish. If I wasn't careful, it could be taken from me—and part of me even wished for it... I had just one other person to see, and was soon knocking on her door. A few moments later, Mel opened it, a wide smile on her face.

"Right on time. Come in," she said, gesturing with her hand.

Once inside, I grabbed her and gave her a hug.

"Whoa! What's this for?"

"When was the last time I gave you a hug?" I asked, my voice low, as my chin rested on her shoulder.

Pulling slightly away, Melanie raised an eyebrow. "Let me think back. Hang on a moment... Oh, that's right, never!" she grinned. "You okay?"

"Actually, I am," I said, heading toward her living room.

"Okay, then why the sudden change? Does it have to do with what I said the other day?" she asked, taking the seat beside my own. "Because if I remember correctly, I said to take control back, not to change your personality."

"Oh, and I did. It has nothing to do with that."

"Is it Angela again? Marcus? There's definitely a switch in how you're acting."

"It's everything and nothing... I don't expect that to make sense, but it's not something I want to focus on right now. I just want to spend some time with you—not as colleague, not as a sounding board, but as a friend."

She sat back into the couch, keeping her head turned toward me. "What did you end up doing today? Wait, let's have a drink! I have a perfectly chilled bottle of Domaine Ramonet Montrachet Grand Cru."

I laughed.

"Since when can you speak French?"

"Since I started drinking French wine." She grinned and went to the kitchen to grab the bottle from the wine fridge. She held it up to me, along with two glasses in her other hand, tempting me with what she had to offer.

"Well, if you're going to present it that way, how can I say no?" Once the glasses were filled, she handed me mine. "Should we toast to something?" Melanie asked.

"Of course. To our friendship," I said, smiling warmly and lifting my glass to her. "Thank you for being who you are. I don't know what I'd do without you."

"Ditto," she said, putting her glass within inches of mine before gently tapping them together.

I laughed. "Nicely put. You wanted to talk about my day, so I'll go first, and then you can tell me about yours."

She nodded, putting all her focus on me.

I told her about my time with Marcus, and she told me of her first slow day in a long while, and of her seemingly never-ending paperwork. When she moved on to a cute new intern, I began to fade out, focusing, instead, on her... how she talked in her soft, melodious voice that would heighten in tone when something excited her; her facial expressions, which always gave away how she felt, no matter how hard she'd try to hide it; and her mannerisms, as she used her hands to help tell her story, drawing me in. What I wouldn't give to be like her. I envied her relative ease at being so open and free, just her general happiness no matter what she spoke about. Two hours with Melanie felt like minutes... it was as though time stood still for us. I wished we could spend more time like this.

My cell phone rang in my bag. I had to answer it.

"I'm sorry," I said, interrupting her. A glance at the caller ID told me what I told Mel: "I really should take this."

She nodded then took a sip from her glass, as I tapped "accept" on the screen. Listening attentively, I felt my body go rigid.

"I'll be there as soon as I can," I said, then ended the call.

She looked at me, worry replacing her previous smile. "What's going on?"

"It's Dean Matthews. I have to go meet with him," I said, placing my wineglass on the coffee table and getting up from the couch.

She stood up as well. "Is there anything I can do to help? I can come with you."

I picked up my bag. "You've done more than enough." I reached over and hugged her again.

"That's twice in one day—within hours. Now I'm really worried," she said, her brow furrowing.

320

"Nothing to worry about. I'll give you a call later." I made my way to the door and left quickly, not giving her opportunity to protest my sudden departure.

As I walked down the hall, I felt the control I'd thought I had slip from my grasp.

This isn't how it's supposed to go, I thought, pressing the elevator button repeatedly. *What's the plan now?*

CHAPTER FIFTY-FOUR

DAY OF RECKONING

ABOUT FORTY MINUTES after Dean's call, I arrived at the shipping yard, hoping I wasn't too late. I jumped the fence and made my way to the loading dock. Slipping through the crack between the floor and the dock's door, I was surprised to find the lantern already lit. As I cautiously made my way through the room, I was alert to what could be lurking in the shadows.

"Dean?" I asked, barely above a whisper, desperate to avoid attention from the rest of the yard. It was just after nine o'clock, and the new security guard would soon be making his first rounds. "Dean?" I called out again.

"That didn't take you long," he answered, coming forward. He looked unhurt, which perplexed me.

"Where's Michael? You said he found you."

"Got you here, didn't it?" he asked, his voice lacking emotion. "The same thing got Michael here too. I told him I had you, that you were trapped. It would appear the two of you have a one-track mind—who could best the other."

I shook my head. "It's never been about that, Dean. It's not a competition. Where is he now?" I asked.

"Don't worry. He's fine for now. I knew you'd want to watch."

He walked over to the tarp, and I was worried what I'd find underneath as he grabbed for the edge. But there he was, his mouth gagged: Michael, attached to the reassembled Saint Andrew's cross... but not like Dean and I had discussed. Through his palms and the tops of his feet, daggers had been inserted so deeply that the handles pressed against his skin. His body was positioned in an "X" formation—to Jonathan's shame, for he was fully nude. In addition to this, Dean had inflicted upon him the same torture he and I had endured in our youth. He was covered from head to toe with lacerations, burns, contusions, and welts. The very same infinity symbol had been deeply carved into his once smooth chest. Michael's eyes were wide, but he remained silent—with the exception of his labored breathing.

"Dean, what have you done?" I asked, looking back at him. I couldn't believe he'd gotten this far without me. I hated that he told me I could watch... I would never watch.

"What was meant to happen, what he deserved!" Dean removed the gag from Michael's mouth, but Michael remained quiet. "You just have to ask him the question."

I shook my head, trying to think straight. "Question? What question?"

Michael suddenly spoke. "The question he asked those girls."

Dean immediately delivered a blow across his face, causing blood to burst from Michael's mouth. "I didn't give you permission to speak!" he shouted at him.

For the first time, I felt genuinely scared of what he might do. I slowly approached, stopping when his posture stiffened. "What are you talking about? What question am I supposed to ask him?"

He took a seat on a nearby crate. "I couldn't save them all, like I saved you. So I gave the ones I couldn't a choice. They could continue to endure the torture the Brotherhood inflicted upon them, or they could answer my question."

It was him. He'd killed them.

A long pause followed. "What question, Dean?" I asked, softly. "I won't know what to ask if you don't tell me."

"'Are you ready to sleep now?' I gave them the choice. They were the ones who made the decision."

"I understand why you did it," I said gently. "You couldn't save them all... But you gave them an impossible choice. In the end, when their will was completely broken, you killed them. You have to—"

He slammed his fist on top of the crate. "No! I didn't kill them. I gave them what they wanted. I put everything behind them and helped them sleep. They asked for it!"

It was a psychotic episode... no amount of reasoning would get through to him. He believed he had saved those girls, not taken their lives. As much as I wanted Michael dead, I had to get Dean under control first.

Then I noticed the gun at his hip... my cast couldn't compete with a bullet.

"Listen to me. The security guard will be by soon. We have to put the gag back in and turn off the lantern. Once he's gone and out of earshot, we can proceed. Does that sound okay?"

He eyed me suspiciously. "What guard?"

"The guard who took over at nine o'clock. I've been casing this place for a week now. I know his routine. He clocks in, makes his rounds, and he goes back to his booth and goes to sleep."

He looked around nervously. "Why should I believe you?"

"Because the last thing you want right now is to be caught, and if you don't do what I say, that's exactly what's going to happen! Do you want to be caught?"

"I-I... no..."

He was starting to panic, so I took control. "There isn't enough time for you to decide if I'm telling the truth or not—but for all our issues, I've never lied to you, and I'm not lying now."

He jumped off the crate. "Okay, Izzy. Turn off the lantern, and I'll gag him," he said urgently. "But once the guard is gone, you'll ask the question?"

"I'll ask the question when the time is right. Now hurry!"

Before turning off the lantern, I watched Dean put the rag back into Michael's mouth and whisper something in his ear. Then all was shadow. I made my way toward the entrance in the dark, where I leaned against the wall beside the door.

Ten minutes later, the beam of the guard's flashlight bounced off the walls. I pressed myself even closer and waited as he made the perimeter of the building. I'd timed it before; it wouldn't take longer than a few minutes. The dock was the last stop on his patrol, and he'd be in a hurry to get back to the booth.

When he was gone, I stood up and turned the lantern back on.

"He's still not far enough away, so we have to keep things to a whisper," I softly called out.

Emerging from his hiding place, Dean stood in front of Michael.

"Will you ask the question now?"

I took a few steps closer. "I'll do it when the time is right."

"When the guard is back in his booth?"

"When the time is right, Dean."

He began to pace around Michael, like a hyena, circling its prey. "You'll have to be more specific than that. For all I know, that's next week."

It was time for me to take control of the situation again, so I took on a firmer tone. "I was saved. You can't put me in the same situation as you did the others."

He shook his head. "I don't understand."

"I don't have to make a choice right now. I'm not in danger, am I?"

He looked puzzled. "No, but Michael has to die. If he doesn't, you'll always be in danger."

"He's fastened to a cross. He doesn't pose a danger to anyone right now. And I don't appreciate being forced to do something." I knew I was pushing it, but I had to put him in a specific state, make him see he was wrong in what he was doing. "Are you trying to force me like they did in the Brotherhood?"

He shook his head fiercely. "No, I'm not one of them. I'm like you!"

"I know you are. That's why this has to be done on my terms. You've completed what you felt was necessary, and Michael's secure. Thank you." Dean was obsessively focused on my face, and I was thankful he hadn't noticed what I'd just heard: someone slipping beneath the door behind me.

326

Suddenly a flashlight shone in his face. Dean grabbed for his gun and was pointing blindly.

"Detective Matthews, lower your weapon," a female voice called out.

"Who are you?" he asked, trying to shield his eyes from the light with his hand.

"Special Agent De Luca. I'll ask you again to lower your weapon."

I took the opportunity to slowly move out of the line of fire. When Dean pointed the gun at me, I stopped. "Dean, do as she says. This will only end badly if you don't."

"You betrayed me, Izzy," he cried out. "You brought her with you."

"I didn't! She must have followed me."

"You're lying!" he shouted.

"Detective Matthews, if you don't lower your weapon, a lie will be the least of your worries. This is your final warning."

Dean changed his target and fired—as if in slow motion, I watched as a single bullet entered Angela's forehead. As she was going down, her weapon discharged… but it wasn't headed for Dean. It went straight through my right triceps, which meant both my arms were compromised.

On the floor, I rapidly made my way to Angela with my casted arm and bruised knees. I grabbed the gun with both hands, and pointed it at Dean. My right arm hurt and I was wearing a cast on the left. I wasn't even sure I could make the shot.

He stared at me, a wounded look in his eyes. "Izzy?"

"Dean, lower your weapon," I said with such force that I didn't recognize my own voice. "I won't give you a second chance."

He looked at me with a desolate smile, and as I perceived him preparing to shoot, I pulled the trigger three times. The kickback from the gun hurt my arms, even positioned where I was on the floor. When I looked toward Dean, I got his blood in my mouth. There was so much of it, and it spread out all across the floor.

I waded through the puddle, splashing blood all over my pants. I kicked the gun away from Dean before checking his vitals. He was dead.

That confirmed, I pulled the rag from Michael's mouth.

He smiled weakly. "My hero," he said between gasps. "Coming to save my life? Gonna take me out on your back?"

"I win, Michael. This should have ended a long time ago."

"So he couldn't kill me, but you can?"

"That's right."

"I'm not even close to the worst of it, and you know it. You take one of us down, three more will pop up. Hell, you and Dean aren't the only ones who want me gone."

"Who else is there?" I pressed.

"This isn't a comic book, Bella. You want all the evil plans from me? You want to save the day my little killer? Pretend you murdered your brother for a good cause?"

I raised the gun. He smiled.

"Like father, like d—"

I spattered the cross with his brains, and fired an extra shot for good measure.

I headed for the door, but stopped over Angela.

"You didn't deserve this," I told her. "I'm sorry."

When I tried to climb down the platform outside, the pain in my arm was too much, and I lost my grip, falling the rest of the way. It wasn't a far drop, but it felt like it was. Placing my back against the wall, I heard sirens and saw a man rush up to me. I pointed my gun.

"Woah there, Isabella. It's Wes..."

With a light toss, the gun was out of my reach, and into the grass nearby. Wes stood over me, concern plastered all over his face. The guard wasn't far behind.

"Isabella, are you okay?" Wes asked. "What happened?"

"Angela's dead." I looked up at him, my eyes watering. "There are three of them in there—Michael O'Reilly, Detective Matthews, and Angela. They're all dead," I said, trying to steady my voice. "Matthews shot Angela. I shot Matthews with her gun. Michael was behind Matthews; he caught his bullets."

He was now crouched beside me. "Who shot you?"

"The bullet was from Angela's gun. It went off after she was shot... How did you know where to find us?"

"Marcus told Angela that both Michael and Dean were here, with you as a prisoner," he said. "She called me when she was on her way."

How did Marcus know? I did everything I could to keep this location a secret. Had he tapped my phone?

"What are you thinking, Isabella?" Wes asked, breaking me from my thoughts.

"Nothing important," I answered. Grabbing my left arm, Wes helped me get to my feet.

I felt dizzy, but he helped steady me as I removed my coat, and lifted the sleeve of my sweater. It was a clean shot. No bullet. It was bleeding, but not profusely, so it must have missed any significant arteries.

Wes grabbed me around the waist and carefully moved me forward. "The paramedics should be here by now. We'll get you to the hospital and have you checked out."

"That's not necessary. You have a lot to do here, and I'll be done by the time you're ready to head over there."

He shook his head. "This isn't my crime scene. I'm coming with you."

I had no intention of staying at the hospital any longer than necessary, but I wasn't going to tell him that. As soon as I was stitched up, I'd be gone. I'd put it off long enough… it was time to open that goddamned box.

CHAPTER FIFTY-FIVE

SMOKE AND MIRRORS

THE BULLET HAD GONE straight through the fleshy part of my right arm, missing all the major arteries. It was just as I'd predicted: a flesh wound. They stitched me up and bandaged my arm. I refused the pain-killers and left the hospital.

I arrived at my townhome around eleven that night, and headed straight downstairs to the basement. From inside a shoebox on the up-permost shelf at the back of the utility room, I removed the metal box. Sitting cross-legged in the middle of the basement, I placed it in front of me. Cocking my head, I stared at it, willing myself not to open it, but knowing I had to. Every time I reached for the lid, I instantly re-coiled, as if upon contact, it would burn my hands. Catching sight of a small latch, I stood back up.

One good kick, and the lock almost instantly disintegrated. Slowly I raised the lid, and let it fall backward to the floor.

It was filled almost to capacity. Taking a single finger, I began to move things around. The first thing I came across was a silver chain. It was a necklace, and hanging from it were two semicircles, sterling sil-ver pendants—ones Anna and I once wore. Though it was extremely tarnished, I was still able to read the black cursive lettering: LIL SIS and BIG SIS respectively.

I remembered how the pendants had come into our possession. Anna was ten years old, and I was thirteen. On our way home from school, we saw them in a jewelry store window. We were instantly drawn to them, and from then on, we saved whatever money we could get our hands on. We'd collect loose change around the house, help our neighbors with yard work, go to the corner store for an elderly neighbor, who wasn't able to do it herself. It took some time, but once Anna and I had saved up enough, we walked into the jewelry store and proudly bought the pendants... Two separate chains. Two half-hearts that could be combined into a single delicate heart. *"Even when we're apart, we're taking the other with us,"* Anna said as though she were sitting right beside me. My eyes started to water as I recalled how we had to conceal them from our parents for fear that they would be taken away. We put them on one chain to keep them together—us together. The day we bought it, was the day we started gathering items to fill the box.

I rummaged through the papers and photos. I wasn't sure what I was looking for, but my hands continued as though they knew.

There were notes Anna and I had written together, our escape plan, and what we would do once we were free. They made little sense. It was hard to be reminded of how much we were still children... And then there were photographs. Lots of photographs: Polaroids of young children, chiefly girls, with ages and dates written on the white bottom trim. No names.

The children were in different stages of dress, and the harm inflicted upon them was obvious. I would do everything I could to find them—if they were even still alive. After putting them in one pile, I picked up another handful of photographs: pictures of the old cabin at Lake Placid, in all its glory; of different men posing with different backdrops, smiles plastered across their faces. Michael was in nearly all the shots.

As I went through all of them, one in particular caught my attention: a group shot, like one you'd see taken at a family reunion, and I tried to zero in on each and every face individually. Then I saw it. The picture almost slipped from my fingers, and I had to tighten my grip to prevent it from dropping to the floor.

CHAPTER FIFY-SIX

THE VOTE

WHEN HE FIRST ENTERED the room, reverberation of whispers and mindless chatter were almost deafening. He straightened his tie, and pulled at his shirt cuffs, making sure they weren't hidden and shining about a half inch below his coat's sleeves. When everything was ready, he made his way up the center aisle created by the rows of seats that had been carefully placed before the meeting began. He climbed three steps onto the wide, wooden platform, then turned to face the men who'd gathered. He lightly cleared his throat, and instantly, the chatter ceased.

"I appreciate that all of you were able to make it on such short notice and at this hour," he began. "As we all know, it was important to have this meeting take place as soon as possible, to dispel the rumors."

The men in the crowd nodded, murmuring words of agreement to one another.

"And I'm truly sorry that I can't do that. It's no rumor. It's been confirmed... Jonathan—or Michael if you prefer—is dead."

The murmurs turned louder, but no voice threatened to take over. Without so much as raising his hand for silence, it returned on its own.

"Even though our leader is gone, it doesn't mean the Brotherhood has been compromised. Things will continue as they always have," he went on. "Better actually. We all know he had grown weak."

Murmurs rose again.

"But before his death, he wrote down the name of the person he wanted to take over, if such a tragic event occurred—and he named me."

A buzz resounded throughout the room. For the first time, he heard the beginnings of disagreement among the men. As the conversations continued, one man stood up. "Will we able to see this document?"

"More importantly," he answered with a sneer. "If the brothers disagree with the obvious choice, they can hold a vote, which we'll hold now."

He pointed to a wooden box, with a slit of an opening in its lid, sitting on a table in front of the stage. "Under your chairs you'll each find a folder containing a copy of Michael's letter, along with a blank slip of paper and a pen. On that paper, write your answer, fold it, then come up to the box to deposit it. At this moment you're directed to write down only 'yea' or 'nay' as your vote. The results will determine whether we need to go any further than that."

Each man took a folder from beneath his chair and read the contents. "At this time, does anyone have any questions?" he asked.

Silence. As orderly as ants heading to their colony, they lined up, cast their votes, and returned to their seats. Once the last had cast his vote, the shiny shirt cuffs made their appearance again.

"I'll now ask Brad and Damien to tally the votes," he instructed, waiting for his order to be carried out. Two men on opposite sides of the room stood up and made their way to the stage. After opening the box, they searched for "Nay" votes. They didn't find a single one. The vote would pass, and not a naysayer wanted evidence of their opposition.

A minute later, the task was complete, Brad and Damien faced the other men. Together they gave the result: "Yea."

CHAPTER FIFTY-SEVEN

BEHIND THE MASK

PICTURE IN HAND, I walked to the torch lamp. Once on, I brought the photograph beneath it and my face closer. The picture was old and faded and slightly creased, which made it difficult to make out who was who, but that wasn't what was holding me back from naming the face I was fixated on. Turning off the lamp, I let the photograph drop to the floor. As I made my way to the stairs, I picked up the necklace and turned off the light.

In the bathroom, I looked into the mirror and put on the necklace, gently positioning the pendant so it was face up. It was dark and blotchy—far from the pretty trinket it once was.

As I stared at the blackened heart over my chest, it reminded me of who I'd become: a girl hardened by the world, forced to wear a mask of false emotion because she was broken—whether by nature or nurture, she was made wrong. Perhaps that was why I was so willing to die for Ember. I wanted to save the other girl who died with Anna all those years ago... and so, was doomed to vicariously save myself, over and over and over again.

But I regretted nothing—not the cast on my arm or the scar on my shoulder. It was the way it had to be. In fighting for those girls, I'd stopped going through the motions of life. For all my inadequacy, and for all the horrible surprises, for the first time, I had a goal that drove me forward. It didn't give me life so much as a chance to utilize what I'd become. It was the same in agriculture: sometimes, the dead crop is used to fertilize the living. Yes, it failed to grow like the other grain around it, but it is finally given purpose precisely because of its death. *Perhaps*, I thought as I eyed the crying girl in the mirror, *that was enough*.

ABOUT THE AUTHOR

Victoria Parks writes dark, mind-twisting, action-packed thrillers. Her characters are clever and fearless, and she loves to intertwine fact and fiction in everything she writes. Her debut novel — The Awakening — is the first book in the series *When the Harvest Dies*.

A Canadian writer, Victoria is currently dividing her time between South Korea and Kansas, while her husband is deployed.

Besides writing thrillers, Victoria enjoys reading traveling, creating different forms of art, and pretending she's the alpha to her three growing puppies.

If you want to know when Victoria's next book will come out, please visit her website at http://www.victoriaparksauthor.com, where you can sign up to receive an email when she has her next release. You can also follow her on twitter @ParksThriller.

www.ingramcontent.com/pod-product-compliance
Lightning Source LLC
Chambersburg PA
CBHW050920250626
47155CB00001B/310